BADD TO THE BONE

A BADD BROTHERS NOVEL

Jasinda Wilder

BADD TO
THE BONE

ONE

Brock

MY BROTHERS AND I WERE SHOOTING THE SHIT, hanging out at the bar, slinging drinks, and keeping the patrons happy. Business was so good these days that all of us needed to be here pretty much all the time. For the hundredth time, I wondered how Bast had managed to run this place all on his own after Dad passed away—even with seven brothers on hand, it was all we could do to keep the bar stocked and the food coming. Much to our collective surprise, it turned out that we were pretty good at it; although, it shouldn't have been *that* much of a surprise, since we'd all grown up in this bar, and we'd all taken turns helping out over the years.

Bast had just announced last call, and I was about to take a break to call Claire when I heard a loud crash on the stairs leading up to the apartment. Bast and I both ducked under the service bar and went running to investigate—we'd only gotten halfway from the kitchen to the stairs when there was another crash followed by a loud volley of drunken cursing. Bast yanked open the door and we saw our brother Baxter lying upside down on the stairs, his feet facing up, his head facing down. There were several holes in the plaster on either side of the stairwell, presumably from his fists and elbows. He was a bloody mess, barefoot and shirtless, wearing nothing but a pair of gym shorts. He had a bottle in his hand, a fifth of shitty tequila which was virtually empty.

Jesus. What now?

"Goddammit, Bax," Bast snarled. "The fuck, dude?"

Bax just moaned, writhing helplessly, and then the bottle went clattering down the stairs, the remains of the tequila glugging out onto the steps.

Bast shot me a rueful grin. "We're a fucked-up bunch of dudes, ain't we, Brock?"

I laughed and nodded. "Sure are. Wonder what the deal is here?"

"Hell if I know. If he's like the rest of us, it could be anything. Who the hell knows what secrets Bax is hiding?" He gestured at Bax with a sigh. "Grab his feet."

Bast trotted down the stairs, kicked the bottle away and grabbed Bax by the armpits. I hefted his feet over my shoulders and braced his legs, lifting and backing up the stairs in an awkward shuffle.

"He's fucking heavy, man. Jesus." Bast grunted under the weight of Bax's upper body.

"He's a monster, all right," I agreed.

We laid him on the couch upstairs, and then we both stood up, panting like girls.

"God*damn*, Bax," Bast breathed as he got a good look at him. "What did you get into, brother?"

Baxter was black and blue from clavicle to rib-cage; a mass of gnarly fresh bruises on his abs, chest, and sides. His nose had been broken and never set, his cheekbone was cut open, and he had another cut on his eyebrow. His hands were taped from knuckles to past his wrists, and the tape was fraying and stained rust-colored over his knuckles.

"He was fighting," I said.

"No shit." Bast reached forward to grab one of Bax's hands, which was clenched closed into a fist.

Bax shot upright, swinging his fists in wild hay-makers. "FUCK OFF! GET OFF ME! LEGGO!"

His breath was potent enough that you could probably get drunk from a single whiff at fifty paces, which led me to assume the bottle of tequila on the stairs probably wasn't the only one he'd downed, considering what we all knew of his tolerance—which, in a word, was inhuman. His fist, the one he had clenched closed, connected with my jaw, and I grabbed his wrist in a Judo hold, spinning him and then pinning him face down on the couch.

"Bax, it's us, it's your brothers," I said. "It's Brock and Sebastian, man. Cool it."

He went limp, and I let him go as he slowly and laboriously flipped over onto his back. "Duuuudes. Whassup?"

Bast wasn't amused. "What the hell, Baxter?"

Bax held up his hand and released his fist, letting a rain of hundred dollar bills flutter onto his chest. "Two words, bitch: prize…fighting."

"Oh, Christ no," Bast snarled. "You have *got* to be kidding me."

"Oh, Christ yes," Bax said with a laugh. "And I…am…*good*. I'm mothafuckin' unstoppable, yo. I pulled down two G's tonight, baby."

"Why?" I asked, genuinely baffled as to why anyone would voluntarily have the shit beaten out of them for a couple of grand.

His glare was dark and furious. "You wouldn't

understand." His gaze flicked to Bast. "Neither would you. Nobody would."

"Try us," Bast growled.

"How 'bout I don't?" Bax attempted to stand up, but flopped back down. "I just need to crash."

"You're a fucking mess," Dru said, standing behind the couch and eyeing him, having obviously heard the commotion. "We should get Mara over here to look you over."

Bax waved a hand dismissively. "Bah. Cuts and bruises. I've gotten hurt worse during practice. It fuckin' tickles, okay?" He scraped up his cash, wadded it in his fist, and rested his forearm on his eyes. "How about we skip the part where you fuckers act like my mommy and just let me sleep."

Dru sighed and tugged a blanket up to Bax's neck. "You can crash, but you better be nice to me. Don't forget what I'm capable of, asshole."

Bax eyed her from underneath his thick forearm. "Yes ma'am, madam badass."

Bast just shook his head and left to go back downstairs.

I joined Sebastian down in the bar; he had cleaned up the tequila and thrown away the bottle. Thank god it was late enough that Xavier, Luce, and the twins had closed the kitchen and the bar while Bast and I dealt with Bax; Bast cut the others loose and he and I sat at the bar drinking beer.

"Underground prize fighting? For real?" Bast shook his head again, sighing in frustration.

"He's always had a violent streak," I said. "He just channeled it into football."

"And now that's gone." Bast nodded. "So he needs an outlet for whatever's eating at him."

"We've all got shit to deal with, but this seems extreme."

"What do we do?" Bast asked, eyeing me. "You know he's gonna keep doing it, and there ain't shit we can do to stop him."

I shrugged. "Someone's gotta go with him. Have his back."

"We take turns, maybe? We can all hold our own."

"I mean, I know *you* can, and I know *I* can, and obviously Zane can. Do we need to involve the others, you think?"

Bast chuckled. "I wouldn't want to meet Lucian in a dark alley, I can tell you that much."

I frowned. "What do you mean?"

"That dude who owned the fishing boat Luce worked on? He was this wiry old Brazilian dude. Hard as fuck, man. Like, he was just one of those truly hard, weathered dudes who you just knew would live to be a thousand years old. I was out for a ride on my bike once, back before I sold it. I saw Luce and the old guy on the deck of the boat, doing...what's that gymnastics kickboxing shit? Where they do the upside spinning and stuff?"

"Capoeira?" I suggested.

"Yeah, that shit." Bast shrugged. "Plus, Lucian's been all over the world, and I get the feeling he's been in some less than savory situations. Luce can take care of himself, brother. And then some, I'm betting."

"I had no idea."

Bast chuckled. "Yeah, well, like I said, it seems all of us have our secrets."

"What about the twins and Xavier?"

Bast shook his head. "I dunno about them. I wouldn't put it past Xavier to have secretly mastered ninjutsu or something, you know? He's the type who would do that, just decide to take up some obscure martial art just because it sounded cool."

"And the twins have spent enough time in dive bars that they're probably pretty decent with their fists."

Another hearty laugh from Bast. "Dude, we're the Badd brothers. We were born shaking our fists at the world. Yeah, those two pretty boys can throw down, I guarantee it."

"I guess I was less interested in their ability to fight as much as whether or not we *need* to involve them in this business with Bax."

Bast tipped his head to one side. "Ahh. That *is* a different question." He mulled it over. "I think you're right. Let's just pull Zane into this, and go from there, keep it between us four for now."

Zane pushed through the door at that exact moment. "Pull me into what?" Zane examined the holes in the drywall. "And how the hell did this happen, anyway?"

"The questions are one and the same," I said. "It seems our dear idiot brother Baxter has decided to try his hand at underground prizefighting."

Zane slid onto a stool beside me. "He *what?*"

Bast took over the explanation. "He stumbled in about thirty minutes ago, crashed all over the stairs, leaving those awesome holes you're fixing. He was fuckin' colossally obliterated, bruised from head to toe and covered in blood, with a fistful of hundreds in his hands."

Zane blew out a shocked breath. "Damn."

"Yeah," Bast said.

"Well, one of us will have to be with him whenever he fights," Zane said. "He needs backup. That shit can get out of hand real fast."

"You sound like you're talking from experience," I pointed out.

Zane shrugged. "Spent some time in Thailand

ᴥ deployments. Me and my squad ended up in
ι   house in the truly abysmal end of Bangkok,
wᴥ   ese Muay Thai guys beat the holy fuck
out   ther. Let's just say that when the wrong
guy lᴥ   an go sideways in a fuckin' hurry."

"Ᵽ   nna like this," I pointed out. "I can
hear hin   don't need you fuckers to babysit
me,'" I sᴥ   growl meant to mimic Bax's
rough, grav

"Tough ᴥ   said. "He ain't got a choice.
He wants to fiᵷ   it with us at his back."

"Do we tell   Bast asked. "I mean, Dru
already knows, anᵷ   ing she'll put up a fuss
about also wanting   ack."

Zane chuckled.   bad idea, actually.
That woman is truly hᴥ   ening when she decides to
throw down."

Bast laughed with him. "I wouldn't *want* her to be
at a prize fight like that, but if she gets it in her head
to be there, I won't be the one to stand in her way."
He laughed again, more ruefully. "I sound like I'm
pussy-whipped, but shit, you know as well as I do that
Dru can hold her own in just about any situation."

Zane nodded. "That's not pussy-whipped, that's
knowing your woman's skills. She can kick ass with
the best of them, and I say that speaking as a trained
killer." He lifted a shoulder. "Mara's pregnant, so she

ain't getting within ten miles of a prize fight, but I'll tell her what I'm doing. Those girls are all so tight that if I don't tell Mara first she'll be super pissed at me."

Sebastian turned to me. "Are you going to tell Claire about this?"

"I want to but, to be honest, with this trip to Michigan coming up, I'm not sure the timing is right. It was all I could do to get her to agree to go and see her dad one last time in the first place. He sounds like a class-A jackass, honestly. I can't help but think that Claire will regret it if she doesn't go and try to make peace with him, though."

"Well, I don't envy you," Zane said. "You guys have basically just met and this is a shitty thing to have to manage. Just know we're here for you, bro."

"Absolutely," added Bast. "Say the word and we'll do whatever we can to help."

"Thanks. I'll only be away for a few days—what could happen in less than a week?"

TWO

Claire

I WATCHED AS BROCK STOOD IN FRONT OF THE MIRROR, shaving, a white hotel towel cinched low around his waist. His whole jaw was slathered with shaving cream, and he was dragging a big, bulky, expensive-looking razor down his cheek and across his jawline in slow, careful lines.

The man is a fucking god. For real. Six-one, one-ninety-five and all of it toned muscle. I'm not super attracted to the macho bodybuilder types, which works, because while Brock works out, eats right, and generally stays fit and sexy, he's not a gym rat, and certainly isn't anywhere near as ripped and jacked as his brothers Zane, Bast, and Bax; those boys are true monsters, especially Bax, which is fine for them, and for those who like that look. Bax is hot, don't get me wrong, but that look just isn't for me.

But Brock? He is truly, deeply, intensely *beautiful*. Sculpted, chiseled features, brown eyes the exact color of creamy milk chocolate, with thick wavy brown hair that he keeps cut in a classic side part, so a few strands tend to dangle in front of those chocolate eyes. One look at Brock, just from the neck up, and I get a case of the dropsies—as in *oops, I drop to my knees*. If he takes off his shirt, I get all sweaty and my pussy gets super moist. Once his pants are off and his dick is brought into the picture, all bets are off. I am a goner. He could ask me for anything, do anything to me, and I'd let him. He has complete and total control over me once he is naked.

But *ssshhhh*—I haven't exactly told him that yet. Let him figure it out on his own.

So yeah, I watch Brock shave, and entertain fantasies of ripping that towel off and blowing him while he shaves. I mean, yeah, we did just finish fucking, and he'd already showered and so had I, and I was supposed to be getting dressed because we were going to William Beaumont Hospital in Royal Oak, Michigan…to visit my dad. Who is dying.

I didn't want to go.

I wanted to stay in this hotel and fuck Brock.

I wanted to be back in Ketchikan, with him and his brothers and my BFF Mara, or in Seattle working.

Anywhere, essentially, but here in Oakland fucking County, Michigan, preparing to visit my dying father, who had disowned me for having a miscarriage.

I felt the knot of tension and anger and sadness boil up inside me, but I shut that line of thought right down. Brock was going to drag me to the fucking hospital no matter what. He insisted I'd regret it if Dad died before I got a chance to at least *try* to see him. I wasn't so sure myself. Brock hadn't met the sorry bastard, and I couldn't imagine that he'd changed one iota since I last saw him.

I let out an irritated breath, and Brock glanced at me, his face half-shaved, the other still white with cream. "What's up, babe?"

"Oh, you know, the usual." I shrugged. "I don't like this, I wanna go home, I don't care if the old goat dies, yada-yada-yada. Same old, same old."

Brock rinsed the razor and brought it to his skin for another pass, twisting his face in one of those weird shaving-man grimaces. Even while shaving, he was so damn pretty my ovaries applauded God for creating him. "We've had this discussion a dozen times, Claire. You know deep down this is the right thing to do."

"It's the sucky, shitty, horrible, painful, stupid thing to do."

"And the right thing."

"Have you even *met* me, Brock? I'm not exactly aiming for sainthood here."

Brock just snorted gently and kept shaving. I stood up, wearing nothing but an orange thong, and sidled up behind him. He stilled, watching me in the mirror, the razor frozen at his cheekbone.

"Claire…what are you doing?"

I slowly pulled the end of the towel free from where he'd tucked it in, and it fell to the floor in a heap of damp, heavy white cotton. "Nothin'."

He'd just blown his load less than thirty minutes ago, but all I had to do was *look* at his cock and he'd start hardening. "Claire. Seriously. We've gotta get going."

I leaned up against him, pressing my tits—such as they were—against his back, and slid my palms under his arms, caressing his chest, and then his stomach, and then down his thighs. He was well and truly erect at this point. The sink and counter came to just below his navel, and his cock stood hard and glorious, a thick, straight marvel of manhood. Brock was perfect. Big enough that he filled me and stretched me and made my eyes bug out in shock every time he drilled into me, yet not so big it actually hurt.

I wrapped my hand around his perfect penis and stroked him gently, peering around his sculpted-from-marble bicep in the mirror, watching my tiny pale little hand slide up and down his huge golden cock. "This is better, isn't it?"

"Claire, damn it."

"Is that like goddammit?" I asked.

He heaved a deep breath and attempted to pretend I wasn't doing anything; he drew the razor carefully down his cheek, rinsed it, and scraped down once more. Then he tilted his head to one side and pulled the razor upward from his neck toward his ear.

"Yes," he grated through gritted teeth. "Claire-damn-it. You can't weasel your way out of this."

"I'm not weaseling." I brought my other arm around his body and did the thing he liked best: hand over hand, slowly, each hand gliding in a tight, slow squeeze from tip to root, one hand and then the other in a rolling continuous stroke. "Does this feel like weaseling?"

"It feels like you trying to distract me."

"Maybe," I admitted. "Is it working?"

"No." He went back to shaving, and he was taking more time with each stroke now, because he had to focus harder. "Not working."

Time to switch tactics. I cupped his balls in one

hand and used my middle finger to massage his taint, worming my way toward his prostate. He wouldn't let me really massage his prostate yet, but I was working on it. I could get my finger close, but then he'd chicken out before I could manage insertion. Someday, though. For now, a nice firm taint-massage would do the trick. One hand gliding up and down his lovely cock, my boobs rubbing against his back, all happening in the mirror where he could watch? Oh yeah.

Hot. Really hot.

Shit, it was hot to me, and I was only doing this to try to get out of having to go to the damned hospital.

"Shit!" Brock snapped, and my gaze lifted to his.

He'd cut himself underneath the jaw, a thin red line beginning to appear. He reached over and ripped a square of toilet paper free and dabbed the spot. "You made me cut myself. Happy now?"

I lifted up on my tiptoes, grabbed his neck to pull him down, and kissed the spot, all without missing a beat in my stroking of his cock. "I'd never be happy about you getting hurt."

"You're not gonna change my mind, Claire. This is important. It's important to you, too, even if you try to deny it."

I could tell he was losing the ability to think clearly, because it took him a while to formulate that sentence, and he spoke very crisply and precisely, as he did when he was trying to keep the drawl out of his voice; case in point, the use of *gonna*, rather than *going to*.

He was flexing in time with the slow movement of my hand, pushing forward as I slid my fist downward. He was close, now.

"If my distraction technique isn't working, maybe I should just quit, then." I let go, and Brock's jaw tightened, his eyes narrowing.

He let out a breath, blinking hard, jaw muscles flexing, abs tensed. "Fine."

I met his irritated gaze in the mirror. "Really?"

"You can't use that to manipulate me."

I rested my cheek against his bicep. "I'm not trying to manipulate you, Brock, I just—"

"Yes, you are. And I get it." He took his gaze off of mine to finish one last pass along his jaw, and then rinsed the razor before setting it aside and bracing his fists on the countertop. "You're freaking out, and you've got a lot of negative emotion tied up in this. Shit, I can't understand completely, and probably won't ever really understand. But I understand this much—you *are* trying to manipulate me, and it's shitty of you."

I sighed, and dropped my gaze. "I'm sorry. I'm just—"

His smile in the mirror was gentle, loving, and understanding. "I get it, Claire. I really do. Just...don't pull that shit with me. I'm not doing this to punish you. I'm doing it because—"

"Why, Brock?" I demanded. "Why *are* you doing this?"

"Because..." He hesitated. "Because I care about you, and I'm not going to allow you to cheat yourself out of this. You're angry, you're scared, you're hurt, and you have every right to be. But your dad is dying. Short of a miracle, he's going to die, and sooner rather than later. If you don't at least *try* to go see him now, even if he tosses you out, you'll regret it." He reached down and took my hand. "I'm doing this for you. You have to forgive him—for you, though, not for him."

"Well, I don't forgive him. I can't and I won't."

"Try."

"I told you—I *can't*. Been trying for years, and I'm too pissed off."

"Forgiveness doesn't mean not being angry about it anymore. It's just letting go of it and understanding that you're just wasting emotional energy hanging on to the hatred."

"Okay Mother Theresa, whatever."

He shook his head. "You'll get it. I know you will." He glanced down. "Now, are you really gonna leave me hanging like this?"

I giggled, muffling it against his skin. "Not much about you is exactly *hanging* at the moment."

But of course I wasn't going to leave him hanging, metaphorically speaking. I grasped him in both hands and stroked him gently and slowly, and we both watched in the mirror as my little hands slid along his huge cock. His six-pack tensed as he neared the breaking point, and his big, meaty chest swelled with each ragged breath he took.

"Normally," I whispered, letting my lips slide against his bicep, "I'd finish you off with my mouth right about now, but I already brushed my teeth."

"And you already took a shower, so you probably won't let me come on your tits."

I shook my head. "Yeah, that's a negative Ghost Rider, the pattern is full."

"Don't you dare quote *Top Gun* at me, woman, or I'll fuck you silly, freshly showered or not."

I giggled. "Take me to bed or lose me forever, Goose."

"That's not even the actual quote." He was clenching his jaw now, and his hips were pivoting as he got closer and closer to orgasm. And then, seconds before I knew he was about to blow, he pivoted, grabbed me by the hips, spun back around, and plopped my ass on the counter.

"Yeah, fuck that noise," he grunted, and tugged my thong aside and drove himself into me.

"Goddammit, Brock!" I snapped.

"You can't get me all worked up and think I'm gonna be content with a simple handjob, Claire."

"It was going to be fun."

"For whom?"

"For me. Watching you spooge all over the mirror."

He snorted as he thrust deep into me. "Only place I'm *spooging*, babe, is deep inside your sweet little pussy."

"You're determined to make me take another shower, aren't you?" I asked, but I was getting breathless, because his slow thrusts were grinding his cock inside me just right and if I wrapped my legs around his waist and tipped my hips forward to tilt my pelvis downward, his shaft would slide along my clit, and— oh. Oh yeah.

Yep.

Just like that.

"Maybe I won't let you take another shower. It's already ten and we haven't even had breakfast yet."

"So you want me to visit my estranged, dying father with your cummies drip-drip-dribbling down my thighs?"

He glared down at me. "Cummies? *Really?*"

"It's a fun word."

"It's demeaning. Makes it seem…juvenile."

"And wanting to come on my tits isn't?"

He was holding back, waiting for me. "You love it when I come on your tits," he muttered. "Don't even try to pretend you don't."

"It can be hot sometimes, but I wouldn't say I *love* it," I lied.

He smirked down at me. "You're a shitty liar, Claire."

"Am not."

He laughed. "Okay, you're actually not, but I can still see right through you."

Thing was, I wasn't lying or even faking. I really would have loved it if he'd have thrown me off the counter, shoved me down to my knees and come all over me. But he would never do that.

He was thrusting raggedly, now, and I knew he wasn't far from coming. Prediction: Brock would come inside me, and then he'd tell me to stay put on the counter while he got a warm, damp washcloth, and he'd kneel between my thighs and he would clean up with sweet, loving, gentle front-to-back swipes.

Sweet, loving, and fucking saccharine.

I didn't know how to tell him how much I hated it when he was all sweet and tender with me like that. I wanted him to be rough and controlling. I wanted him to fuck me like his own personal whore. I wanted him to use me and take advantage of me and do dark, dirty things to me. I wanted to take a bath in his hot salty come. I wanted to have bruises on my tits from his teeth—shit, I wanted bruises from his teeth on the insides of my thighs. On my clit itself if he was so inclined.

But instead he treated me as if I was more precious than diamonds, and more fragile than porcelain. He catered to my every whim. He took care of me, served me, and he loved me like no one ever had.

No, we didn't say that word yet, and I certainly wouldn't be saying it first or even in return anytime soon. But I knew he was in love. And so was I.

I hated it.

I didn't want it.

But I couldn't and wouldn't give him up.

Because even his sweet, saccharine, tender *lovemaking* was better than all the hard and brutal fucking, better than the hours of dirty bondage and edging and light S&M. Better than all the random hook-ups, better than any glory hole or back-alley BJ. Obviously, it was better than all that.

I'd been fucking Brock for months and wasn't tired of him, so *obviously* the sex was pretty damn amazing.

But it was *vanilla*.

And I wanted more.

I just wasn't sure Brock had it in him.

"God, Claire. I'm gonna come."

"Well I'd hope so, since that's kind of the point."

"Are you close?"

"No," I lied.

"You are, aren't you?"

"Fine, I'm close."

"Why lie?"

"Because I don't want you to stop. It feels too good having your dick inside me."

"I'm holding out as hard as I can. You feel so good, Claire."

"Can you just take your cock off and leave it inside me?"

"You're so weird."

"You know you dig it."

He was grunting now, and his thrusts were harder and rougher than ever before.

"Harder, Brock."

He picked up the pace, but not the roughness. "Like this?"

"Not faster—*harder*. Fuck me hard, Brock," I growled, "Fuck me like you mean it."

And, for once, he sort of listened. He pulled me to the edge of the counter and held on to my ass and pounded into me.

"Fuck, yes, Brock, just like this—" I held on to his strong neck with both hands and hooked my ankles tight around his lower back and met him thrust for thrust, slamming my pussy against him as hard as I could, taking his pounding and loving every single second of it. "Yes, yes, Jesus…YES!"

Our pelvises bumped, our bellies slapped, and I came like a lightning bolt smashing down out of a clear blue sky. I screamed and sank my teeth into the meat of his pec, clinging to him, screaming around a mouthful of his skin and muscle as I came and came and came.

And then I felt him let go, snarling in my ear, his strong hands clawed into my ass. He lifted me off the sink and spun me around, slamming me up against the wall, his hands clutching my ass cheeks and his weight pinning me to the wall, his crashing thrusts nailing me to the wall.

The harder he fucked me, the harder I came, and I kept coming as he kept fucking me.

My throat went hoarse from screaming as he drilled me over and over and over, and I felt his come shoot into me in hot spurting bursts of wetness, filling me until I felt myself leaking around him while he continued to thrust into me in stuttering, ragged movements.

Finally, he stopped, and pulled out. He twisted in

place, pivoting to put me back on the counter. "Stay put for a second," Brock murmured. "I'll clean you up."

He stood up, grabbed a washcloth, rinsed it under hot water, wrung it out, and then returned to kneeling in front of me. He gently, tenderly touched the washcloth to my pussy, using two fingers to hold my thong aside and spread my labia apart, drawing the cotton downward toward my butt. I watched, my heart hammering weirdly, my throat seized. He was so fucking *sweet* it drove me nuts.

I didn't know how to tell him I *wanted* to spend the day walking around with his come dripping down my leg. I was afraid he'd find it gross, or stupid.

Basically, I was afraid to tell him a lot of stuff that I thought about and wanted, and felt, because if life has taught me anything, it's that guys don't really want the raw truth from you. They wanted steady sex, a high libido, lots of blowjobs, anal once in a while, and for you to keep your girly, emotional shit to yourself. Fine by me. It's what I know, and what I do best.

Brock seems different, but I enjoy being with him too much to risk losing what we do have, so I'm currently settling for vanilla. And the occasional creampie.

I was on birth control, obvs, but Brock usually

used a condom as well, since neither of us was in any way interested in an accident of the kind Zane and Mara had experienced. Their pregnancy seems like it's gonna work out for them, but I personally would shit myself it that ever happened to me. I'd haul ass down to Planned Parenthood faster than I could spell P-R-E-G-N-A-N-T, because I am *NOT* mommy material. I don't have a nurturing bone in my body. I became a combat nurse because the sight of blood didn't move me in any way whatsoever, and because I could handle gnarly shit without flinching, or letting annoying shit like emotions get in the way. Maternal instincts? I've got those about as much as I have testosterone and big swinging balls. In other words, I have none.

I may act like I've got big brass balls, but I'm all woman, trust me—just not the bouncing babies and changing diapers kind.

I let Brock clean me up and then I hopped off the counter, pressing myself up against Brock's front, and lifting up on my tiptoes to kiss him. "*That*, Brock Badd, was some damn fine fucking."

I turned away from him, only to feel a swift, sharp swat to my ass. "It was more than just fucking, Claire, and you know it."

"Yeah, yeah, yeah," I said, breezily. "Semantics. Point is, that's exactly how I like it best."

I went to the bureau and pulled out a pair of

skinny jeans and a mint tank top, with a white floral print three-quarter sleeve cardigan over it. As I shimmied into the jeans, I caught a glimpse of Brock, gazing at me thoughtfully while he swiped on deodorant.

"What's the look for?" I asked, tugging the tank top on.

He was still naked as he rubbed a dab of hair paste onto his palms, and then worked it into his hair. "That's exactly how you like it best?"

I nodded, leaving the cardigan off for the moment, hunting for my favorite pair of leopard print Tieks in my suitcase. "Yes sir."

"Hard and rough?"

I found them and leaned against the bedframe to tug them onto my bare feet. "The harder and rougher the better. Fuck me so hard my pussy is sore for days."

"Really?"

I dug in my suitcase again, this time for my bag of jewelry, rummaging for my fake pearl teardrop earrings and Alex and Ani bracelets. I found them and switched places with Brock in the bathroom, as he started getting dressed and I put in my earrings and did some light makeup.

"Really, really," I said, in a shitty Scottish accent, going for Shrek and ending up sounding something else that was mostly just embarrassing. "The fact that every time we fuck I shout *harder, harder, harder* hasn't clued you in yet?"

He stepped into a pair of khakis, tugged on a PRL polo shirt, dark blue with a huge orange logo on the left side of his chest. "But for real, the harder the better?"

"Yes, really, Brock." I paused halfway through applying eyeliner. "Why?"

"So when it's not hard and rough—"

I stifled a groan, because this conversation was exactly what I hadn't wanted to have. Not now, especially. "Brock, don't. Don't be like that."

"Like what?"

I shrugged and went back to applying eyeliner. "All insecure and shit. Any sex with you is good sex. Hell, *bad* sex with you would be better than the best sex I've had with anyone else. I always like it. I'm never left unsatisfied—I'm too selfish to let you get away with that."

"But?" He jerked on socks and shoved his feet into a pair of Red Wing boots.

"But nothing."

He stared at me for a long moment; I pretended not to see his stare, not to feel it, even though it was all I was aware of. I messed up the eyeliner and had to start over, cursing under my breath.

"There's a but."

I put away the eyeliner and dug through my

collection of lip stain. "Yes, Brock. There's a but. A *big* one." I glanced at him, wiggling my eyebrows suggestively. "And if you're really nice to me, I may let you play with it later."

He laughed, but shook his head. "Not what I meant."

I finished my lips, dusted on some foundation and blush, put everything away, and turned around. "I know." I pressed myself up against Brock's big hard body, wrapping my arms around his broad shoulders as I lifted up to kiss him again. "Brock, quit worrying. You fuck like a god. Now, unless you're letting me off the hook, let's go already so we can get this visit over with."

He snagged my purse off the bureau and handed it to me, letting the strap dangle from his index finger. "And no, I'm not letting you off the hook."

I tossed the strap over my shoulder and draped my sweater over my forearm. "Fine, then. Let's go… hotcakes."

He just rolled his eyes and huffed as he led the way out the door.

I was acting casual and unaffected, but inside, I was a wreck. Total tumult. Complete chaos.

I did *not* want to do this. Not one bit. And if it weren't for Brock, I wouldn't be here at all.

THREE

Brock

A S I SLID BEHIND THE WHEEL OF THE RENTED MUSTANG, I wondered if Claire thought she was fooling me with her easy-breezy casual attitude. She probably did. Claire routinely assumed she could fool me with her bullshit, and I routinely let her get away with it, because I couldn't quite figure out what lay beneath the bullshit, or why she wouldn't just be upfront with me. I could see and sense when she was full of shit, but I couldn't read her mind, so I couldn't figure out what she really thought or wanted. It was quite a conundrum, knowing she was lying but not being willing to pull the trigger on the accusation:

You're lying, Claire.

Oh really? About what?

I'm not sure, but I know you're lying.

Yeah, that'd go swimmingly. She'd absolutely love that conversation. I'm sure we'd be together for a *super* long time after that.

I glanced down at Google Maps on my iPhone and followed the directions from the Townsend Hotel to the William Beaumont Hospital almost on autopilot, letting my brain chase down the endless maze of rabbit holes that was my relationship with Claire.

She blew my mind on a regular basis, she constantly surprised me, and she never ceased to amaze me. She always kept me on my toes. But she also had walls a mile high and a mile thick, and sometimes I felt like I'd never really find my way through them. Which was the point, I supposed—I couldn't get through them, or over them, or under them…she had to let me in on her own, and I just wasn't sure she was capable of that. We'd been together for going on four months, now, which was an eternity for both of us. We spent every available moment together. We fucked like teenagers who had just discovered sex. We talked nonstop, about *everything*. She'd told me a lot of her sordid past. On paper, it seemed like she trusted me. Yet I still got the feeling she was holding back, keeping something in—there was some part of herself she wasn't sharing.

Sexually, she was freaky, which was hot. I mean, I thought I'd liked sex, but she took it to a whole new level. She was insatiable, to the point that I sometimes wondered if she was, clinically speaking, a borderline nymphomaniac. I wasn't complaining, hell no. But… it was constant. My sex drive was healthy, my refractory period nice and short, my stamina good. I could keep up, and I knew how to please her.

But…

I just felt like there was a but.

She never admitted to wanting anything I wasn't giving.

Until this morning: *The harder the better. Fuck me so hard my pussy is sore for days.*

I'd been worried I was going to hurt her, nailing her like I had. She was so small, so dainty and delicate. But she was also fiery, feisty, and strong. I knew she was strong, stronger than any other woman I'd ever met—emotionally and mentally. But physically, I was just scared I was going to lose control and hurt her. I stood six foot one and weighed in at nearly two hundred pounds. None of us Badd brothers were small men, thanks to Dad's genetic gifts to us. And Claire? Five-five at the most, and probably one-ten after a full meal, soaking wet. Slender, svelte. Bird-bones, delicate features. *Stunning* features. Like, my breath caught sometimes, looking at her. Like right now, she was staring out the windshield so she was in profile to me, and the sun caught her pixie-short hair—which she'd recently had dyed a sort of silvery blonde, which just worked with her pale skin and virulently green eyes. And, god, I just couldn't quite breathe right because she was so fucking beautiful, like just...*lovely*. Those cheekbones, that mouth? God, that mouth, literally and metaphorically. Sassy, biting, wickedly sharp, sarcastic. Vitriolic and cutting, yet also prone to insights and truths, and hilarious and unexpected turns of phrase. And, literally, that mouth. Wide, with plump lips in a perfect cupid's bow. Those lips could kiss my lips, and they could slide across my chest, and they could wrap around my dick. Those lips, though. I stared at her mouth more often than I'd like to admit. Especially when she put on that bright red lipstick that contrasted so brilliantly against her creamy peach skin.

"You're staring at me," she remarked, still staring forward.

"Can't help it," I said. "You're just so damn beautiful."

"You were looking at my mouth."

"Yeah."

"Why?"

"Because your mouth is…I don't know. One of my favorite features of yours."

She glanced at me, a wry twist on her lips. "My mouth? Really?"

I shrugged. "Yeah, really. Why, is that weird?"

"A little." She pulled down the visor and flipped open the mirror, turning her head this way and that, making a moue with her lips, faking a cutesy smile, a pout, then baring her teeth. "Why my mouth?"

"You have a beautiful mouth. Your lips, the way you smile…it's just…beautiful. I'm attracted to your mouth."

"Literally speaking, you mean." She closed the visor and turned to watch my reaction.

"And metaphorically."

"Growing up, my—my dad used to say I packed the attitude of three people into the frame of half a person."

I couldn't help a laugh. "Sounds about right. You're all attitude, and I like it."

"Even when my attitude gets in the way and makes problems?"

"You? Problematic? Never."

She snorted. "Nice."

"Hey, I'm a stunt pilot. I do stupid, crazy shit in an airplane for a living. Safe to say I don't like boring."

"Well, you'll certainly never be bored when I'm around."

"Exactly." I reached out and took her hand. "Notice how we haven't spent more than half a week apart since we met?"

She rolled her eyes and shook her head and turned to stare out her window, brushing off my words like she always did when I said something sweet or romantic or cheesy. Yet I saw the hint of a smile at the corner of her mouth, and the pleased glint in her eyes, before she shut it down again.

"Whatever. You're just crazy."

"Guilty as charged. You have to be crazy to intentionally stall out a plane at two hundred feet."

"Didn't you once lecture me about the difference between stunts and tricks, and aerobatic maneuvers? And how everything you did was carefully calculated and practiced obsessively?"

I laughed. "And all that is still true. But in this case, I'm just proving a point."

"And what point would that be, pray tell?" She rested her elbow on the window frame and propped her head up with three fingers to her temple, eyeing me with a half-smile.

"That I'm not interested in boring or safe. I like things crazy and interesting."

She stared at me hard for a long moment. "Well,

you've certainly got that in me, then."

There was more, but she wasn't going to say it. I could see her wheels turning though, see her thoughts spinning.

"Do you even say half the things you think?" I asked.

She frowned, as if the question was unexpected. "Half? Nah, not even. As unfiltered as I may seem, I hold back at least eighty percent of the crazy nonsense that goes through my head."

"Why?"

"Because I get enough shit as it is. If I vented *everything* I thought, I'd be locked up." She glanced sideways at me. "Why? Do you say everything you think?"

"Not even close. But I get the feeling there's always more that you're thinking but not saying, and I always wonder what it is."

"Hey look, we're here," she said, as I pulled into the parking area near the hospital's main entrance.

She pointed out a parking spot a few rows from the doors.

"*Avoi*ding," I murmured in a singsong, under my breath.

She laughed, but her heart obviously wasn't it in it. "I'm not avoiding, I'm putting a pin in it. For later." She jabbed the air with one hand as if driving a tack into a corkboard, making a popping sound with her lips.

"Nice," I said, as I slid out of the Mustang.

Claire got out and circled the back end to wait for me, and then took my hand. "Can you not, Brock?"

"Not what?"

"I'm stressed, okay? And it feels like you're trying to pick a fight."

"I'm trying to distract you with conversation."

She shook her head, irritated. "Well...don't. You're just making it worse."

I sighed. "Sorry."

"You wanna know what I'm really thinking?" she asked, as we entered the hospital and angled toward the check-in desk.

"Absolutely."

"I'm fucking terrified right now. I haven't seen my dad in over six years. The last time I saw my mom, I screamed at her for being a pussy and a pushover and giving in to whatever Dad wanted. And now my dad's dying, and I don't want to be here, but I know deep down you're right, that I have to at least make the effort, because this is probably the last time I'll ever see him, and even though I fucking hate him, he's still my father." She let out a shaky breath, shook her hands as if to dispel their trembling, and stepped up to the reception desk. "Hi, I'm here to see Connor Collins."

"And you are?" The woman behind the desk was middle-aged, harried looking and severe, but her voice was solicitous and kind.

"Claire Collins. His daughter."

The woman tapped at a keyboard and then glanced up with a smile, but not a bright one, considering where we were, and where she was about to send us. "Oncology, fifth floor. You'll both need to sign in and wear visitor's badges."

We signed in, stuck the bright neon stickers to our shirts, and followed the signs to the elevator bank. The elevator was crowded, so Claire burrowed in against my side, standing stiff and tense under my arm. It took us a full five minutes of walking to reach the correct part of the hospital, and then we had to check in at another desk, where Claire identified herself once again as his daughter, and was then directed to a specific room.

The hallway was wide and smelled of antiseptic, our footsteps echoing loudly. Miscellaneous hospital equipment lined the hallways here and there, and the occasional barely intelligible announcement came over the PA system. We found the room Claire's dad was in and found the door closed. I heard the low murmur of voices on the other side.

Claire stood in front of the door, chewing on her lower lip. Her fingers were tangled together in a knot, squeezing until her knuckles went white. Her chest rose and fell rapidly, and she was blinking hard.

I tucked her against my side, lowered my mouth near her ear. "You can do this, Claire. I'll be with the whole time, no matter what."

"I can't," she breathed. "I can't."

"Yes, you can."

She shook her head. "I can't go in there. He doesn't want to see me, and I don't want to see him." Her voice was barely audible, and shaky.

I'd never seen Claire like this, not even remotely. She was rarely emotional about anything. Excitable, manic, crazy, wild, fun, weird, sarcastic, quirky...but never emotional.

I felt her trying to pull away, and I held on to her waist. "Deep breath, honey. You can do this. It's going to be okay."

She twisted to look up at me, and didn't even call me on my use of the cliché endearment—which was how I knew she was really and truly freaking the hell out. "You won't leave my side?"

"Not for a single second," I promised, trying to keep a serene and comforting smile on my face.

"Swear to me." She gripped my shirtfront in trembling hands. "Swear, Brock."

I took her hands in mine, cupped her tiny, shaking hands in my palms. "I swear to you I won't leave your side."

She nodded. She let go of my hands, stepped back away from me, and shook hers out again. Then she rubbed her face with her palms, rolled her shoulders, and let out another harsh breath. "Okay. Okay. I can do this." This wasn't meant for me, though, but for herself.

Another moment's hesitation, and then Claire knocked on the door. The voices quieted, and I heard a reedy male voice. "I wonder who that could be?" He had a hint of an Irish accent. "Moira, would you see who that is, please."

A ghost of a squeaky footstep, and then the door swung inward. A sharp intake of breath. "Claire, my goodness. You're here?" She said this quietly, in a near-whisper.

The woman was around Claire's height, and it was obvious that Claire got most of her looks from this woman, her mother. Thin, straight blonde hair, slim figure, striking features. She was exhausted looking, with bags under her eyes and pain in her expression, now mingled with surprise.

"Uh...hi, Mom." Claire shifted from foot to foot, clutching the strap of her purse with one hand and my hand in a death grip with the other.

The woman, Moira, stared at Claire, and then at me. "Who's this, then?" Moira, too, had a faint Irish accent.

Claire glanced up at me, then at her mom. "This is...um...my boyfriend, Brock. Brock, this is my mom, Moira."

I let go of Claire's hand long enough to shake Moira's hand. "Hi, Moira. Nice to meet you, although I'm sorry it's happening under these circumstances."

Moira's hand was cold and clammy and she barely shook mine before letting go. "This is a surprise." She eyed me up and down, scrutinizing me. "Nice to meet you, Brock." She said the words as an automatic reply, but I could tell she was stunned by my presence, or by Claire's use of the word *boyfriend* when introducing me, which had, honestly, taken me by surprise, too.

"Who is it, Moira?" called out the male voice, which I assumed belonged to Connor, Claire's dad.

Moira sucked in a deep, fortifying breath, held it, and let it out again. "Come on in, then, the both of you."

She turned and led the way into the room, which was a private room like any other, white walls with a floral-print border halfway up, a TV in one corner hanging from the ceiling, a bathroom, a tan rolling adjustable tray over the bed with the detritus of breakfast still on it. Imitation leather chairs stood on either side of the bed, and there was a nightstand and a remote control/speaker attached to the bed. A medicinal smell mingled with the scent of sickness, and it was obvious from the odor alone that Claire's father was very ill.

I held Claire's hand but trailed a step behind her as we entered the room. The man on the bed was... well, sick. Obviously dying. Thin, pale, haggard. Unnaturally bald, with sunken cheeks, yet his eyes were a bold vivid blue, sharp, fiercely intelligent, proclaiming an undaunted spirit despite the weakness of his body. Hooked to an IV and a myriad of wires, he was barely a lump beneath the sheet and the thin white blanket. I guessed he would stand a few inches taller than his wife and daughter, but not by much, and I guessed that he had probably never struck a large figure, physically. His gaze was fearsome, though, as it landed on me, searching, judging, examining, and dismissing before skipping to Claire.

His gaze wavered on Claire for a long, long time, a living, roiling silence enveloping the room. I was aware of two other people in the room, two more women, both younger than Claire. One was a girl barely out of her teens, if that, and the other a few years older, maybe twenty-one or twenty-two. They both strongly resembled Moira, as Claire did, although the younger had brown hair, and Connor's blue eyes, while the older one had Claire's green eyes and hair somewhere between Moira's blonde and what I assumed was Connor's brown—Tabitha, I knew, was the older of the girls, while Hayley was the younger. Tabitha and Hayley both looked like a mixture between Connor and Moira, while Claire resembled only Moira; I saw nothing of Connor in her features at all, except perhaps her slightness of build, which was also true of Moira.

Claire stood stock-still in the middle of the room, clutching her purse and my hand as tightly as she could, barely breathing, staring at her father.

"Dad." It was all she managed, and even that was a broken sound.

"Claire?" Connor blinked. And then his jaw set and his head lifted. "Didn't expect to see you."

"I—I know."

He eyed his wife, then his other two daughters. "Who was it that told her?"

Hayley's jaw set, just like her father's had. "I did, Daddy."

"Why? I said not to."

"She deserved to know."

"That wasn't yours to decide, Hayley." He glanced at me, then at Claire again. "And this is your latest fling, I assume? What is it I've heard the kids say…? The flavor of the month?" He said the last word *moooo-nth*, a sharp ascension on the first syllable.

Claire let out a hurt breath. "Jesus, Dad."

"Do *not* mock the name of the Lord in my presence, girl."

I stepped forward, extending my hand. "My name is Brock Badd. I'm Claire's boyfriend."

He stared at my hand as if it were a snake, and then took it. He squeezed hard, probably as hard as he could, which…wasn't very hard. "Connor Collins."

I wasn't pleased to meet him, not after what he'd done to Claire, and I saw no point in faking the phrase. "Sir." It was all I said, taking my hand back and dipping my chin at him.

Connor flattened his hand on the blanket at his side, and then plucked at the loose threads. "Well, since you're here, I'm assuming Hayley filled you in."

"Only that you were sick."

A scoffing breath. "Sick, she says. Oh yeah, I'm sick all right. I'm dying, is what I am."

Claire blinked hard. "Dad—"

"Terminal cancer. Started in my left leg, in the bone. Spread from there." He flipped away the blanket to reveal that his left leg had been amputated at mid-thigh. "It took my leg, and now it's pretty much everywhere."

"Dad, I'm…I—shit." She rubbed at one eye with

the underside of her wrist.

"Even now you can't be respectful, can you?" Connor bit out.

"Sorry for cursing, I just—when Hayley said you were sick, I know she said cancer, but…"

"Not the man you remember, eh?"

Claire scoffed, much as he had moments ago. "Oh no, you're still very much the man I remember."

Connor's eyes narrowed. "And what's that supposed to mean, then?"

"Just that you're still you, that's all."

"And who else should I be? You think just because the Lord has seen fit to take my life like this that I'm suddenly going to just…*forget* everything? That you can just waltz in here unannounced and that you would just be forgiven?"

Claire laughed openly, mockingly. "Forgiven? *I* would be forgiven?" She shook her head in disbelief. "I don't know what I thought."

"I'm sorry to say, Claire, if it's a reconciliation you're looking for, you won't find it here simply because I'm on my deathbed."

"I don't know what I thought I was looking for," Claire admitted. "But you're right, I should have known nothing could ever soften you. Why should you apologize, or learn compassion, or understanding? Even now, why would you show any of that to me? Stupid of me, as usual."

"*I* should apologize? *I* should learn compassion and understanding?"

"*YES!*" Claire shouted, a sudden, startling, deafening bellow too big to have come from her tiny frame. "I did think maybe you could just…let it all go. I thought maybe staring death in the face might teach you a little *fucking* humanity for once!"

"Claire Brigid Collins—"

"Oh come off it, Dad! Like a couple of F-bombs are going to change anything at this point? It doesn't matter what I say or what I do, you won't ever—" She cut off and shook her head. "Never mind. There's no point."

Hayley and Tabitha were watching this exchange with wide, frightened eyes, and Moira looked as if she was in too much pain to even speak.

"Ever what, Claire?" Connor's voice was low, quiet. "I won't ever what?"

"Nothing." She turned away and tugged at my hand. "Let's go, Brock."

I remained where I was, and she caught up short as I held on to her hand, stopping her. "Not yet."

She stared at me as if I'd betrayed her. "Not yet? You see what I'm dealing with, and you think I should just stick around beating my head against the same wall I've been banging it against my whole life? Why,

Brock? For what? I told you this was a stupid, futile idea. I'm leaving." She yanked away forcefully.

I hauled her back to me, pulling her in close until I could cup her face in both hands. Normally she hated any kind of lovey-dovey touching, but for some reason she allowed this. "Say it, Claire. Tell him." I lowered my voice so only she could hear me. "You won't ever get another chance. Just...*say* it. Any of it—all of it."

"Why?" she breathed, eyes misting. "It won't change him."

"Maybe not, but it'll be off your chest, out of your soul. You've got a lot of shit buried real deep, Claire. I see it. I'm not ever going try and pull it out of you, but I see it." I brushed her cheekbone with my thumb. "Just...say what you came here to say, no matter how hard it may be."

"I fucking hate you."

"I know."

She shook her head. "No, for real, we're fighting."

"Okay. I can accept that. But you're here, so you may as well get it all out there."

"Yes, by all means," Connor said, obviously listening in. "Get it all out there."

Claire hesitated, looking from me to her dad. Then she straightened her spine, lifted her head, and hardened her jaw, a gesture clearly inherited from

Connor. "Fine."

She pulled a chair up to the side of the bed, sat down, and crossed one knee over the other, settling her purse on her lap. I stood behind her, my hands in my hip pockets. "Fine. But no bullshit, and I'm not censoring myself."

"As if you ever have," Connor muttered.

"Oh, I have. You have no idea how much I've censored myself around you." She sucked in a breath, held it, and let out slowly. "Okay, well, the first thing I'd like to say is *fuck you*. You're an arrogant, controlling, heartless bastard, and I hate you." She laughed shakily. "Wow, I've been wanting to say that for years."

Connor seemed stunned speechless. "I knew you harbored some hard feelings, but—"

Claire laughed acidly. "Hard feelings? Yeah, you might say I harbor just a *few* hard feelings, Dad. My whole life I was never good enough. You wanted a son, and you got a daughter, which was the first strike against me. And then I wasn't all nice and sweet and compliant like Mom, which was another strike against me. I have—and have *always* had—a mind of my own, and that didn't fit in with your high and mighty ideal of how a holy and righteous family should be. I should be seen and not heard, sit still and listen, do what I'm told without question, that's what you always said. Hell, when I was…what, twelve?…we got in an argument about something, something I did that you didn't agree with. Which, let's be honest, was everything. I told you I was just thinking for myself. And you know what you said? You told me, you actually *said* in so many words that I shouldn't think for myself. I should just follow along with all your stupid, petty rules like an obedient robot."

"I was trying to teach you right from wrong," Connor interjected. "I was trying to train you up—"

"'Train a child up in the way he should go, and when he is old, he will not depart from it,'" Claire quoted. "Yeah, I remember. What was the other one from Proverbs you liked so much? Oh yeah: 'Spare the rod, spoil the child.' The problem is, you weren't training me, not at that age, and not as I got older. You were *controlling* me. There was no way but *your* way. No choice but what *you* allowed. And it didn't work very well, did it? You tried to train me up in the way *you* thought I should go, and what happened?" She paused for effect, but Connor remained silent. "Yeah, I fucking departed from it, didn't I? And that really steamed your corn, didn't it?"

I tried my damnedest to stifle the snort, but couldn't quite manage it, and everyone turned to look at me. "Sorry, but...Claire, what the heck does that even mean? Steamed his corn?"

Claire craned her neck to glare at me. "Oh shut

up, Brock. Nobody asked you."

I raised my hands in surrender. "Shutting up."

"I blame myself," Connor said, after a moment. "I always have."

"Good. You should."

"I wasn't...I didn't do a good enough job. You didn't learn any of the lessons I was trying to teach."

Claire sat back in the chair. "Even now, you still don't get it, do you? No, I didn't learn any of the lessons, Dad. The only lesson I learned was that you didn't care what I wanted, you didn't care about how I felt. I don't know what you *did* care about—I didn't know then, and I don't know now, but it wasn't me, that's for damn sure."

"Of course I did—"

"Well then you sure had a crazy way of showing it. If I made my bed wrong, I got in trouble. If I got less than an A on any assignment ever, I got in trouble. If I was one single minute late coming home from a friend's house, I got in trouble. And not, like, a talking-to or even a lecture. The tiniest infraction, and you'd beat my ass with that fucking stick of yours."

"It's called spanking, Claire—I hardly think that counts as beating you up."

"I can see spanking being acceptable in tiny doses, for the most major of infractions, and even then the research shows it has a detrimental effect on children. But you *whaled* on me with that stick for the littlest thing, Dad." Claire shook her head, whether disbelieving or merely trying to express the depth of her emotions I wasn't sure. "Every little thing, you spanked me for. And then when I got too old to spank, you grounded me for everything you didn't like. If I dared to so much as express a differing opinion, I was grounded for a week. No friends, no TV, no computer, nothing. What do you think I did all those hours and days and weeks I spent alone in my room, bored out of my fucking head? I sat there stewing, *hating* you."

"You make it seem like all you did was dare to have your own opinion and I locked you in a dungeon," Connor argued. "You cursed at me, you shouted at me, you refused to listen to the slightest thing I said. If I told you to pick up your room, you made a worse mess. If I told you to stay away from a certain boy, you dated him to spite me. You did literally the opposite of everything I said, no matter what it was, or why I may have said it."

"Yeah, because I hated you at that point, because I'd been spanked and grounded and shouted at and lectured to and made to feel inconsequential, like a nuisance. You never hugged me, never sat me on your lap and read me stories. You sat me on the couch and preached at me. You read fucking Second Timothy to me, as if a six-year-old girl is supposed to care about any of that. I wanted to play Barbie's, or read a *kid's* book with my dad. Or play. And you wanted to lecture me about grace and mercy and the fruits of the damn spirit."

"That's hardly fair—"

"It's more than fair! I was a little girl!"

"I was doing my best!"

"Then your best was complete shit, and you shouldn't have had kids."

Ho-ly shit. I winced as Claire said that, because even from her, that was harsh.

"Claire, now *really*—" Moira started.

"Shut up, Mom," Claire snapped. "You don't get a say in this. You never stood by me, you never tried to soften *anything* he ever said or did to me, and you never even *tried* to mitigate the insane punishments Dad handed down, no matter how minor my fuck up was."

Moira's jaw snapped closed and she stared at Claire, taken aback.

"Yeah, I'm pissed. Brock wanted me to clear the air because he thinks it might…I don't know, soothe my troubled spirit or some shit." She glanced at her mom and then her dad. "So yeah, I'm gonna unload with both barrels. I told you, I'm not censoring myself."

"That hardly seems a reasonable excuse for the vile language you're using."

"Yeah, well, deal with it. You lost any input as to how I talk when you disowned me for having a miscarriage."

"It's far more complicated than that," Moira said, "and I don't think we need to bring that up right now."

Claire jabbed a finger at her mother. "I told *you* to shut up. And yes, we *do* need to bring it up. Although you're right, it is far more complicated than that. It wasn't the miscarriage; it was everything to do with who I am…who I was. That miscarriage was the end of everything. Right when I needed my parents the most, you kicked me out on the street. I needed love and support and understanding…I'd just experienced one of the worst things a woman can go through, and you never even stopped to find out what fucking happened. You just tossed me out of the house without so much as a how-do-you-do. I was still fucking bleeding, and you packed me a backpack and told me to leave.

"I walked, alone, still bleeding, to the hospital, and told them I'd had a miscarriage. I was given a D-and-C, *alone*. Nobody to hold my hand, nobody to tell me it was going to be okay." She choked, gasped, and had to breathe a moment. I held her hand over her shoulder, squeezing as she began again. "I was twenty years old, and it was my birthday."

"Claire—" Connor began.

"*No*," Claire snapped, her voice a rattlesnake hiss. "You shut your *goddamn* mouth."

Connor's mouth closed abruptly, and he blinked hard.

"You wanna know how I got pregnant? I messed up, Dad. That's how. I was nineteen years old, and I went to a party, got drunk, and had sex with a guy I didn't know. I don't even really remember it. It was a stupid, innocent, childish mistake. It was a mistake people make all the time. A simple, stupid mistake, and it changed everything. It fucked up my whole life and I don't even remember it." Claire let out a breath, pausing to collect herself once more.

"I told myself it was fine," she eventually continued. "I pretended I was fine. Pretended it never happened. And then a few weeks later, I realized I was pregnant. I was a virgin and I didn't have a boyfriend, I'd had no plans on sleeping with anyone, so I wasn't on birth control. I didn't know what to do. I couldn't tell anyone. I—I was terrified. I didn't want it, I—what was I supposed to do? I couldn't afford an abortion. I know, I tried—I couldn't get the money. I even tried to steal it from you guys, but you didn't have enough cash. I couldn't—I couldn't do anything. So I hid it. I'd sneak trash bags into my room and puke into them as quietly as I could in the morning. I...*fuck*—I cried myself to sleep every night. Every night, for weeks. For *months*. I was totally alone.

"And then...on my twentieth birthday, you guys all went to mass, and I stayed home. I was sick. I actually was sick, too, but it was just morning sickness, not a virus like I'd told you. I was three months pregnant, and I couldn't handle going to church, not after what I'd been through, what I was *still* going through, and that morning I just...I felt like total hell. So I stayed home. So then at one point I went to the bathroom, and I felt this cramp, and then it got worse, and I started bleeding everywhere. I couldn't stop it, and it hurt—" She faltered, her voice breaking. "It hurt so *fucking* bad. I bled everywhere, for so long. I thought I was gonna die. And then you guys came home, and I couldn't even get off the floor. I could barely move. It hurt, it hurt, god, it hurt so bad. I still remember how bad it hurt, and I've never felt anything that bad before or since. I was relieved, too, but I was scared I was dying, and I was in complete and total agony. And then you came home, found me on the bathroom floor, and you realized I'd had a miscarriage."

"Claire—"

"*I'm not finished,*" Claire snarled, her voice a low, cold, vicious hiss. "Did you comfort me? Did you help me get cleaned up? Did you ask what happened? No.

You told me to get out. You called me a *whore*. You called me a *slut*. You threw me out of your house. You didn't let me get so much as a word in. You just threw me out on the street."

Connor had tears running down his cheeks.

"You'd better cry, you *bastard*," Claire snapped. "Your little girl, your oldest daughter—you called me a whore and disowned me, and threw me out on the street. I'd lost so much blood I was dizzy, and you kicked me out! I walked alone to the hospital, blood still coating my thighs, still in agonizing pain, and got a D-and-C. I slept in the hospital that night, and at Lindsey's house the next night. I didn't tell her what happened, just that I couldn't go home."

"Claire, please—" Connor started.

She shook her head, standing up abruptly. "No. You don't get to talk to me." She jabbed a finger at him. "*That's* what really happened. That's why I became the person I am today. I turned to heavy drinking and casual sex, because I figured if my dad assumed I was a slut, I obviously was one, so I might as well become one. So I did."

"Claire—"

"I just don't even understand how, seeing me in a *pool* of my own *blood,* you wouldn't comfort me, or help me, or show me love, or at least to stop and ask a few simple questions. Like oh, hey Claire, looks like you're bleeding to death. As your mother and father, how can we show you the bare minimum of human decency and kindness? I mean shit, Dad, you're a fucking *deacon* in the Catholic church. I'd think you of all people would be required to act like a human fucking being. But no." She stood up, staring coldly down at her father. "I'd have gotten more mercy and compassion from Satan himself than I got from my own parents that day."

Connor covered his face with his hands. "Claire, I'm sorry."

She snorted derisively. "Yeah, you are. You're a sorry piece of shit, Connor."

I slid the chair out of the way and wrapped my arms around her. "Claire."

She snapped her gaze up to mine. "What, you still think I should forgive him? After what you just heard?"

I swallowed hard. "Yes. I do."

She blinked at me in shock. "How can you say that, Brock?"

"I told you from the very beginning that this wasn't about him, or for him. It's about *you*, for *you*."

"I don't get you, Brock." She shook her head. "I thought you'd understand."

"I do. As much as anyone can, I do."

"Then how can you want me to forgive him for

what he did?"

I pulled her aside and murmured my words so only she could hear me. "Because you don't forgive people for them, but for yourself. You can't move on with your life until you do. You'll always hang on to the hurt, the anger, the pain." I sighed and wiped my face with both hands. "I know I sound like Yoda, or the Pope, or something, but it's true. Anger will consume you. It *has* been consuming you. And now with your dad terminally ill, you're out of time. I'm not saying you should hug it out or try to start some lovey-dovey daddy-daughter relationship. Just that you make the conscious choice to forgive him, for your own peace of mind. And that's it."

"You go to church, Brock?" Claire asked.

I shook my head. "Nah. Never been. This isn't about God or the church or the Bible, or even being a good person or anything like that. It's about finding a peace of mind I don't think you've ever had since that bitter day, and you may not ever have it if you don't move past this."

She rested her head on my chest. "And this is the only way?"

I nodded. "The only way I know."

She pushed off me, and stared past me at her father. For a long, long time, she just stared at him, and he stared back, his gaze open, tears running freely down his face. Claire's mother sat staring at her hands, and her sisters were huddled together, looking shell-shocked.

Eventually Claire stepped past me and stood over her father's bed. "I can't. I just can't. I don't know how—I just don't know how to get to a place where I can forgive the way you completely and totally betrayed me. I probably never will be able to. You ruined me, Connor."

"Claire—" he sobbed. "I—please, just—"

"No. You lost any right to speak to me ever again, to call yourself my father." She whirled around, away from him. "You can go fuck yourself, Connor Collins." She pushed past me. "Let's go, Brock."

I followed her out of the room, and down the hall to the bank of elevators. She jabbed the call button several times, furiously, and I stood near her but not touching her. I heard running footsteps on the tile floor behind us, and saw Tabitha approaching.

"Claire, wait," she called out, as the elevator doors opened.

Claire stood in the doorway so the elevator couldn't close. "Hey, Tab. Sorry you had to hear that."

Tabitha slammed into her sister, wrapping her arms around Claire and clinging to her fiercely. "Don't leave, Claire."

"I can't be around him, Tabby-cat. I just can't."

"He's *dying*, Claire. Another week or two at most."

"Call me when he dies. I'll come to the funeral."

Tab blinked at her sister. "You're really not going to come back?"

"Why? I see him, and I—I'm back there, in that bathroom, hearing him call me whore and slut and telling me to leave and never come back. That's all he'll ever be to me." Claire pushed her sister away, out of reach. "At least this way we can have a relationship again."

"I love you, Claire. I'm so, so sorry you went through that."

"Yeah, me too, Tab. Me too." Claire moved her foot so the elevator doors could slide closed between Tabitha and us. "I'll see you."

Tabitha's last look was at me and, unless I was mistaken, it was a silent plea for me to try to convince Claire to go back before her father died.

That would be easier said than done.

FOUR

Claire

HE STOOD BESIDE ME IN THE ELEVATOR, HIS SHOULDER brushing against mine.

I wished he could see how badly I needed him right then. I was crumbling inside. Collapsing. Shattering.

Seeing Dad—seeing *Connor* had brought everything back, had unearthed the boiling maelstrom of emotions and turmoil I'd worked so hard for so long to repress. Talking about what had happened...it was wrecking me. I was incapable of expressing that, however, and Brock didn't seem to see it.

"Claire, babe—"

I felt myself resorting to anger, because I had nothing else to rely on. "Oh shove it, Brock," I snapped. "I don't wanna fucking hear it."

"Claire, just listen to me for a second."

I wanted to listen to him—god, I wanted to. I wanted to crawl into his arms and let him carry me, let him hold me, let him tell me it was gonna be okay. But I couldn't say that. I just didn't know how. I was scared and all I had was anger, the same anger that had festered inside me for so long. My anger was my shield, but it was my nemesis, too. I had to feed it or the tenuous control I had on life would be gone forever. My anger was propping me up inside, and if I let it all collapse, I'd never recover. So I used the anger and let it flow through me, as Emperor Palpatine might have said.

I whirled on Brock and glared up at him. "I don't want to hear one fucking word from you, Brock. I didn't want to come here. I didn't want to see him. I didn't want to talk about this shit. Yet here I am, and what have I gotten? Nothing but more hurt, nothing but being told, again, that I am worth nothing. These people have turned me into someone I barely know and, for the last fucking time, I don't want to talk about it."

He stayed silent, following me to the parking lot

and to our rental car. I rounded the hood to stand on the driver's side. "I'm driving."

He eyed me for a long moment, and then tossed me the keys. He said nothing, just sank into the passenger seat as I cranked the engine. He barely had the door closed before I was backing out of the space and then peeling rubber to fishtail out of the parking lot. Brock appeared relaxed, even as I swung far too fast out of the hospital lot and onto Thirteen Mile Road. I didn't have far go before I reached my first destination; Tip-Top Liquor. I skidded to a halt diagonally between two parking spaces, threw the vehicle into park, and leaped out. Brock waited, seeming to know better at that moment than to follow me. I bought a fifth of Patrón Silver and tossed it to Brock as I slid behind the wheel again. More squealing tires as I peeled out of the lot and onto Thirteen Mile again, heading for Woodward Avenue. I barely slowed down and certainly didn't look as I skidded sideways around the right turn onto Woodward, and this time even Brock held on to the oh-shit bar and braced as we barely missed a Smart Bus and then two pedestrians crossing the street.

"Slow down, Claire," Brock said through gritted teeth. "This isn't going to help anything."

"Shut up, Brock."

"You're going to get us killed at worst, pulled

over at best. Slow down."

I ignored him, weaving through traffic with the pedal mashed down. It wasn't even noon on a weekday, so when we got to Scotia Park, not far from where my parents still lived, the park was empty. I parked the Mustang, snatched the bottle from Brock, and stormed across the park to the set of mini-bleachers placed randomly near a towering pair of maple trees, which shaded the metal bleachers from the worst of the sun. I sat down on the bleachers, uncorked the Patrón, and took a giant four-gulp swig straight from the bottle, hissing as I swallowed the last gulp.

Brock joined me a few seconds later, leaning back to brace his elbows on the riser behind us. "Not saying I don't understand, but getting day-wasted isn't going to change anything."

"Nope," I agreed. "But then, I'm not trying to change anything."

"Then what is this about?"

"This is about me wanting to get completely obliterated so I don't have to remember any of this in the morning."

"Also not going to work."

"Yeah, since when are you an expert in any of this?"

He breathed out a long, heavy sigh. "There are few things I haven't told you, or anyone."

"Like what?"

He eyed me. "Cork the bottle and open up to me a little, and I'll tell you."

I pulled on the bottle again, twice more. "Fuck you."

"I know what you're doing, Claire."

"Oh yeah, smart guy? What's that?"

"Trying to hurt me. Push me away. This is all too much for you to handle, and you're freaking out, and you don't know what to do." He slid closer to me. I stiffened, because I could smell him and his smell always made me want to burrow into him. "You hold so much in, Claire. Talk to me."

Fuck. The tequila was having its way with me, singing through my blood and erasing my inhibitions as swiftly as only tequila could; I should have gotten a bottle of Grey Goose instead...vodka wouldn't betray me like this.

"I don't trust you," I said, hating how the words toppled out of me, evading my attempts to keep them in as the tequila pushed them out. "And I trust myself even less."

"Why don't you trust yourself?"

I shook my head. "Oh no, you're not gonna take advantage of me like this."

"What do you mean, Claire?" He sounded so puzzled.

"You know what tequila does to me."

"Actually I don't. We haven't gotten tequila hammered together yet."

"It makes me all...truthy." I could feel my head swelling, my brain fogging—I was feeling the six or seven shots I'd had in less than five minutes. "It also does like it says in that one song. You know which one I mean?"

He laughed. "'Tequila Makes Her Clothes Fall Off?'"

I nodded, and knew I was already sloppy. So fuck it, right? I took another shot or three. "Yep, that one. It does that. And it also makes me prone to say pretty much anything."

"Like what?"

I shook my head. "Oh no. No way, José. Nice try."

Another chuckle, and I realized he'd somehow managed to pull a fast one on me, sneaking the bottle away from me. Probably for the best. I didn't pack much mass, so it didn't take much for me to get blitzed, and I'd had a lot very quickly.

"You're gonna have your hands full pretty soon, Brocky-baby," I said, laughing. "I'm a lunatic when I'm tequila wasted."

"Oh joy," Brock deadpanned.

"Like this one time, Mara and I were at this bar, our favorite bar in San Francisco. Someone bought a round of tequila, and that led to another and then all of a sudden I was topless in the bathroom, going down on two guys at once. Not even sure how I ended up there, honestly, it was just…one tequila, two tequila, three tequila—and then *bam*, dicks in my mouth. But I was like whatever, and I finished them both off."

"Jesus, Claire."

"Not sure even he can help me, at this point." I glanced at him, and if this was a cartoon, Brock would have steam spouting from his ears and his face would be beet red. "Oh, are you jealous?" I asked, mocking. "Poor Brock."

He growled. "You've never been anything less than honest about your past, and I've never been anything less than totally accepting."

"Oh, I'm supposed to apologize for being a slut, now? That's not even the worst story I could tell you. There's the time I took a week off of work and went down to Acapulco by myself. I don't think I wore clothes at all that week. I don't remember much except being wasted the whole time and doing a lot of blow and sucking a lot of cock." I watched his reaction. "You don't like these stories, do you?"

"No, Claire, I don't." He stared hard at me. "I don't like hearing about you sucking off other guys, whether it's one or a hundred."

Brock lapsed into a stony, pissed off silence.

Whatever.

"Actually, I think there's a video of me from that week up on YouPorn. One of the guys recorded some shit and put it up with the amateur stuff. I checked it out later. Can't really tell it's me though, because I had my hair dyed bright neon purple and I had a shit-load of makeup on." I laughed. "It's kinda hot, actual-ly. I was wearing a push-up bra, so with the downward angle of the camera, it actually looked like I had tits for once."

"Claire, come on."

"What? I'm sure you've seen that shit before."

He shrugged. "Sure."

"Never done it, though?"

He frowned at me. "Hell, no." A shake of his head. "That shit is degrading."

"Not if she's into it. If she lets it happen voluntarily."

"That just smacks of self-esteem issues to me."

I snorted. "Well, no shit. Obviously. That's the entire point. She does that shit because it feeds her need for attention. She likes guys doing that shit to her because then it's at least guys finding her attrac-tive. And if they want to blow their load on her face, then fine, but that's her choice. It's not degrading if she chooses it."

He hesitated before answering. "I don't know if

I agree."

I stared at him—my view of him was spinning, now. "So then, that time in Seattle in my apartment, when you came all over my chest, that was you degrading me?"

"That's different."

"How?"

"It wasn't your face, and it was just me."

"So it's different when it's four guys and I get come on my face rather than my tits?"

"Yeah, it's different. I value you, Claire, which is more than those guys did."

I was really dizzy now and the world was spinning around me but I did manage to ask a question I'd asked myself many times before now. "If I'm not worth shit to my own father, who should I be worth shit to?"

"Me?" Brock asked.

"Yeah, *now*."

"Yeah, now," Brock echoed. "And no story you could tell me is gonna change that."

"Not even if I tell you I got DP'd?"

Brock winced. "No, Claire."

I was so dizzy, now. "I've been a bad girl, Brock. Done a lot of bad, bad things. And you're saying none of it matters to you?"

"Of course it matters. It matters a lot. I wish to

fuck I could go back and make you see your worth so you wouldn't have done any of it. So you'd have some self-respect."

"Yeah, well…you're too late. None of that self-respect mumbo-jumbo matters to me. I'm just little ol' slutty Claire Collins, whore-extraordinaire."

He palmed my cheek, and I opened my eyes to see his close to mine, burning with sincerity. "No, Claire. It's never too late."

"Oh, you're gonna save me, is that it? I'm a pity project. Save Claire, the slut with a heart of gold." I took on a deep, mocking tone of voice. "'I'm Brock, and I'm gonna love Claire so good she'll stop being a whore and have some self-respect for once in her whore life, because I'm fucking *magical!*'" I blew a raspberry. "Get over yourself, Brock. I'm un-save-able and not worth saving."

He didn't have an answer for that.

I tried to sit up, and discovered that superdrunki-ness had snuck up on me while I was babbling about my whorish past. "Damn." I grabbed at Brock. "Can you help your drunk whore of a girlfriend to the car?" He stood up, bent over, and scooped me up in his arms. I nuzzled against his chest, unable to stop my-self. "Wanna know a secret?" I mumbled.

"Yes."

I felt him bend and lower me into the car—I

wasn't sure how he got the door open while holding me, though. I grabbed onto his neck so he couldn't stand upright, and I whispered into his ear. "I know I act like a hard-ass bitch, but I'm not. I just don't know how to stop pretending I don't give a fuck." I bit his earlobe, *hard*, and he grunted in surprise. "Another secret, since I'm all truthy on tequila? I really, *really* want you to fuck me like the dirty slut I am, and do every dirty thing there is to me. I need it, and I'm scared you won't give it to me. And I also want you to keep doing all those sweet, tender, princess-y things for me even though I act like I hate them. I don't—I love them. I just hate that I love them, because I'm not worthy of them, or of you." I kissed his earlobe where I'd bitten him hard enough to leave an angry red mark. "I'm gonna pass out now, and when I wake up I'm gonna pretend I never said any of that."

"I know."

"Will you forget?"

The car was moving, and the window was open, letting in a sweet, cool breeze. "Not a chance," I heard Brock say.

"Promise?"

I felt him take my hand in his, and I let myself hold on to him, for my heart's sake, not because I was so dizzy the world felt like it was wobbling like a spinning top losing momentum. "Yes, Claire. I promise I won't forget."

"I'm gonna be a pain in the ass about this, I hope you know."

"I know."

I rested my head on the side of the door, next to the open window, closing my eyes, feeling myself sliding into unconsciousness. "Hey…Brock?"

"Yeah, honey?"

"I'm sorry."

"For what?"

"This."

"Don't be."

"I am, though."

"I'll let you make it up to me."

"With blowjobs?"

He laughed, squeezing my hand. "I'll think of something."

I sighed, and focused on not puking. "'Kay. Bye."

Hello darkness, my old friend.

⌣

Oh my god.

I knew this would happen.

Ouch. My head hurt so bad I could hardly open my eyes.

Shit, goddammit, and motherfucker.

Ow, ow, ow, ow.

I slowly cracked my eyes open. I was in the hotel room, so that was good. In bed, also good. Still in my clothes. A glance at the window showed darkness beyond, and a glance at the clock showed that it was 5:55 a.m. Why the fuck was I awake at 5:55 a.m.? I never wake up this early; I'm a computer programmer and I do my best to work late at night.

Brock was in bed beside me, knees drawn up, turned away from me, spine curved into a broad, hard arc. There was a bottle of mineral water on the bedside table, a packet of aspirin, and a handwritten note beneath my cell phone. I took the aspirin with half the bottle of water, and read the note.

Claire,

I really, really, REALLY like you. A lot.

Also, I'm not trying to save you.

Furthermore, I'm not trying to change you.

Additionally, you're sexy. Even passed out drunk, you take my breath away.

And finally, you can totally make this up to me with lots of random BJs. Or, if you'd prefer, we can just agree that shit happens, and that there's nothing to make up for. Either way, I'm in this with you, good or bad, no matter what. So don't freak out, okay?

Okay, so there's maybe one more thing: It's going to be fine, I promise.

Yours, because I want to be,

B

I read the note three or four times and tried to convince myself that I wasn't crying. But I was just bullshitting myself. I was crying. In fact, I was bawling my eyes out. Get a grip, Claire. You don't do crying. What is it about this guy that brings all this stuff out of me?

On top of it all I felt like shit because I was hungover as all fuck, and also upset at myself, and at Connor—since I refused to acknowledge the bastard as my father ever again—and at Brock for being so damn sweet when I just wanted him to either fuck me like I want to be fucked, or just get it over with and leave me already.

Having been hungover like this a time or two before, I'd discovered one surefire way of getting rid of a nasty hangover; it sucked, but it was effective. I changed into my workout clothes—a pair of tight red yoga shorts that didn't really even cover my ass all the way, and a yellow sports bra. I laced up my Brooks, and headed down to the gym.

I did leave Brock a note, however, written on the back of his, and tucked it under his cell phone:

Brock,

Running away from my hangover. (In the gym, I mean.)

We can talk about the contents of the reverse side of this note when I get back.

Yours, assuming you still want me to be,

C

I found the gym and the treadmill, turned on my running playlist, cranked the speed up as high as I could handle it, and ran like a girl running away from problems, and herself, and the world, and her mixed-up and stupid feelings for her man, and all the other bullshit. So, yeah, you can't get very far away from that shit on a treadmill, but that's not the point. You can't get very far from your problems even on a jet, because your problems are inside you. Unless your problems have something to do with the law or the mafia, in which case running might do SOME good.

Running while hungover really sucks. It hurts, you wanna puke the whole time, and you're never quite sure you're not gonna actually just die. But the longer you run, the more you sweat, the better you start to feel, in a backward sort of way. Eventually the hangover is replaced by the normal pain of *why the fuck did I decide to run ten miles?* It's stupid, but it works.

When my Garmin told me I'd hit ten miles in an hour and a half, I smashed the stop button and slowed to a stop as the belt halted under me. I stood on it gasping, clinging to the handles as I caught my wind, dripping sweat, and no longer quite as hungover as I'd been when I first got here.

Stumbling back to our room, I found Brock still asleep, this time on his back, arm over his head, mouth slack, his hair a mess, and a monster hard-on bulging the front of his underwear. Shit...if I wasn't a sweaty disaster, I'd have woken him up with the first of my apology BJs.

I spun on the hot water, stripped out of my running clothes, dragged a brush through my hair, and then squirted toothpaste onto my travel toothbrush and went after my furry teeth. As is my habit, I wandered around as I brushed my teeth, since I get restless just standing at the sink staring at myself in the mirror. I ended up at the window, the curtains pulled open a few inches, enough that I could see out onto the dark, empty Birmingham street below.

I didn't hear him, didn't even sense him until his hands slid around my midsection. I jumped about a foot, and squealed while trying to keep the foamy toothpaste in my mouth. "Gah-dammmmih, Brock!"

He laughed, a low amused chuckle in my ear. "Startled you, huh?"

"No shih, a-hoh."

His hands slid up to cup my tits, and I moaned as he lavished attention on them, squeezing, kneading, and thumbing my ultrasensitive nipples. And then he shifted closer, and I realized he was naked now, and still as hard as a rock.

I went back to brushing, and then stopped after a few brushstrokes. "Brock? Whah are you doing?"

"Showing you that I absolutely want you to be mine."

"I'm bruffing my teeh," I protested.

"So?"

He used one hand to continue playing with my tits, and the other slid down to my pussy, two fingers finding my clit, flicking, and then slipping into me, curling, gathering the gush of wetness that was suddenly but not unexpectedly flooding through me. His cock was a hard rod against my ass, hot and thick and soft. His hands worked me into a furor as swiftly as only Brock could, bringing me to knee-weakening climax in a minute, two at the most, and he pushed me over the edge, pinching my nipple between his finger and thumb and squeezing in sync with my gasping groans of release.

I had a mouthful of toothpaste, which was now dribbling down my chin and onto my chest, and onto my wrist, and I was still holding my toothbrush.

Brock laughed and guided me to the bathroom, pressed me up against the sink, and I bent, spat, and rinsed my mouth, then used a washcloth to dry my face.

I waited for Brock to take me to the bed, but he didn't. He kept me pinned up against the sink. "Brock?"

I was still quivery from my orgasm, and his eyes were fiery with need, his cock a tease between the upper swell of my ass cheeks.

He slid his fingers into me. "How about one more, first?"

I gripped the edge of the counter. "I wouldn't argue."

He went more slowly, this time. Teasing my clit, tweaking my nipples, sliding his fingers into me, then out to circle, never giving me a rhythm I could sink into. This time, as I drew closer, he slowed and changed his pattern, keeping me from the edge. Again and again, he got me to the point of flexing my hips and whimpering, and then he'd do something different.

"Brock, please."

"I like it when you ask nicely," he murmured, meeting my eyes in the mirror.

I smiled at his reflection. "Oh yeah?" I slid my ass against his cock. "Please, Brock. Please?"

"That's hot." He had me almost there again. "Please what, though? Some specifics might be helpful."

"Let me come," I breathed, grinding into his fingers as he squelched them in and out of me, letting his thumb rock against my clit.

"Just let you come?" he teased, pressing his cock against me suggestively. "That's all you want?"

"No, no…I want to come around your cock. Put it in me, Brock. Right now. Please."

He kissed my shoulder, a soft, sweet, gentle gesture that had my heart twisting and leaping. "Put it in you, and then what, Claire?"

I felt my heart skip a beat. "Fuck me, Brock."

He kissed my other shoulder. "You taste like sweat."

"I was running."

"I know." He kissed the back of my neck. "I like this, taking you like this, while you're all sweaty."

"It's not gross?"

"Would you fuck me after a workout, if I was the one all sweaty?" he asked.

"Without hesitation," I answered.

"There you go, then." He kissed behind my ear, his tongue flicking, tasting. Another kiss, to my nape, and I shuddered. "So you want…this?"

He put both hands on my shoulders and pressed me downward, toward the counter. I went willingly, and he kissed me as I bent over, his lips and tongue sliding over my skin, tasting my skin and my sweat. And then I felt him slide two fingers against my pussy, seeking my opening. I felt him touch the broad, hard head of his cock against my slit, and I arched my back and groaned as he slid into me, slowly.

"This is what you want, isn't it, Claire?"

"Fuck yes. Just like this."

He pulled me backward by the hips and I grabbed onto the edge of the counter, pushing back against him as I bent over the counter. I swallowed hard and gasped in pleasure as his massive cock filled my tight pussy. God, oh god. So good. So fucking good, the way he felt. His hands slid up my body to cup my boobs, and now, with his dick inside me and at the edge of orgasm, my nipples were more sensitive than ever, and my nips were always insanely sensitive.

He met my eyes in the mirror. "Fuck me, Claire. You do it. Show me how you like to be fucked."

I closed my eyes momentarily, relishing the ache of his cock inside me, stretching to a burning throb, and then opened them, meeting his eyes. And then I did what he said: I showed him how I like to be fucked. I used the counter for leverage, shoving my ass back against him, taking him deep and then twerking away to slide him out. Starting slow, I built up speed steadily until I was undulating against Brock as hard and fast as I could. His hands clutched my tits the whole time, and yet he didn't move with me. He just let me fuck him.

And then, as I neared the edge all over again and felt him shuddering and heard him gasping, he grabbed my hips and halted me. "Wait," he murmured.

"What?" I demanded. "I was close."

"Me too." He growled as he pulled away from me.

"Then what are you doing?" I felt desperate, needing in this moment at least that connection with him, to keep at bay all the shit I was refusing to think about.

"Making you wait."

"Why?"

He just smiled at me, a secret, amused, thoughtful

little smile. He pulled out of me completely, spun me around, and brought my hand to his cock. I slid my fist around him, eying him. "You wanna come on my tits? Is that it?"

"Could be fun."

He was up to something.

"How about my face?" I remembered yesterday's drunken admissions all too well; maybe that's what this was about. I dropped to my knees and stroked his cock with both hands. "You wanna shoot your load all over my face?"

He let me touch him, but he didn't answer. And I was losing the edge of my orgasm; this wasn't what I wanted. I wanted to be touched, to be fucked, to be held, to be taken, to have Brock all around me, blocking out the world.

"Is this what you want, Claire?" he asked, almost as if he could read my mind.

I kept stroking him with both hands and didn't answer.

"Is it?" he repeated.

"No."

He lifted me to my feet, grabbed my wrists to slow my touch. His other hand went between my legs, and he touched me. I widened my stance so he could access my clit, and access it he did, flicking and stroking until I was at the verge again, involuntarily squeezing and stroking his cock as I flexed my hips with the rhythm of his flicking fingers.

"What do you want, Claire?" he asked, slowing until I started to lose the edge.

"Don't stop, Brock, please."

"Then tell me what you want." With one hand he gripped my wrists, keeping me from caressing his length, and with the other he teased me, edging me, keeping me from coming but always near the edge.

"Tell you what I want?" I leaned back against the edge of the counter. "Why?"

"I want to know."

"Why do you want to know?"

"Because I want this to be more than just good fucking, Claire. I want this be *real*. And if you never tell me what you really want, then it can't ever be real."

Oh god. Oh god. I was so close, and I had an image of what I wanted, but the words were stuck. He would hate it. He would think it was stupid, and embarrassing. He wouldn't do it. He would call me a freak, a slut.

"Tell me, Claire."

"No."

"Why not?"

"Because you won't want to do it. And you'll—"

"Try me. Have I judged you for anything yet?"

"No, but—"

"Then try me, Claire." Three fingers then, finger-fucking me, giving it to me hard and fast, squelching in and out wetly, curling just so, pushing me to the edge of what I was sure was going to be an actual squirting orgasm, and he knew it, too, because that's exactly what he was going for.

"I'm scared to tell you," I whispered.

"Why?"

I couldn't answer. Didn't answer.

He leaned against me, sucked my breast into his mouth, flicked his tongue against my nipple, rocking his hand against me so his fingers fucked me and the heel of his palm struck my clit just the way I needed it.

"Why, Claire?"

I felt it break over me, then, and I couldn't help answering, the words were just ripped out of me as the climax battered through me like a tornado. "Because I'm afraid of falling in love with you, goddammit!" I shouted. "And I'm afraid if you know the things I want, you'll leave me!"

I felt myself break open on his hand, everything inside me clamping and clenching as a wall of blasting heat crashed through me, and I felt my orgasm wrench something free, something wet that I was afraid was pee squirting out of me beyond my control. I sank my teeth into Brock's shoulder to muffle a scream as I came like a lightning bolt searing through me, and he didn't relent, but kept driving me through the orgasm, kept me in it, weltering in the primal, coruscating ecstasy of an orgasm like no other.

"Tell me what you want, Claire," he murmured, his lips nuzzling my ear.

"Open the curtains and press me up against the window and fuck me," I whispered. "Fuck me as hard as you can. Fuck me until you come inside me, bare, and then force me down to my knees and watch me lick your cock clean."

"Holy shit," he breathed.

"Yeah. I told you, I like—"

He put his hand over my mouth, and his fingers smelled like my pussy. "Claire? Shut up."

He whirled me around and gave me a surprisingly forceful shove toward the window.

HOLY SHIT.

Oh my god, holy shit, and kill me dead—he was going to do it? No way, no way, no way.

Yes way.

I reached the window, and he shoved the curtains aside. Below, the city was waking up, a few early risers passing back and forth on their way to work. My heart was crashing in my chest, and not just from the intensity of the orgasm. I was still shuddering from it, and it would only take the slightest touch to set me off again.

The window was huge; nearly floor to ceiling, and our room was on the second floor.

He pressed me up against the glass, my tits smashing flat against the cold window. I reached up to hold the frame, and then lost my ability to breathe as Brock slid himself into me, grinding deep, impaled to the hilt inside me. Oh…fuck.

This was real. Up against a window, in broad daylight. Brock behind me, the city before me, a wakening city full of lots of wealthy people—this was Birmingham, after all, one of the wealthiest towns in Michigan. His cock drilled into me, and I groaned in bliss.

"Like this?" he demanded, pounding into me.

"Fuck yeah, god yes, Brock, just like this."

He reached up, took both of my hands in his without missing a beat, and pinned my wrists behind my back with one of his strong hands, using the leverage of my arms to press me harder against the window, and then pulled me a few steps away from the window so I was bent forward against it, just my face and tits against the cold glass. He grabbed my hip at the crease and pulled me backward into his thrusts, keeping my hands pinned hard. Not painful, but firm, and with no chance I could get away.

Oh, Jesus.

I whimpered as he fucked me, and the whimpers became shrieks, and then the shrieks became outright screams. Because he was fucking me so good, so hard, harder than he'd ever fucked me, and he was doing it up against a window.

"Brock!" I screamed.

"You like this, Claire?"

"So fucking much."

"You gonna come again for me?"

"Oh yeah, baby, I'm gonna come again, so hard..."

"Look out there," he murmured. "All the people walking by. What if someone looks up right now?"

I groaned, the image turning me on even more.

"Oh god, oh god—oh *fuck*," I groaned, and I felt it shear through me, another blistering, boiling orgasm. "Brock, keep fucking me. Come with me!"

I felt his grip tighten and his thrusts took on renewed power, and then he released my hands and I immediately reached up to grab his hair, and his hands cupped my breasts, and then one slid down to my pussy, and his touch was unnecessary but incredible, pushing me past mere orgasm into something else, into a screaming paroxysm I couldn't control, and he was grunting in my ear, snarling, fucking me with relentless fury, pounding into me so hard our slapping flesh was audible even over my screams and his hoarse grunts.

And then I felt him come, felt him drive into me with sudden grinding power unlike anything before from him, and I felt his come shoot into me, flood through me, and he fucked me again with another spurt of wetness and heat, and again, and again. He lifted my thigh, sliding his touch down to behind my knee as he raised my leg up, and he braced my foot against the window frame, and kept fucking me, twice more, three times, grunting in my ear.

"Pull out, Brock," I breathed.

He bent at the knees, drawing himself out of me, and I stood like that, one foot braced on the window frame, and Brock's come dripping out of me.

And then Brock put his hands on my shoulders and pressed me down to my knees. Brock: naked, cock still hard and jutting up, rigid and glistening wet, his abs furrowed and his chest broad, his shoulders round, his biceps carved from marble, his face out of a magazine, his hair messy. I stared up at him, saw him like that, and I nearly came again, just looking at him. He was, very literally, a god, or an angel. Fucking gorgeous beyond belief. So beautiful my breath caught.

I cupped his heavy balls in both hands and licked him from root to tip, tasting his musky come and my own tart, smoky scent. I took him into my mouth, and then backed away, and licked him again. A bead of come seeped out of him and slid down the side of his dick, and I licked that away, too.

I knelt in front of him and tilted his cock forward, and I took him all the way into my mouth, looking up at him.

He met my eyes, and then wrapped a palm around my ass and jerked me up against him, smashing me hard against his muscular body. "Was that what you wanted?"

I searched his eyes. "Yes," I said, not seeing judgment or anger, only satisfaction and lust…and something else, something hot and possessive and thoughtful and intense. "You?"

"That was new for me," he said. "But it was hot as fuck."

"It was new for me, too. That's why I wanted it."

His lips met mine, and now he tasted our mingled essences, transferred from his cock to my lips to his mouth. The kiss was demanding, deep and drowning, until my breath left me.

"Brock…" I gasped.

"What, babe?"

"Thank you."

"For what?"

"Everything," I said. "For—"

I broke off, realizing I'd been hearing something

for a while now. A buzzing sound. I glanced over at the bedside table, and caught the end of my phone's on-silent vibration pattern. Who would be calling me before seven in the morning?

Oh.

Right.

Brock fetched my phone and brought it to me without looking at it. Respecting my privacy, the wonderful, crazy, absurd gentleman.

My heart scudded in my chest as I thumbed through the barrage of notifications filling the screen: *Missed call: Tabitha (4)*; *Missed Call: Hayley (5)*; *Missed Call: Mom (2)*; *Message: Hayley:* **Dad took a major turn for the worse this morning. Come see him now!**; *Message: Tabitha:* **Dad is going to go today. PLEASE PLEASE PLEAASE come.**

"Fuck." I breathed the word.

"Your dad?"

I nodded. "They're saying he's going to go soon. They're begging me to come."

"Go get dressed, and we'll head over to the hospital."

I rinsed off in the shower as fast as I could and pulled some clothes on, and the irony wasn't lost on me that, yet again, I was going to the hospital with Brock's come still seeping out of me. I wondered if there was a meaning in that, somewhere.

Probably not.

And if there was, I don't think I'd like what it said about me very much.

Why was I going? To watch him die? Or because, deep down, I still wanted him to, just once, tell me he loved me, that he was sorry? I don't know. But I was going, and I didn't want to go, but I couldn't help it—I knew I had to, like it or not. I thought about my little sisters and knew I was doing this as much for them as I was for any other reason.

I was going. I *had* to.

Thank god Brock was at my side.

FIVE

Brock

LIKE LAST TIME, CLAIRE STOOD OUTSIDE THE HOSPITAL room, hand on the door, hesitating. This time she sucked in a deep breath and, after only a moment's hesitation, she pushed in. I wasn't sure if I should go in with her, especially with such a deeply personal thing happening, but Claire had my hand in a death grip and she wasn't letting go, so I followed her in.

Connor was there on the bed, but his eyes were closed, and his chest was barely rising and falling. The heart rate monitor beeped very slowly: *beep......* *beep......beep.* So slow. Too slow.

Tabitha rushed across the room to her sister. "Claire, thank you for coming, thank god—thank god you're here." She hugged her sister tightly and sniffled against Claire's shirt. "I don't think he's going to last much longer."

Hayley came over and the three girls hugged, both Hayley and Tabitha crying, while Claire remained stoic and dry-eyed, but I could tell she was glad to be with her sisters. Her mother was sitting next to the bed, her forehead pressed to Connor's hand, her shoulders heaving.

The beeping slowed even more.

Tabitha let out a deep breath, sniffled, and then grabbed Claire's shoulders. "I know you and Dad—" Her voice shook and then broke, and she started over. "Please say goodbye, Claire. Tell him you're here. Tell him you forgive him."

Moira lifted her head to peer at her daughter through tear-hazed eyes. "Last night he just kept repeating, 'I didn't know, I didn't know, I didn't know.'"

Connor coughed, a slow deep rattle, and the beeping slowed even more.

I put my lips to Claire's ear. "Say goodbye, honey. Let him know you're here."

She shook her head. "I can't...I can't—"

But she took a tentative step forward, toward the bed, releasing my hand only reluctantly. Another step.

She was visibly shaking, and her hands were trembling like dry leaves in a cold fall wind. She sat in the chair and took her father's hand. "I'm here, Dad," she whispered. "I'm…here."

It was all she could manage before her voice gave out.

"Tell him," Moira said.

Claire glanced at her mother. "Tell him what?"

"That you forgive him. It's what he's waiting for, Claire."

"What if—what if I don't forgive him? What if I *can't*?"

Moira shuddered as if Claire's words physically hurt her. "You *have* to, Claire. Please. You have to." She stood up and circled around the bed, kneeling on the tile floor beside her daughter, clutching Claire's arm in supplication. "We made mistakes—he did, I did. You have every right to hate us. To hate me. You're right about everything you said yesterday. About him, about me, about how I was never there for you. And for those things I am deeply sorry. But…this is it, Claire. It's the end. Your father is about to—to—" She couldn't say the word. *"Please*…Claire. Please."

"Why is this all on *me*?" Claire demanded, her voice a desperate, agonized hiss. "I was the victim in all this, and yet *I'm* the one who has to forgive?"

"It's what God—" Moira started.

Connor gasped, coughed, and the heart rate monitor spiked, a sudden series of frantic beeps. "Unhhhh..." he moaned. "—Didn't...I didn't know..."

Claire sobbed at the sound of her father's faint words, and she clutched his hand. "Dad, I'm here."

His eyes fluttered. He tried to open them and I was sure he wanted to look Claire in the face and give her his last words of forgiveness.

But he was too weak. It was all he could do to take a breath.

The beeping slowed—*beep.........beep.........beep...*

Claire's shoulders shook as she clutched her father's hand in both of hers. Her words were nearly inaudible, meant only for Connor. "I...forgive you, Dad."

Connor sucked in a deep breath, and his lips moved, but no sound emerged. I stood behind Claire, my hands on her shoulders and I was certain she understood what he was trying to say.

Moira sobbed, and Hayley and Tabitha clustered around her, all of them clinging together.

The tense, throbbing silence was punctuated by an isolated beep now and then, irregular and very slow.

And then the silence changed, altered by the soft

steady tone of the sound of a flatline.

Moira went to her husband and laid her head on his chest, sobbing, and Hayley and Tabitha hovered behind her, each crying silent tears, their shoulders shaking.

Claire let out a soft breath. I squeezed her shoulders, and her head bent forward, her chin dipping to her chest.

She stood up, breathing slowly, her thin shoulders rising and falling, her spine straight, and her head high. She stood there for a long moment, staring at the scene before her—the still form of her father, her grieving mother and sisters.

And then Claire turned around, and she gazed steadily at me for a moment, her eyes clear and serene. "Let's go, Brock."

I wasn't sure what to say, to her, or to her mother and sisters, so I said nothing. I simply took Claire's outstretched hand and led her toward the door.

"Will you stay for the funeral?" Tabitha asked.

Turning to Tabitha, Claire said, "I'll stay in town until then, Tab. Lynch and Sons, right?"

"Yes," Moira said, her voice tear-thick. "He's going to be buried at Rosewood."

"Just text me with the details."

"A text message, Claire? Do you have no heart?" Moira asked.

"No, I don't," Claire snapped. "I lost it six years ago."

Despite the anger in her voice, she opened the door softly and closed it just as gently behind her. She said nothing as we made our way to the elevator, and her eyes were dry and distant.

On the elevator, I turned to her. "Claire, I'm—"

"Don't, Brock," she interrupted. "Please, just don't. I don't want apologies or condolences or sympathies. I just want to go back to the hotel and go to bed."

I kept silent, holding her hand as we walked from the elevator to the car. She grabbed my hand again in a vise-grip as soon as we were seated in the car and she didn't let go or relax the strength of her grip all the way from the hospital to our room at the Townsend. As soon as we were in the room, she put out the "Do not disturb" sign, locked the door, and pulled all the drapes closed so the room was darkened.

She stripped naked and climbed into the bed and pulled the covers up to her ears, lying on her side. I stood in the doorway of the bedroom for a long moment, watching her, wondering what I should do, and how I should comfort her.

"Brock?" Her voice was tiny, soft.

"Yeah, baby."

A quiet pause, and she twisted under the blankets

just enough to glance at me with one eye. "Can you... will you hold me? Skin to skin. Just...hold me." Her voice shook.

"Yes, of course."

I shed my clothes and slipped into the bed behind her, wrapping my arm around her midsection. She tucked her butt against me, and wriggled her shoulders against my chest.

A long, long silence. I thought she'd fallen asleep, but her breathing never quite slowed enough for that. Eventually, I heard her whisper.

"I didn't mean it."

"Mean what, honey?"

"When I said I forgave him, I didn't mean it. I just...I only said it because I felt like I had to."

I wasn't sure what to say to that. "Claire, I—"

"I think that probably makes me a terrible person, but I'm not going to lie to you. He's dead, and I can't cry about it. I don't know if I'm even sad. I watched him take his last breath, and I just—I feel numb."

"It's a lot to process," I said.

She rolled a shoulder. "Probably." She turned to look at me. "I notice you didn't deny that I'm a terrible person."

"Don't be stupid, Claire—of course you're not a terrible person. You can't undo the kind of anger and the feelings of betrayal that you have for your dad overnight, after one conversation, or even just because he got sick and died. It's too much to expect to think you could just…erase it all, or to let it go that easily."

"Do you…are you disappointed that I can't forgive him?"

"Disappointed?" I searched myself. "No, I'm not. After hearing the whole story, I…I'm having trouble with what he did, too. I don't know how anyone could behave that way. If I found my worst enemy bleeding in a bathroom, I'd still probably try to help."

"Well, that's because you're a genuinely good person, Brock." She sighed. "I'm…not."

"Yes, you are, Claire. Stop berating yourself."

"I'm really not, Brock. I'm just being realistic and honest about who I am. I've turned into a callous person. I feel absolutely no sympathy for my mother because she never protected me. I know I'm supposed to be sad for her that she lost her husband. They were together for thirty-two years. They met when they were sixteen, in primary school in County Clare, Ireland. She was with Dad her whole adult life. He loved her, she loved him, and I—I know those things, the love they had—I know it was real. But why didn't they love me? They treated Tab and Hayley different than they ever treated me, they could do no wrong."

Claire swallowed hard. "If I got a C, I got grounded for a week. If they got a C, they got a mild talking-to and a hug, and were told 'I know you can do better.' If I came home past curfew, I couldn't go out again for a month. Tab once didn't come home until the next morning, *on a school day*, and they didn't even bat an eye. And she was fucking sixteen. I was eighteen and still had an eleven o'clock curfew. It's never made sense to me."

A thought occurred to me, which I wasn't sure I should even share, not now. Maybe not ever. But it struck me, and wouldn't let go.

"What?" Claire asked. "What is it?"

"What do you mean?"

She shrugged. "You just...you tensed. It feels like you thought of something. I don't know. I'm just getting a weird vibe from you."

I let out a breath. "I'm not sure I should even say anything."

"Well now you have to." She rolled over, pushed against my chest until I lay on my back, and then she settled her head on my arm, her hand on my diaphragm; she wasn't exactly a cuddle-bug, so this was unusual for her. "Out with it, Brock."

"Well, it's just conjecture, okay? Just my own observations and nothing else."

"Quit stalling."

I brushed a lock of her short silver-blonde hair behind her ear. "You don't look anything like your dad," I said. "You've got your mother's eyes, her hair, her cheekbones, her build. I can see your fierce attitude and independence and all that coming from your dad, but that's not...that stuff isn't necessarily genetic. Nature versus nurture, you know?"

Claire froze, to the point that I wasn't sure she was even breathing until she spoke. "What are you saying, Brock?"

I considered my words with extreme care. "Nothing, for certain. Just...suggesting the possibility that there might be some things in your parents' past that you don't know about, which might help explain the disparity in parenting styles."

She was quiet a while. "I never thought about that, but you're right. Tab has Mom's eyes and her hair is a little of both of them, kind of brown and kind of blonde. Hayley has Dad's eyes and Mom's hair. I'm all Mom, *only* Mom." She blew out a breath. "Holy shit, Brock. Tab and Hayley also both have a birthmark only Dad has, a little splotch of red on their left side, just above their hips. I don't have that."

"It could be nothing, Claire. Genetics are weird, and there's always the possibility of some weird genetic fluke where your mom's DNA just won out over your dad's. It's just a thought that struck me when I first met everyone. It doesn't necessarily mean anything."

She shook her head. "No, it makes perfect sense. Except the fact that they've been married for so long, and I just can't imagine Mom cheating on Dad."

"It could be nothing, like I said."

"Or it could be everything."

"Are you going to ask her?"

Claire didn't answer right away. "I can't ask her at Dad's funeral, but yeah, I'm gonna ask. I *have* to know."

"Are you sure?"

"Absolutely. I have to know, now. I'll go crazy until I do." She sighed. "Fuck. I didn't need any of this."

"I'm sorry, Claire."

She tilted to look up at me, and then shook her head. "What are you sorry for? You're the only reason I'm even halfway sane right now, let alone sober."

"I just mean my speculation probably isn't helping anything."

"Oh. Well, no. But you know me, I'd always rather have the messy, painful truth than a bullshit lie to spare my feelings."

"Me too."

She let out another breath. "You okay if I take a little nap? I woke up too early and I'm exhausted."

"Of course." I kissed her shoulder. "I might get

in my own workout after you're asleep."

A minute or so passed before she answered. "You don't have to...wait for me...to fall asleep."

She rolled away, curling into a ball, and was soon snoring softly, an adorably girlish little *snurk... sigh* sound that made my heart twist in a weird, possessive, protective way. I tucked the blankets higher around her shoulders, and found myself staring down at her face, soaking in her beauty. Just...staring at her, feeling so damn lucky that I had met her, and that we were together. I was so proud of her for doing what she did and, deep down, I was sure that things would only get better for Claire. If anyone deserved to feel happy and safe and loved, it was Claire.

I changed into workout clothes and headed down to the gym, where I worked my way through my regular routine, starting with some light barbell lifts to get warmed up; it felt good to push myself and sweat out some of the stress.

My thoughts turned to Claire, and even though we'd only been together for about four months, my feelings for her only grew stronger with each day. She was so smart, and during her time as a combat nurse she had seen some pretty tough stuff so it was no surprise she'd left nursing to work in programming. She'd taken a few courses in Seattle after leaving the Army and had ended up loving it. The Badd brothers' business ventures were going so well that I knew we could use someone with Claire's skills to keep the business side of things organized. Of course, that would mean she would have to move to Ketchikan...

And I had to admit it would be so great to have her there on a permanent basis. We could do lots of fishing and flying—she'd said she'd like to learn to fly, and it'd be fun to teach her the basics Soaring above the clouds, feeling beautifully alone in the world, no noise except for the faint drone of the propeller muffled by headsets. I let that image play out in my head as I powered through three sets of twelve double kettlebell cleans, until my arms were jelly and I was gasping. A quick break, and then I knelt on the weight bench and braced one hand on it while rowing with the other, and tried to pull up the image of flying again.

Except now Claire was in the plane with me, giggling as I did a long, wide barrel roll. Of course, thinking about Claire in the plane with me only led me to remembering that time on the way up to Ketchikan from Seattle, when she'd taken off her shirt and told me to put it on autopilot. I'd informed her that the airplane I was flying didn't *have* autopilot, and she'd then told me to just make sure I didn't kill us...and had set about opening my jeans and spending a solid fifteen minutes going down on me.

Fuck, that had been a day to remember.

I wiped down the handles of the kettlebells I'd used, put them away, and turned on the treadmill, trying in vain to banish thoughts of Claire and her mouth as I did a few sets of interval sprints.

Proof positive that a guy can take damn near anything and make it sexual: the interval sprints made me think about when we'd gone hiking together outside Seattle, and she'd pulled me off the trail a good quarter of a mile in and I'd bent her over a fallen tree and fucked her from behind, and her screams of orgasm had shaken birds free from the branches above us.

Damn it, damn it, damn it—we'd already fucked once this morning, and I was raging for round two. What the hell was wrong with me? I'd always had a more-than-healthy libido, but something about Claire just left me constantly horny, always ready to take her again.

I finished my interval sprints and went gasping and heaving back up to our room, sweating, sore, and still rocking a semi. Claire was still asleep, so I hopped in the shower. I had barely started lathering shampoo into my hair when the shower door opened, and Claire stepped in.

"Thought you were napping?" I asked.

"I was."

"Did I wake you up?"

She shook her head. "Nah. I woke up thinking about you, heard the shower, and…" She shrugged, reaching for my cock, which had finally subsided a little. Not all the way though. "Looks like you were thinking about me, too."

I grinned. "Damn straight I was. Made it hard to work out. Kept thinking about you, so I had to cut my workout short and come back here for a shower."

"All roads lead to Claire, huh?"

"Pretty much."

I rinsed my hair and started washing my body, watching as Claire stroked me.

She knelt down in front of me, the spray hitting my back so only errant droplets touched her, just enough to dampen her hair and bead on her naked chest.

"You're so sexy, Claire."

She shrugged a shoulder in a cutesy, sarcastic gesture. "You're just saying that because I'm on my knees with your dick in my hands."

"Well, I'm not gonna lie, you're extra hot like this, naked and wet, but you're always sexy, babe."

She only smiled up at me again, and then grabbed the small bottle of complimentary conditioner, tapped a glob into her palm and rubbed it on both hands, and then slathered it along my shaft, so her sliding strokes were slick and slippery, squishing and squelching. I braced a hand on the wall to my left and watched, chest heaving as I felt the pressure build in my balls. I couldn't hold still, had to move, had to thrust into her hands.

I tugged at her arms. "Stand up and face the wall, Claire."

She made a sassy face. "No."

"No?"

She shook her head. "Nope. I'm staying right here, just like this."

"I can't hold out much longer."

"Good."

I growled as I struggled to push back the need to come. "What are you after, Claire?"

"I said I wouldn't mind a shower, Brock." She tilted my cock away from my body, toward herself. "Maybe I wasn't talking about the water."

"Oh."

There was a shadow behind her eyes, though. A hardness to her features, an element of seduction and distraction to this. Her father had just died. Why was she doing this? What was she really after?

"Claire—"

Her eyes met mine, searched me, and then narrowed. "Don't, Brock. Quit fucking analyzing me."

Her fists moved in a blur, and I was pivoting at the hips helplessly, her touch slick and hot and firm, and I felt the urge to release become too much to resist.

"I'm not analyzing you, Claire."

"Yes, you are. You have that look, the one that says you're trying to figure me out."

"So?"

"So what if I don't want to be figured out right now? What if I don't want to cope? What if I just want this?"

"This being what?"

"This being you. This being *this…*" she slicked her fists in a tight sliding squeeze around my crown down to my root, "—your big hard cock."

"You can have me whenever you want, babe, you know that. But it doesn't have to be like this."

She stared up at me, her expression revealing only lust, her thoughts inscrutable. "It doesn't *have* to be, no. But it's how I want it right now."

I growled again. "Fuck, Claire. Jesus, I'm gonna come."

She slowed her strokes and switched to a slow hand over hand motion, and my hips flexed forward and locked like that as my orgasm tore through me. "Give it to me, Brock," she murmured, angling my cock toward herself with one hand around the head and stroking my shaft with the other. "Make a mess all over me. You were right, before, you know. I do love it when you come on my tits."

"That's what you want right now? My come on your hot little titties?"

"Fuck yeah, Brock." She shifted closer, kneeling right underneath me, angling me at her chest. "Come on me. Right now, all over me."

I groaned, thrusting forward, barely able to keep my eyes open as come blasted out of me. It shot in a thick white ribbon all over her chest, and she bit her lower lip, watching raptly as I growled and snarled and thrust into her jerking fist. And then she leaned even closer, shifting downward and opening her mouth, resting the tip of my cock on her chin as she stroked me hard and fast at the base; I squirted another stream of come, this time a web of liquid white lace burst all over her upturned face. It coated her from chin to forehead, and she kept caressing me as I gasped through the last of my orgasm. She laughed, grinning, as my come dripped down her face, on her lips and tongue and nose and cheeks, blinking it out of her eyes...

"Jesus, Claire."

She swiped a finger across her tits and popped it in her mouth, remaining on her knees in front of me, my come still all over her face. "Did you like that, Brock?" She twisted and swayed in a sultry dance, still clutching my cock in one hand. "Watching yourself shoot your hot load all over my face and tits?"

I felt conflicted, is what I felt. Mixed up and un-sure. On the one hand, fuck yeah, it was hot. The whole thing was hot, the way she entered the shower and grabbed my cock and jerked me off all over her face and breasts, yeah, that was hot as hell. I'd actu-ally jerked off to that exact image, when I was stuck working in Ketchikan and Claire was stuck working in Seattle. I'd never have done it, though, and honest-ly, when I'd imagined it, I'd felt guilty afterward for even mentally using Claire like that, to come on her face.

It was a common thing in porn, obviously, but it wasn't something I'd ever done in real life. Porn wasn't real life. Nothing about it was real, or believable, or realistic. It was dumb. Once I was inside Claire, I nev-er wanted to leave. I wanted to stay buried as deep inside her as I could get, for as long as I could stay there. I didn't want to pull out for anything. I wanted to bury myself deep and come inside her.

But this, what she'd just done…fuck yeah, it was hot. But I wasn't sure if I *liked* it. I *enjoyed* it, yeah, but did I *like* it? The two weren't necessarily the same thing. She'd done it of her own volition…but why? It's not like I'd shoved her to her knees and jizzed on her face without warning. She'd come into the show-er with the purpose of doing exactly what she'd done.

Was it for me? Or was it for her? What enjoyment did she get out of it? But then, maybe it wasn't enjoyment she was after...

All that flashed through my head in the space of a few seconds; the water was still beating hot on my back, and Claire was still kneeling on the marble shower floor in front of me, her face covered in my come. She was smearing it around her chest with one hand, and then wiping it off her face with her other forefinger and licking it off. We'd done some freaky, dirty stuff together, but this was the freakiest, by far.

I lifted her to her feet without answering, grabbed a washcloth off the rack, got it wet and wrung it out, and then wiped her face clean, starting at her forehead and wiping around her eyes, down her nose, her cheeks, her lips, her chin, then down to her breasts, and I wrung the washcloth out again before gently and lovingly wiping her breasts clean. When I was finished, she was staring up at me with an expression I couldn't quite fathom on her face. It was a combination of anger and confusion, mixed with tenderness and the love we both knew was building between us, but which neither of us had expressed yet. There was so much in that expression, and I wasn't sure what any of it meant.

"What, Claire?" I whispered. "What does that look mean?"

The water was soaking into her hair now, strands sticking to her cheeks. Her skin was pebbled with goosebumps, so I pivoted us until she was beneath the hot water. She leaned up against me, her erect nipples poking against my chest, and she clutched my ass, staring up at me still.

"I just don't get you."

"Why? What don't you get?"

She leaned away, took the washcloth from me and scrubbed soap onto it, then used it to scrub my skin, starting at my chest and working around to the rest of me at a leisurely pace. "I just…I thought that would make you crazy. I thought you'd like that. But you…I don't know. It doesn't seem like you…like you want me like that."

"The hell are you talking about, Claire?" I took the soapy cloth from her and scrubbed her breasts. "It was hot."

"But?" She saw through me as easily as I did her, that was for damn sure.

"But nothing."

Why was I lying to her? There was a *but* to this; I sighed. "That's not exactly true."

She lathered soap onto her hands and scrubbed her face and then rinsed off. I shut off the water and we got out, then handed her a towel and dried myself off with another. Claire wrapped the towel loosely around herself and went into the sitting room and sat down on the couch. I followed her, sitting next to her, and she let the towel sag open—Claire had a thing for "air drying", sitting naked and still dripping wet. She'd towel off her hair a little and make a few cursory swipes over her body, but she let the rest of the water evaporate as she strutted around naked, putting on makeup, doing her hair, picking out an outfit, sometimes even working from her phone. If she was at home for a while after a shower, she'd still be naked more often than not hours later. This was something I very much appreciated.

At the moment, though, it was distracting me from all the thoughts whirling through my head, which I was hoping to discuss.

"Talk to me, Brock."

"I'll talk to you if you'll talk to me," I responded.

She rolled her eyes at me, and sassed back in a droll, dry, sarcastic tone. "Well yes, Brock, that *is* how typical conversations work, dear. I talk, you talk, we talk."

I snorted, reaching over to pinch her nipple. "Smart-ass. You know what I mean."

She whacked at my hand, trying to stop the pinch. During sex, she loved having her nips played with, but at any other time she hated it, because they were insanely sensitive. "Don't! Brock, I swear, do *not* pinch my nipples!"

"How can I not?" I said, imprisoning her wrists in one hand and flicking her nipples with the other hand. "They're right there, all nice and hard and just begging for a little pinch."

She struggled, thrashing, and then tried to bite me. "Unless you're gonna go down on me, you better leave my goddamn nipples alone!"

"Fine by me," I murmured, and moved to slide off the couch.

"No, no, no." She grabbed me and pulled me back up, and actually wrapped the towel around her chest to shield herself. "As much as I want you to do that, no. We're talking. Talk now, cunnilingus later."

"Why did you do it, Claire?"

"I wanted to. I woke up horny, thinking about you. I heard you in the shower, and decided I wanted to jerk you off."

"Yeah, but why? Why that? Why not sex? Or a blowjob? Why...*that*?"

She shrugged. "I dunno. I just...I wanted to feel you. I wanted your come."

"Come on, Claire. Dig a little deeper."

She sighed in frustration. "Why? Does it really matter?"

"Yeah, it does, kind of," I said.

"You tell me why it matters, and I'll tell you why

I wanted to do that."

I spent a second organizing my thoughts. "Okay, here it is. I have mixed feelings about what happened in the shower."

"Mixed how?"

"It was hot, and obviously it felt incredible. The way you just sort of walked into the shower with me and jacked me off? It was hot. And a part of me did find it hot how you wanted me to come on your face and all that. We've both been around the block, right? We've both had a lot of experiences, but that's the first time I've ever done that. On someone's face, I mean. Tits, yeah, sure. Not often, but hell, it's kinda hot, I think any guy will agree to that much." I paused to think, then continued. "With you, though…I'd always rather be inside you. Like, fuck yes, I *love* the way your hands feel, and I *love* the way your mouth feels. But nothing can compare to the way it feels being inside you."

"I understand that, and I feel the same way for the most part, but I'm not seeing the conflict."

"For the most part?"

She sighed and shrugged. "I'll explain later. Keep going."

"Okay, well…there's also this part of me that finds it…degrading to come onto your face. I dunno. I mean, I know you chose to do that on your own, for your own reasons. I want to think you'd never do anything you didn't want to do, just because you thought I might enjoy it. Would you?"

She shook her head from side to side. "There's nothing I wouldn't want to do with you, let's just put it that way for now."

"Vague, but okay, I'll go with it. Like, why would you want *that*? Why on your face? I don't get it."

"Haven't you ever fantasized about doing that to a girl? Me or someone else? Be honest."

I nodded. "Yeah, of course. But I never actually considered doing it, though."

"Who was it? When you fantasized about it?"

"You, as a matter of fact. A month or so ago, during the week. You were in Seattle and I was in Ketchikan."

She seemed pleased by this. "You fantasized about coming on my face? Did you jerk off to it?"

"Of course."

"I'm kinda mad you didn't text me and tell me."

"Really?"

"Not, like, *mad* mad, just…slightly miffed at worst because I wish you'd shared. I mean, guys jerk off, it's totally normal, and I'm glad you jerked off to me." She eyed me. "Honest now, have you ever jerked off to anyone else since we've been together?"

"No."

She scrutinized me. "No? For real?"

"For real. Why would I need to or want to? We haven't been apart for more than a week, and then not even a full week. And I've got plenty of material to think about when it comes to you and us, so if I'm at home alone and feeling like I need to blow off some steam, yeah, I'll think about you and jerk one off."

"Do you jerk off when we're together?"

I shook my head, laughing. "Hell, no. We have far too much sex for that to ever even enter the equation." I glanced at her. "What about you?"

She ducked her head. "I sort of masturbate all the time, when I'm in Seattle by myself. Like…a *lot*. And yeah, I always think about you, at least, since we've been together. And no, if we're together, I don't need to. I've got you. If I'm horny, I find you. Much more satisfying than getting out my Womanizer Pro."

"Your what?"

She waved a hand. "A sex toy. Or, well, a personal female clitoral stimulator, if you want to be specific. An amazing, incredible device that every woman should own. I can come in literally a minute or less with it."

I gaped at her. "Jesus. I want to see that."

She smirked at me. "A trade, then."

"A trade?"

She nodded. "Yeah. Next time you're in Ketchikan

and I'm in Seattle, you record yourself jerking off, and I'll record myself masturbating, and we send them to each other."

"What do you think would happen if we just didn't masturbate at all?"

She stared at me in consternation. "Holy shit, I'd go insane. I'd be crawling the walls by the end of the week."

"Me too. That's the point though."

"I am kind of jealous of your come, now that I think about it. I want it all for myself. Like, I hate the thought of you coming all alone, shooting all that lovely stuff down the drain and wasting it."

"Exactly. When you come, I want your orgasms to be for me and only for me."

Claire poked me, suddenly. "How'd we get so far off topic? I still don't understand what your hang up is about coming on my face if I want you to."

"I don't know. I just feel weird about it."

"Tell me about your fantasy."

"Pretty much exactly what you just did. I was in the shower when I was thinking about it, so obviously I just pictured you in the shower with me, all wet, on your knees, sucking me off, and then instead of swallowing, you took it on your face and tits."

"Well maybe next time you take a shower, we'll do that again, only this time I'll use my mouth more."

I grinned. "That's up to you, babe."

She eyed me curiously. "Why? Why is that up to me? That's the part that I'm having trouble with. If you want something, make it happen. Like, if you want me to suck you off, tell me you want me to suck you off. Better yet, *show* me."

"Just, like, whip my dick out and slap you with it?"

She shrugged. "If a cock-slap turns you on, then yeah, sure."

"I'd never do that."

"Again, why not? I love your cock, and even as big and hard as it is, you can't really slap me with it hard enough to actually hurt. If anything, I'd think it would hurt *you*."

"So if I legit smacked you across the face with my dick, you'd be like *hell yeah*, and start sucking?"

She nodded. "Absolutely." Claire's gaze was steady, open, and scrutinizing. "I'm not sure how well you really understand me, Brock."

"What do you mean?"

A sigh. "I'm a perpetually horny girl—not sure if you've noticed. I like sex, a *lot*. I want it literally all the time. I used to joke with Mara that not only am I built like a boy, I think about sex as much as a boy."

I tugged at the towel, and she dropped it so I could thumb her nipple. "You are *not* built like a boy.

You're all woman, Claire."

"You wouldn't prefer someone built more like… oh, say, Mara, for example?" She cupped her tits, hefting them as if they were several sizes larger. "Big bouncy titties and an ass that don't quit?"

"Mara is an attractive woman," I conceded. "But she's got one fatal flaw."

"What could that possibly be? Her face is just as beautiful as her body."

"No, that's not it. Yeah, she's a lovely girl in every way." I hesitated, for the sake of drama. "Except that she's not you."

Claire glanced at me askance. "Oh my *god*, Brock. That sounds like something out of a romance novel."

"But true all the same."

"What about your other girlfriends? Were any of them like me?"

"What you mean, like you?"

Claire gestured at herself, a sweep of her hand from head to toe. "Short and skinny and not very well-endowed."

"Claire, do you remember how we met?" I asked.

She frowned, and then nodded. "Well yeah, of course."

"Who initiated contact?"

She rolled her eyes. "You did."

"And who was the first one to suggest leaving the

bar and going to your hotel?"

She bit out the word as if admitting it was painful. "You were."

"Have I ever, *ever* given you any indication that I feel absolutely *anything* but total and genuine attraction to you?"

"No, but—"

"But nothing. What the other girls I've been with look like doesn't matter. They're not you—*you're* you, and I'm attracted to *you*. No, you don't have the biggest tits in the world, but so what? I get off on touching them and seeing them and putting them in my mouth. And yeah, it was hot seeing my come splattered all over them."

She shifted in place, swallowing. "Don't bullshit me, Brock."

"I would never bullshit you, Claire." I gave it a moment, and then went with my question. "So, why did you do that, for real?"

She shrugged, a tiny lift of one shoulder. "I wanted to. That was one reason, and it was a real reason. I really do think about your cock all the time, and want it all the time. I think about you coming, and it turns me on. Seeing you naked turns me on. Seeing you wet turns me on. So you in the shower, naked and wet, having a big messy orgasm? Yeah, it turns me on."

"So then why didn't we have sex?"

"Because sometimes I want other things." She paused, glancing at me almost shyly—there wasn't usually a single shy molecule in Claire's body, so this was something new, something deep. "I've—I've never had sex with the same person for as long as I have with you, and…it's weird. Usually with other guys, I'd get bored. We'd fuck, and it would be over. But you… you hold my interest. I never stop wanting you. But I don't want to just *fuck* you every time I'm horny. I like the full range of experiences. And with you, it's always different, it always feels new and just as hot, just as erotic."

"That makes sense."

"But it's…I don't exactly know how to put any of this into words, but I'm trying. For you." She ruffled her hair with one hand, brushing errant strands away from her eyes and then wiped her damp palm on the towel. "Being with you as long as we've been together, I'm learning there's…what's the word? There's a—a rhythm, I guess you could say. To us.

"Like, for real, we fuck *all—the—time*. And I absolutely love that about us. I've never had so much sex in my life, and it's amazing. As much as I was a slut before—and still am, I guess, but now I'm a slut for you…there's a rush in the unexpected and the different. With you and me, though…I still want all that. I want to blow you, because I do genuinely like doing it to you. Do I derive sexual stimulation from it? Of course not. Sex isn't always about *just* receiving stimulation. I like giving the stimulation just as much, *being* the stimulation—I like knowing I can make you feel good, make you crazy, make you want me, make you come so hard you can't walk straight."

"I've never talked this openly about sex with anyone else." I eyed her, searching, thinking.

Claire stared back, and then frowned. "You look like you're about to psychology me."

I nodded, shrugging. "Well, yeah, I guess so. I mean, I'm trying to put all this into the frame of some of the things I've learned about you lately."

Claire rubbed her face with one hand. "Goddammit. I don't want to talk about that shit. It's old news, Brock."

"No, it's not. It's relevant, whether you want to admit it or not."

"How so?"

"I mean, you said it yourself: you figured if your dad thought you were a slut, you might as well earn it."

"That was just a dig."

"A dig, yes, but not *just* a dig."

Claire stood up, paced away—I shamelessly stared at her tight, round little runner's ass as it wiggled with her steps. "Do we really have to go here?" It was a rhetorical question, though, because she started answering before I could speak. "Fine, yes, that was a true statement. Before that night, at that party, I'd only messed around a little. There'd been about a half dozen guys that I sort of dated—more just…hung out with at most. We'd go to parties and mess around in their cars and shit, mostly innocent teenager stuff. Lots of kissing and heavy petting, letting them cop a feel, letting them put their hand in my pants and see if they could make me feel good. Until that night at the party, I'd never even made a guy come, never let a guy make me come, and I'd never been totally naked alone with a guy. I'd been skinny dipping once, but that was with a lot of other people so it was different."

"Damn. So you really were a virgin in pretty much every way."

"Sure was. Never even sucked a dick before." She clutched the towel to her breasts, facing away from me, letting it hang loosely at her sides to frame the graceful sweep of her spine and the taut bubble of her ass. "Then that party happened, I got wasted, and I ended up getting kicked out of the house for making a stupid mistake."

I found it hard to breathe. "Goddammit," I snarled. "The thought of what happened to you makes me so angry I could break someone."

She gave me a soft, reassuring smile over her shoulder. "Don't, Brock. I'm glad you feel that strongly, though." She turned away again. "You know what's weird, and kind of a good thing? I don't really remember what happened. Just…vague impressions of a guy, things being…clumsy and awkward and not what I expected it to be."

A pause, then. Claire stared into space, thinking.

"So, yeah, I don't remember it. The real pain, the really deep, long-term fucked-up pain comes from how my parents treated me regarding the miscarriage and, really, throughout my life. They called me a slut and a whore, and kicked me out. I mean, yeah, I went to a lot of parties and got drunk a lot, smoked, did drugs with my friends, and it was a pretty safe assumption on their part to think I was having a lot of sex, too. I get that. I was a problem child, a rebellious, angry teenager. But that was their fault, the way they parented me. I just wanted attention, you know?

"Basic psychology, I guess. And I was angry, I wanted my space, my freedom. I wanted to be treated like an adult, like someone with value, but my parents didn't seem to think I had any. They automatically assumed the miscarriage was a result of me going out and fucking a lot, and was just punishment for my sins. It was the last straw, as they saw it. Well, after that, I was alone. Lived with my friends, but that welcome ran out after a while because I was all kinds of fucked up, for obvious reasons.

"Going through that miscarriage was absolute hell on its own. Agony and terror—those words don't do it justice, Brock. That was the worst moment of my life, before or since. Being disowned for it was a close second, though."

She sighed deeply, and then continued. "I told you about how I joined the Army, and how I was gonna kill myself. Somehow, that scary decision was a turning point. I decided to live, to own my past, to own myself, to own everything, including the pain, the hate, and the anger. I joined the Dark Side, you might say. I just gave into it. I fucked a guy from another unit during basic, and that kind of…opened me up to sex. It was harsh and rough and not sexy at all, and I got off on it. I mean, real talk, now? The guy totally used me to get off and then bailed the second he shot his load. But while it lasted, as short as it was, I liked it. So I tried again with a different guy from a different unit, but I made him wait until I'd gotten close, which he found hot, and we both came, and that was like…it was a light bulb moment.

"I made sex about *me*. Guys could use me—guys *would* use me, I knew that. But if I used them back, that was a game changer. See, I discovered most guys don't give a shit if you're only using them for sex, as long they get the O. So I used guys for sex. I got what I wanted, and I spent a lot of time and effort figuring out what I wanted."

She paused yet again, and when she spoke once more it was very quietly, almost inaudible. "And deep, deep down, so deep I don't think I've ever thought about it like this until now…yeah, it was about Dad. It was a fuck you to him. Call me a slut? Call me a whore? I'll show you what a slut is, old man. It was more than that, but whatever 'it' was, was buried deep in my subconscious. And, yeah, that was part of it, too."

"And now?"

She didn't answer for a very, very long time, and I remained quiet, giving her the space and time I knew she needed. "I honestly don't know, Brock. I think a lot of it will depend on what Mom tells me. I also think…I feel like things are changing for me, *inside* me, and it scares the hell out of me."

I stood up and crossed the space between us, slid my hands around her, wrapping my arms around her middle. She dropped her towel, and I dropped mine, so there was nothing between us.

"I'll be with you through it all, Claire," I whispered. "No matter what."

"What if I change into someone you don't like?"

"Impossible."

"You don't know that."

"I mean, unless you turn into some simpering, useless airhead, yeah I do know."

"Like, ohmygod, as *if*." She said this in a scarily accurate *Clueless* impression, and then laughed. "Okay, no, there's literally no chance of me turning into *that*."

"Then we'll be fine. You'll just have to trust me."

"Easier said than done." She twisted in place and put her chin on my chest, staring up at me. "But I'll try."

"That's all I'm asking, honey."

SIX

Claire

IT WAS LATE AFTERNOON AND WE'D SPENT THE DAY IN THE room, ordered up a fortune in room service, and fucked. I was hormonal and needy—this whole week was the part of my cycle where I was one giant ball of sex-crazed hormones, which I affectionately referred to as "fuck me stupid week."

Brock got it, I think, and never called me on it. Never said a damn word about the fact that I hadn't shown even a hint of sorrow over my dad's death. He just went with it, because I think—I hope like hell—he understands that I don't know what I'm thinking or feeling right now, and that I'm going to need serious time to figure it out. I also hope he understands that when I do finally to come to grips with the fact that Dad died and how I feel about it, it's going to get messy.

So we lazed about and avoided heavy conversation.

By late afternoon I was getting antsy, because I can't stay cooped up for long, even with Brock.

The TV was on, playing a trailer for a movie, and Brock was dozing, lying on his back, arm over his eyes, cock flaccid against his hip, completely spent from having just bent me over the side of the bed and fucking me until I saw stars. I was sitting next to Brock, toying with the remote, and trying to decide what I wanted to do.

"You're fidgety," Brock mumbled.

I laughed. "I'm always fidgety, haven't you noticed?"

"Yeah, but you're extra fidgety at the moment. What's up?" He slid his arm up so he could look at me.

"I'm just antsy. I need to do something."

"Okay. What sounds good?"

I shrugged. "I don't know. I know I'm supposed to be in mourning or whatever, but…I can't cope with everything right now. I need time to process things, and it's all on hold until I talk to Mom anyway. I just know the way I feel right now is crazy and inappropriate for the day my dad died, but I just want to go have fun. Play pool in a dive bar somewhere, or go to a club, something. Anything."

Brock laughed. "Somehow, that doesn't seem any more inappropriate than how we've spent the rest of the day."

"You have a point, sir." I went into the bathroom to freshen up, deodorant, makeup, a little scrub-by-scrub to my hoo-ha. "So we're gonna get dressed and go get in trouble, then?"

"Sounds good, babe," Brock said, sliding gracefully off the bed.

I put on my favorite pair of teeny-tiny khaki booty shorts, wearing them commando, and then tugged a forest-green camisole over my bare breasts, slipped my feet into my TOMs, and grabbed my purse. "Well, I'm ready."

He had watched the whole thing. "Damn babe, commando *and* no bra? What are you trying to do to me?"

I wiggled my hips side to side. "Drive you crazy, of course."

He got a washcloth wet and cleaned himself, applied some deodorant, and then dressed in what I would call golf shorts, pastel green and white in a plaid pattern, hemmed knee-length, the kind of thing that are so ugly they're *almost* cool, pairing it with a white Izod polo. He looked preppy and cute and ridiculous. Brock normally wore jeans and polos, or jeans and a tee, or maybe a button-down for a nicer date, and for the rarest of rare dress-up dates, he wore dress slacks and a dress shirt. I'd never seen him in shorts, and didn't know he owned anything like…that.

I couldn't help a giggle. "What are you wearing, Brock?"

He frowned at me, and then down at his outfit. "What's wrong with it? Thought I'd try a new style."

I eyed him, laughing. "I mean, babe. You look adorable. You could wear JNCO jeans and a shirt with wolves and flames on it and look hot, but this…I don't know. Gel your hair up and put on a pair of loafers without socks, and you'd be a straight up country club douche-bag."

He frowned at me again, dug in his bag, and tossed a pair of brown loafers onto the floor in front of me.

I bust out laughing even harder. "Brock, honey. *No.*"

"No?"

I shook my head. "No. Nope. No way."

He looked…puzzled. "I thought it looked kinda cool."

I laughed again, this time softly and affectionately, sidling up to pat his chest. "It does look cool. You totally pull it off. That's not the problem."

"You're gonna have to enlighten me then."

"It's not *you*. I mean, with a name like *Brock*, you wear that outfit…you could walk into any country club and get in without a membership. You just look…I don't know. With your looks, it's just too much. It works *too* well. You look too much like you'd absolutely fit in in Bloomfield Hills. And that's not you. You're from Alaska. You're a stunt pilot. You own a bar. You're a Judo expert. You're tough and masculine and manly, and if you wear that, you wouldn't be you. It's fine for other guys, just not you."

He chewed on his lip, staring down at me. "Well, okay, if you think so." Another beat of silence, and then he gestured at his bag. "You pick."

I sorted through his bag, found my favorite pair of his jeans, old and faded light-wash denim, soft and worn, the pair that cupped his ass like a glove, and then a plain, stretchy gray V-neck with his thick black leather belt. I handed it all to him. "Wear that. But go commando."

"Why? I never go commando. It's weird."

I grinned. "It'll be fun. Neither of us will be wearing underwear, and we'll both be super aware of it. You never know when I might get a hankerin' for a little somethin'."

Brock laughed, snickering at me as he shucked his clothes, and pulled on the outfit I'd chosen. Except he tucked in the shirt all the way around.

"No, no, no." I untucked it except for right behind his belt buckle. "Like this. Casual, but still sort of dressy. Now put on your boots and we'll go check out the town."

We took the elevator to the lobby and then had the valet bring the car around.

"Brock, you are so hot it should be illegal," I said, as we waited. "Just thought you should know."

He grinned at me. "No longer a country club douche-bag?"

"No, but even then you're so sexy it's sinful."

"You're pretty damn fetching yourself, Claire."

I tossed my hair. "Fetching, huh?"

"And gorgeous. Sexy. Adorable. Lovely. Stunning. Breathtaking—"

"Okay, okay," I broke in, laughing—and also blushing, truth be told. "I get it. Thank you."

"You sure? I got more."

"One more, then."

He tapped his chin. "Hmmm. Only one more? I'll have to make it a good one." The car came, and we got in, Brock tipping the valet. "Where to, local girl?"

"How about Ferndale? I heard it's gotten nice

since I left. Just head south on Woodward. It's close to the Dream Cruise, so we might see some cool hot rods, too." I eyed him. "So, one more compliment. Think of a good one, yet?"

His smirk was arrogant and pleased. "Yes, I believe I have."

"Hit me with it, hot stuff."

"My fantasy."

I hadn't meant for it to *actually* hit me like it did; my heart twisted and my tummy lurched. "Your fantasy, huh?" I barely choked out the words, whispering them.

"Yes ma'am." He heard it, saw it, how his compliment had hit me, but he didn't call me on it. He also didn't let up, either. "If I fantasize, it's about you. When I think of the perfect woman for me, what she looks like, sounds like, fucks like, kisses like…it's you. You're my fantasy, Claire."

I blinked hard. "Damn. That *is* a good one."

"I mean every word."

"Okay, you can stop now."

"Why should I? You like the truth, don't you? Not all truths have to be unpleasant. Some can be good truths. Like this one." He reached out and took my hand.

"You're ridiculous."

"Yeah, probably. That's irrelevant, though."

"Pretty sure I'm no one's fantasy, Brock, but it's sweet of you to say so."

Oops, wrong response.

He jerked the wheel, pulling off Woodward into the parking lot of a small strip mall. "You think I'm lying, Claire?" Brock's gaze was hot and furious.

"No, I just—" I cut off, shrugging. "I'm just not… *that*."

"Yes, you are."

"That's stupid."

He flinched, literally, physically flinched. "Why? Why is stupid of me to have you as my fantasy?"

I blinked hard, but salt threatened hot at the corners of my eyes anyway. "Just is," I whispered.

I crossed my arms over my chest and stared hard out the window, trying to breathe, and trying *not* to figure out why I was reacting so strongly to this, which even I knew was idiotic.

A long tense silence, broken eventually by Brock. "Claire—"

"Ignore me. I'm being dumb." I smiled brightly at him, flicked the radio dial so the latest Bruno Mars song blasted loud. "Let's go have fun, okay?"

Brock stared at me, unblinking, his expression hard to read. Eventually, he softened, and took my hand. He didn't say anything, just pulled back out into traffic. Then, when we hit a red light, he lifted my hand to his lips and kissed the back, slowly and softly, with a genuinely soft and affectionate and loving look in his eyes, saying more with that look than he could with words.

Whatever you need, is what that look said.

I see through your bullshit, but I'm letting you off the hook, that look said.

We hit Ferndale and walked around, stopping for a coffee and then checking out a local bar to see how it compared to Badd's Bar and Grill back in Ketchikan. We had a few beers there and agreed it was good, but not as good as the Badd brothers' place. We shot a few games of pool and then asked the friendly bartender for a recommendation for dinner.

By the time we finished our steaks at Ruth's Chris in Troy, it was still kinda early so we left the car with the hotel valet and caught a movie at the Palladium in Birmingham, finishing off the night with too much to drink at an authentic Irish pub, which had a live band playing. We got plastered together, is what we did, absolutely shitfaced. At least, I did. Brock was pretty drunk too, but stayed sober enough that he could take care of me, making sure we found our way back to the Townsend and into bed.

The room was spinning so bad I had to put one foot on the floor to make sure I didn't fall off the world, and my brain was shooting out all sorts of crazy nonsense, and I just knew at some point before I passed out that I was going to say something stupid.

Brock lay beside me, just looking at me, dozing off.

"Brock?" I slurred.

Oh, yep, here came the drunk-Claire verbal diarrhea.

"Yeah, babe."

"You're aware a shit-storm is coming, right? I'm going to completely fall apart sometime soon."

"Yes, Claire. I know."

"It's gonna be bad."

"I know."

"I'm gonna do something really stupid. I'm gonna be a horrible, horrible, terrible, stupid person."

"No, you'll be a person who's grieving and hurting and confused, that's all."

"No no no. You don' understand." I rolled to face him. "I'm unpredictable. I'm crazy."

"Yes, and I love those things about you."

I put a hand over his mouth. "Sssshhh! Don't use that word yet. It's too soon. You don't know what I'm capable of."

"I won't let you do anything too crazy, and I'll be there through whatever you have to go through."

I shook my head, because he was making promises I wasn't sure he could keep. "Just...just make me one promise, okay?" I peered at Brock, at the three of him that were currently rotating in front of me; I closed one eye so there were fewer of him.

"Anything I'm capable of."

"Don't let me break up with you."

"Why would you want to do that?"

"I'm not saying I'm *going* to, just that I might try. For stupid reasons, because I'm stupid."

"You're not stupid."

"I'd be stupid to break up with you."

"I agree."

I tried to make sense of the barrage of thoughts in my head. "Right, and when the hit shits the fan—I mean, I mean—shit, you know what I mean. Just…I mean—I might try."

He tugged me to himself, cradled me in his arms, on his chest. "Get some sleep, Claire."

"You didn't promise."

He kissed my temple. "I promise I won't let you break up with me, Claire."

I snuggled closer to him, feeling a bit better. "Okay. Good. I just wanted you to be warned."

He laughed, although I wasn't quite sure why. "It's going to be fine."

"You're crazy."

"Yep. Crazy about you."

"Cheese-ball."

He patted my ass. "Sleep, Claire."

"I'm trying. My brain won't let me."

"Maybe you're not tired out enough."

I snickered. "Gonna tire me out, Mr. Badd?"

"Why yes, Miss Collins, I think I will."

I wasn't expecting him to actually do it, but he slid out from under me, tugged my shorts off, stuffed a pillow under my back, and kissed his way from belly to hip to thigh to thigh to hip to belly, and finally, god finally to my clit, flicking, circling, and his tongue was *holy JESUS*—whoa…what the fuck? I came so hard I cried out, the orgasm hitting me like a ton of bricks out of nowhere, and he didn't relent, only slowed a tiny bit in his assault on my clit, sliding fingers into me. I had to close my eyes and arch off the bed and clutch the pillow behind my head, and then I reached down and found Brock, and his hair was much more satisfying to hold on to than some stupid pillow.

A second, followed a few minutes later by a third, and then it was too much, his fingers inside me and his tongue on me, so drunk I couldn't think, the room still spinning even though my eyes were closed, holding on to Brock for dear life, half-terrified I might let go of him and be thrown off the world by the spinning, like a kid on a merry-go-round whirling too fast who can't hold on and lets go and is tossed like a doll.

And then, oh…and then the dirty beautiful man

added a finger, but this one didn't go in the pink, oh no, this finger, his pinkie, went right into my ass and god*damn* it was glorious, the slow dirty slide in and out of his fingers, three in my pussy and one in my asshole and his tongue on my clit and more fingers on my nipples, and fuck man, how many fingers did he have? Jesus.

The next time I came it was a maelstrom of heat and pressure flooding through my pussy and my belly, seizing me, and I heard myself screaming so loud someone banged on the floor or ceiling or walls, I wasn't sure which and didn't care, because Brock whipped me through the orgasm into a place of sobbing paroxysms.

I finally pushed him away from my overloaded pussy and tugged him up to me, kissed him sloppily so I could taste myself on him, and then shoved him into place: under me, draping his arm around me.

Now I was done, totally done. Darkness rose up to meet me.

"I don't know how to be your fantasy," I mumbled.

"It's easy—you just have to be you."

"What if that's not so easy?"

"Then we figure it out together."

"Okay."

"Now, *sleep*, Claire."

I nuzzled against him. "Okay."

Brock and I spent the last couple of days exploring the area a little more, and I met with my sisters to go over the funeral plans. I hadn't planned on doing that, but Tab called and suggested we sisters meet for coffee. Since I had nothing but love for them, I figured I should probably go hang out with them at least once; and actually, we ended up having a good time, even though it was shadowed by the knowledge of Dad's—Connor's—death.

The day of the funeral was a bright, beautiful, sunny day.

The ceremony was solemn, held at the church where Dad had worked for twenty years. His friends and colleagues said warm, genuine, wonderful things about him. My sisters said loving, wonderful things about him. Mom tried, but couldn't get anything out without sobbing, so her best friend Mrs. Shaughnessy helped her off the stage, and then it was my turn to say something.

Except, I couldn't.

I couldn't go up there.

Tab and Hayley tried to push me up, Mom gestured at me, but I just burrowed into Brock and shook my head.

But my reasons for not saying a few words were

not what I hoped people assumed: I didn't go up because I wasn't crying; my eyes were dry, and I didn't
have anything warm and wonderful and kind and loving to say about him. He really did seem like he had
been a wonderful man...to everyone except me. And
I just couldn't go up there and talk a bunch of bullshit
about a man I didn't love. So I remained seated.

He was buried in Rosewood Cemetery, near a
huge spreading oak tree. A priest who had known
Dad read appropriate Bible verses and rambled the
appropriate platitudes, and then Dad's coffin was in-
terred and everyone tossed a rose onto the casket.

I did not throw a rose.

I did not throw a fistful of dirt.

I watched it all but I did not cry. I held myself
straight and clung to Brock's arm, staring in stony silence as Mom and Tab and Hayley had one last moment over the coffin of the man they had loved. They
held hands, shoulders shaking.

"Do you want to go over there, Claire?" Brock
asked, nudging me.

I shook my head. "That's for them."

He didn't push it.

After a while it was only Mom and the girls and
Brock and I left at the graveside.

Mom took careful, tentative steps across the grass
toward me, stopping in front of me. "You couldn't

spare a single word for your father at his funeral?"

I fought for the right words, but failed to find them. "No, Mom. I couldn't." I bit down on the questions whirling through my head. "I didn't have anything nice to say, so I didn't say anything at all."

Mom closed her eyes as if my words physically hurt her. "I see." She opened her eyes, searching me. "You're going back to Seattle right away, I assume?"

I shook my head. "Not Seattle, and not right away, no."

"You don't live in Seattle anymore?"

"No, I do. But now I'm splitting my time between Seattle and Ketchikan, Alaska…where Brock lives."

"Oh."

I hesitated a moment. "I have a few things I'd like to talk to you about before I go home, but I know today is probably not the day."

"How generous of you," Mom said, sarcasm dripping from her tone.

"We'll come by tomorrow. Probably around midmorning."

"Very well, then."

I hugged Tab and Hayley, waved at Mom, and then we left the cemetery. I felt Mom's gaze on me as I walked away. I wondered if she suspected what our conversation was going be about, and if she was afraid of it. But I didn't really care—this was going to be about me.

The next morning, after a late breakfast, Brock drove me to my parents' house—Mom's house, I suppose it was now. She answered my knock, and admitted us without a word. Tab and Hayley were both gone, which was a good thing, as this didn't really concern them. Mom was still in her bathrobe, wearing her slippers, cat's eye glasses on her nose rather than the contacts she usually wore; the fact that she was still undressed at nearly noon was a testament to her grief, as Mom was always fully dressed with makeup on and her hair immaculate by seven in the morning, no matter what, even on Saturdays. And she'd certainly never have let a complete stranger see her in such a state of undress.

After letting us in, Mom led us into the living room, and then left to go a make a pot of tea.

The house was much the same as it had always been: a single-story ranch, a little dated, low ceilings, a compartmented floor plan. The living room was the brightest room in the house, with a picture window taking up much of the front wall of the room, admitting sunlight. There was a lot of religious iconography on the walls, as one might expect from the home of a Catholic deacon, a painting of what I always thought of as Pansy White Jesus, a lot of crucifixes, some half-burned Yankee Candles, a shelf full of thick tomes of Biblical analysis texts and a few select fiction titles, and a new flat screen TV on the ancient wooden TV stand from my own childhood. The couch was the same scratchy cloth in an ugly blue-green paisley, with a mismatched love seat and a truly ancient La-Z-Boy recliner, Dad's favorite spot to sit and read and drink tea.

Brock and I sat on the love seat, and when Mom returned, she poured the tea and sat down opposite us on the couch. She tucked her legs beneath her on the couch, and wrapped a fleece throw blanket over herself, then cupped her huge mug of tea in both hands. "So. You have something you want to talk about?"

I took a moment to gather my thoughts. "I don't really know how to ease into this, or how to ask nicely, so I'm just going to come right out with it." I hesitated, sucking in a deep breath, and then let it out. "Am I the biological daughter of Connor Collins?"

Mom's eyes slid closed slowly, and she let her mug rest on her knee, covering her mouth with her palm. "Claire, I—I…"

"Am I?"

"That's not a simple question, Claire."

"Actually, it kind of is. There's a one-word answer, here—yes or no."

Mom opened her eyes and looked at me, and her

eyes were full of tears. "No. You're not his biological child."

"But Tab and Hayley are."

Mom nodded. "Yes."

I felt a bizarre and complicated tangle of emotions rippling and roiling inside me. Relief, hurt, confusion, and anger were chief among the emotions, but it was all mixed up together. "Were you ever going to tell me?"

"No."

"So you were just going to let me go through my whole life never knowing the truth?"

"Your father raised you, Claire. He loved you, he—"

"Mom, come on!" I shouted. "He did *not* fucking love me. He didn't. He never told me he loved me. Not *once*. He rarely hugged me. He was never kind or sweet or loving with me, not like he was with Tab and Hayley. I was a burden to him."

"Your father loved you, Claire," Mom insisted.

"He...*did*...*not*," I snarled. "There is absolutely no reason for me to think that he did. You don't love someone and then do to me what you two did to me."

Mom sobbed, a short choking sound. "Claire, that's not fair, we—"

"Not fair? Not *fair*? I nearly committed suicide because of what you and—and *Connor* did to me. If it wasn't for an Army recruiter, I would have killed myself. It's no thanks to you or *him* that I'm alive right now, let alone even close to stable or well-adjusted. Which, I'm not, really, truth be told. I'm *not* stable. I'm *not* well-adjusted. I'm fucked up, Mom—I'm a mess."

Mom shuddered, and had to set aside her tea so she could wipe at her face. "You don't understand, Claire."

"No, you're right, I don't. How about you enlighten me, then?"

Brock held my hand, sitting as close to me as he could, and remained silent, a strong support beside me. I couldn't have handled this conversation with Mom without him next to me, I knew that much.

"Your father and I married very young. Eighteen, and barely out of school. We'd dated for only a brief time before we married, and it was against the wishes of both of our parents." Mom let out a slow, thoughtful breath, staring into space. "We barely knew each other, but we knew we loved each other. Or…that's what we thought, anyway. Your father—Connor, he…he wanted to go to seminary, and so I went with him."

"I thought you met at sixteen or something?"

"Oh, well yes, sort of. We met at sixteen, but only started properly seeing each other a few months

before he started his post-primary schooling. We got
married just before we moved for him to go to seminary college." Another pause. "Those were long,
lonely years, while Connor was at seminary. I was
so young, and I'd never been away from my family
and now suddenly I was in a different city, alone, with
little to do. I had no friends, I wasn't in school, and
Connor was gone all the time, at his classes. I made
the best of it I could, I suppose. I found a job at a bakery, joined a ladies group...anything to pass the time
and not feel so alone."

"Spare me the Hallmark sob story, Mom," I
sniped.

Brock squeezed my hand. "Let her tell the story
her way, Claire."

"Thank you, Brock." She managed to not make
that sound snarky, but I could tell it took effort. "It is
relevant, I promise. I began to doubt whether I'd done
the right thing in marrying Connor. I had no purpose.
You don't understand, growing up here in America
and in this generation as you have, since things are
so different...but then, in Ireland? There were fewer
options."

"I can see how that would be difficult," I said.

"It was...well, hellish, really. I barely saw my husband, and when I did it was in passing, so to speak. He
would come home to sleep, to eat, and then go back

to school. I was a young woman, and I had—desires, to put it bluntly. And he didn't seem interested. We'd been barely able to keep our hands off each other up until that point, and I'm sure you don't really want to hear this, but it's relevant, so hear it you shall. He stopped touching me, in basically every way.

"It took the loneliness to a new level, especially because then, at that time of my life, I didn't exactly share his faith." She paused, then, and took a sip of her tea, then resumed her story. "Three years. The prime of my youth, and it was spent mostly alone, working at a bakery, and playing bridge with a bunch of old matrons and mothers. I had no children, because Connor was too busy with school and we weren't in a financial position to start a family. I wanted children, desperately, just so I wouldn't be alone, so I'd have some purpose in my life, but he refused, and we still rarely…came together…in that way. I think I went a little crazy, to be honest."

"I guess I can see where this is going."

"I suppose you might, at that." She let out another sigh. "There was a young man who came by the bakery regularly. He was handsome, and he seemed to find me attractive. It was nothing but smiles at each other as I handed him his bread in the morning, but it felt like…the attention I so desperately needed. Three years, and all I ever did was smile at Brennan. And then one day I was leaving the bakery after it closed. Late in the evening, it was, and I knew Connor wouldn't be home for hours yet, studying in the library most like.

"I walked home, not really hurrying. I very literally ran into Brennan, not far from home. He was leaving a pub, and I wasn't really paying attention, and we collided. It was…one of those moments. You know? A moment where you know you're faced with a choice, and you know what's right, but that's not what you want, and what you want is just…far too strong? It was…well, you said it yourself—it was a moment from a Hallmark movie.

"I collided with him and ended up with his arms around me, looking up at him, and he looked down at me like he'd never seen anyone so beautiful, and I hadn't felt wanted like that in so, so long. I knew I was supposed to pull away and go back home, but I didn't. Brennan lived above the pub…we'd collided right outside his door. He pulled me into the stairwell and he kissed me, and…I couldn't stop, after that. If it's the truth you want, then I'll tell you I didn't even *try* to stop. Even with Connor I'd never felt such all-consuming…*passion*. Like a fire I couldn't put out, a fire that only burned hotter no matter what I did."

Mom stared into nothingness, probably seeing Brennan, seeing that moment.

"I slept with him, right there on the stairs."

I boggled. "Holy shit, Mom."

She blinked, glanced at me. "This is the first I've spoken of this since it happened."

"Did Dad know? Did he ever find out what happened?"

Mom dipped her head to one side. "It wasn't just the once, Claire. I had an affair with Brennan for over a year. He knew I was married—it was the first thing I said to him, after that first time."

"Holy shit." It was the only thought running through my head—*holy shit, holy shit, holy shit*.

"It all came to a rather abrupt end. Connor had finished his schoolwork for the day, and since he was nearly done with his degree, he decided to come home earlier than usual. Four years, and he'd never once come home early. I don't know what would have happened, had he not come home early that day. Honestly, I think about it sometimes, and I wonder."

"Was it just sex, with Brennan?" I asked.

Mom took a sip of tea, and shook her head. "No. It was more. I cared for him. I was thinking of leaving Connor, actually." She seemed startled, somehow. "I don't think I've ever said that before, right out loud. I was thinking of leaving Connor to be with Brennan. He took care of me. Gave me the attention and affection I needed, seemed to genuinely enjoy my company. We both knew what we were doing was wrong, but I saw Connor so rarely it was almost like he didn't exist. I'd leave the bakery, go to Brennan's flat, and we'd…you know. We'd eat together, talk, read books, listen to the radio. I'd go home around midnight and go to bed, and Connor would come home eventually and sleep, but he'd wake up and eat and leave for school before I woke again. I saw him on the weekends, but even then he'd often scarper off to the library for more studying. And I never understood it— why was religion so important to him? Why it was more important than me? I…with Brennan…I *mattered*. He *liked* me. He listened to me."

"And then Dad came home early."

She nodded. "He saw me leaving the bakery, which was on the way from the university to our flat. He followed me, but didn't announce himself or catch up. I don't know why, maybe he was thinking to surprise me or something. Well, instead of going to *our* flat, of course, I went into Brennan's. Connor followed me in, and caught Brennan and I in the act."

"Damn. That had to have been intense."

Mom laughed, strangely. "Actually, no. He just stood there staring at us, naked in Brennan's bed, and he didn't say a word. We stared back for a moment, too surprised to do anything else, really, and then Connor just turned around and walked out. I was rather relieved, actually."

"So you went after him?"

Mom didn't look at me, but gazed into her tea. "No. I was planning to leave Connor, remember? I stayed with Brennan."

"Damn. That's kind of cold."

"Perhaps. But I thought it was over. Why would I want to go back to him, and why would he want me back?"

"So what actually happened?"

"Brennan…" She let out a shuddery breath. "Brennan was involved with the IRA. I don't suppose you know much about that, but…well, it was a violent time. Brennan had ties to the IRA, family and friends who were very active in the movement. And he, um…he told me had to take a trip. Down to Dublin, he said. For business. And he never came back. He was involved in a bombing in London, and was killed."

"Wait, go back. This was *after* Dad found out?"

Mom nodded. "I stayed with Brennan until he left for London. Connor just…he was going to let me go, I guess. Then, about two months later, Brennan left for his trip, and never came back. While he was gone, I discovered I was pregnant. I was alone again, and I had no idea when Brennan was going to be home again. This was before cell phones, obviously, so I had no way of contacting him."

"Oh my god."

"Indeed, yes. It was…very difficult. I stayed in Brennan's flat, alone, for days. I went to work, came back, went to work, came back…and I heard nothing. A week passed, and I began to feel afraid he wasn't coming home. Had he left me? I didn't think he would have done that, not when we were talking about me trying to get a divorce so we could be together more openly.

"Then, one day, I was at work. A man entered the bakery, and handed me a letter. It was from Brennan. He'd been fatally wounded in the bombing, but hadn't died immediately. He wrote me a letter. He knew he was dying, and he…" She shuddered, sniffed. "He told me he loved me, and that he was sorry it had happened this way, that he wasn't leaving me intentionally. So I was pregnant with another man's baby and that man was dead, and I hadn't seen my legal husband in over two months, almost three at that point."

"Oh, Mom."

"I went back to our flat, the one I'd shared with Connor. I…" She laughed. "I actually knocked on the door. I didn't know what else to do, or where else to go. Connor let me in, and I told him everything. That Brennan was dead, and that I was pregnant with Brennan's baby."

"And he took you back? Dad—Connor took you back?"

She nodded. "He said it was his duty to forgive me, and so he would. I made it very clear why I'd had the affair, and told him if he was going take me back, that if we were going to do this, then he couldn't just abandon me again."

"You cheated on him, went back to him with another man's baby inside you, and you had the audacity to make demands of *him*?" I laughed. "That took some serious confidence."

"I felt justified in what I'd done. He had, for all intents and purposes, totally abandoned me. It wasn't right, what I did, I'm not saying that—it wasn't, it was wrong, it was a sin, and one I've struggled with every day of my life. But I had good reasons for doing it."

"So you and Dad got back together, and you had me."

Mom nodded. "It wasn't easy. We had to learn how to be together all over again, on top of getting past my affair with Brennan and being pregnant." She paused a moment, drank more tea. "You were born in Belfast, and then six months later, Connor received an opportunity to come here, to America."

I took a moment to absorb all that. "Tell me about Brennan."

"Why?" Mom asked. "He's gone."

"I'm just curious."

She didn't answer for a while. "He was...very kind. But he had an edge to him. I only rarely saw it, since most of the time we spent together was at his flat. But a few times we'd pop down to the pub for a drink, and I caught a glimpse of...another side to him.

"You look a lot like him, actually. He wasn't a large or intimidating man, but he had a lot of presence. He had blond hair and dark eyes, and he was very, very attractive. I think you're much like him in many ways, really. He never showed it to me, but he had a temper. Sometimes he'd have black eyes or bruises from fighting, but with me he was never anything but gentle and kind." She stared off into space, fiddling with her tea. "He was...how do I put this? He was a man of insatiable appetites."

I couldn't help laughing. "Well I certainly got *that* from him."

Mom blushed, but looked directly at me. "And how do you know you don't get it from me, too? He wasn't the only one with an appetite that wasn't easily sated, you know."

"Was Connor that way too?" I asked.

Mom looked away, but shook her head. "Oh, no. Not really."

"You were never satisfied with him, were you? With Connor, I mean."

Mom frowned. "I don't see how that's any of your business, Claire. I loved Connor with all my heart."

"I know, Mom. I've never doubted that." I hesitated, and then continued. "It's *him* I doubt. Connor. I don't look like him at all, and now I know why. But I'm also not...I'm not like him in any way. And he never loved me, so this just...it explains it."

"He tried, Claire," Mom said, through tears. "He tried. He was there the day you were born. He signed the birth certificate. He was there when you said your first word and took your first step. He taught you to ride a bike, gave you your first communion. He...he tried. He *tried*."

"It wasn't enough, Mom," I said. "I never received equal treatment from him. Everything I did was wrong, and nothing was ever good enough. I grew up wondering what was wrong with me, why my daddy didn't love me. I knew it from an early age, Mom. I think I was...nine, or ten maybe when I first really realized that Dad—that *Connor*—didn't love me. I'd gotten straight As, the best grades I'd ever gotten, and he barely noticed." I mimicked Dad's voice. "'Good job, Claire. Do better next marking period.' Nothing was below a ninety-three percent, and yet it wasn't good enough. Tab got worse grades than me, and you guys took her out for ice cream to celebrate.

You took Hayley with you, but me—you made me stay home and study."

Mom cried, and didn't wipe away the tears. "He was never able to look at you without seeing Brennan. It was a reminder of his failure as a husband, and my failure as a wife. You were a constant reminder that I'd sought solace and companionship in the arms of another man. We couldn't just forget and put it behind us, because you were always there, reminding us."

"But that wasn't my fault!" I shouted. "*I* didn't do anything wrong! I was a *child*, a little girl who just wanted her mommy and daddy to love her. But you didn't, and I could never figure out what was wrong with me that made my parents hate me but love my sisters. They could do no wrong, and I could do no right."

She looked at me then, tears shining in her eyes and dripping down her face. "I'm sorry, Claire."

I stood up. "Yeah, well…being sorry doesn't give me my childhood back." I tried to think of something else to say, but couldn't. "But thanks for telling me. It makes sense of everything I've never been able to figure out my whole life."

She didn't answer. Brock stood up with me and we made for the door. I stopped, the storm door propped open. "What was his full name?"

A long silence. "Brennan Patrick O'Flaherty."

I soaked that in, filing it along with the rest of the information I wasn't sure how to process. "Bye, Mom."

"Goodbye, Claire." She said it with a sense of finality. She was staring into space, lost in the past, lost in thought. I wasn't sure I would ever see her again.

As I was angling into the passenger seat of the rental, Tab and Hayley rounded the corner, just finishing a jog together.

"Claire?" Tab, the more observant of the two, stopped beside me, eyeing me. "You're leaving already? What's wrong?"

"Nothing." I stood back up and hugged her. "And yeah, I'm going home."

Tab frowned, and touched my cheek, then showed me her index finger, damp. "You're crying."

I wiped at my face with both hands. "Oh. Um." I shook my head. "Never mind. It's nothing I want to talk about right now."

Hayley stepped in for a hug. "When will we see you again?"

I shrugged as I let her go. "Maybe you guys can come visit me in Ketchikan. You'd like it there."

"Oh, that would be fun! Could we?" Tab asked.

I tried to smile. "I'll call you and set something up."

They both hugged me at the same time. "We love you, Claire," Hayley said. "Please remember that we're here for you."

"I know." I whispered it. "I love you guys too."

And I did. They'd never understood why Mom and Dad—it was hard to break the habit of calling him that even though I didn't feel he deserved the title—had treated me so differently, and they had always done their best to make up for it by loving me all the harder, and I'd never resented them for the difference in treatment, since it was no more their doing than it was mine.

I let them go and got into the car. Brock drove off, and I didn't look back. We were pulling up the hotel a few minutes later, and I grabbed Brock's wrist before he could get out. "Take me home, Brock."

He sank back into his seat. "Home?"

I nodded. "Ketchikan."

He gazed at me steadily. "Ketchikan is home?"

"Yeah, I feel like it is."

He reached up and palmed my cheek. "Home it is, then."

SEVEN

Brock

IT'D BEEN A LITTLE OVER A MONTH SINCE THE FUNERAL, and Claire was being…weird. As in, we hadn't discussed anything she'd learned on the trip down to Michigan. Not once. She told me she needed time to process, that she wasn't ready to talk about it. Okay, fine, I kinda get that. So I've been giving her space. Our relationship progresses apace; we fuck like teenagers who have just discovered sex, and we still don't really use the bed. We spend a lot of time together, we talk, we hang out with my brothers and Mara and Dru, and life is good. She's spending more time here than in Seattle, and I'm starting to think she's considering moving here full time, but she isn't quite ready to actually pull the trigger, or isn't sure how to broach the subject.

I haven't forgotten her warning, though: a shitstorm is coming. I can feel it. I can see it in her. It's... inevitable, it seems. I mean, you don't lose your father and then discover he's not actually your father within a week and remain totally unaffected by it. And when Claire thinks I'm not paying attention, I see her staring off into the distance, deep in thought. But she never shares.

And the sex...? It's hot. It's wild. It's adventurous. It's nonstop. We fuck standing up, we fuck against walls and in the shower and on the floor and on our hands and knees, we 69, we finger each other's assholes, she sucks me off when I least expect it, and I eat her out until she's quivery from too many orgasms. On the surface, it's incredible. A dream come true.

Yet...there's just...there's something off.

I don't know. I don't know how to frame it, how to look at it. Is there something missing? I don't know. What could be missing? I don't know, I just don't know. I get the feeling there's still so much Claire isn't telling me. And I don't know how to get it out of her.

It was two in the afternoon on a Wednesday, and I was sitting at the bar watching sports highlights while

Zane repeatedly tossed a long black knife in the air so it flipped several times, caught it by the rope-wrapped handle, and hurled it at the wall behind the bar to sink an inch deep into the wood, which was now heavily pockmarked from Zane's boredom-killing activity.

"You're stewing on something," Zane said, as he retrieved his throwing knife from the wall.

"Yeah, I'm thinking about how you're completely fucking up that wall."

He laughed. "It is kind of messed up, isn't it? Meh, I can replace the boards in about thirty minutes, and you can't see it unless you're behind the bar anyway." He hopped up to sit on the bar next to me. "Talk."

I sighed, took the knife from him and fidgeted with it. "It's complicated."

"You wouldn't be stewing on it if it was simple."

"I guess you're right." I slid off the bar to stand where Zane had been, and hurled the knife at the wall; it thunked butt-first into the wall and fell to the floor. "You make that look easier than it is."

Zane retrieved the knife and stood beside me. "You have to keep your wrist locked and throw with your whole arm so you impart proper spin to the blade. Like so." He demonstrated, and I watched his posture, the way he held the knife, the way his arm moved. "So…what's the deal?"

I tried again, and this time I got it to stick, but

only sort of. "It's Claire."

"Problems popping up?"

"Well, sort of. More that problems *haven't* popped up. Among other things, her dad died, and she discovered he wasn't her biological dad. How does that not fuck her up a little? Yet she seems fine."

"Seems like you're looking for problems when there aren't any. Are you having second thoughts about being with her?"

"Hell no. She means the world to me, But, I just have this feeling that…I don't know, that she's just suppressing things, and I don't know how to get her to talk about it without pushing her."

Zane watched me throw the knife again, and then adjusted my grip slightly, and showed me a sloweddown version of the arm movement. "Stupid question, maybe, but why not just flat out ask? Sometimes you have to push people, I think."

I shrugged. "I don't know. I don't want to make waves right now. She's been through a lot, and I want her to be able to figure it out on her own."

"Well that's fucking stupid."

I frowned at him. "Why do you say that?"

He gave me a *duh, you're a stupid-ass* glare. "Because you're her *boyfriend*, fucknuts. It's kind of your entire job to help her figure her shit out. That's why we date people, bro: for help when life gets shitty. Company during the good times, yeah, and for sex, and someone to sleep with at night, and wake up to in the morning. All that shit is nice. But…if you're not being a source of help when shit get shitty, then what's the point?"

I laughed. "You have such an eloquent way with words, Zane." I let out a frustrated breath. "But you're right. There's gotta be more than just being there through the shitty shit, as you put it."

"Damn right there does. She needs you to show her the way through, man. I don't mean that in any kind of sexist, women are meant to depend on men kind of way, just…if she doesn't know how to sort her shit, it's your job to help her."

"I don't know the way through, though. I don't what she's struggling with."

"Then that's where you start. Get her to open up."

"How, though?"

"Fuck, dude, I don't know, a can opener?" He slapped me on the back. "By talking, dumbass. Only way there is."

"Oh."

Zane chuckled. "For a guy who's supposed to be one of the smart brothers, you sure are a dumbass, sometimes."

"Fuck you."

"Yeah fuck you back, turd-biscuit."

"Fuck you back harder, floppy cunt waffle."

Zane chortled. "Dude, that's a good one! Floppy cunt waffle? Damn, son."

I laughed with him. "I've been saving that one for a special occasion."

He stared at me expectantly. "So? Go! Go talk to her."

"Now?"

He quirked an eyebrow at me. "Um, yeah, now. The longer you wait, the harder it gets."

"Since when are you wise about this shit?" I asked.

"Since it's not my relationship we're talking about. It's easy to give someone advice about their business, but it's always a hell of a lot harder to make sense of your own shit."

"That's the truth." I shot him a look as I tossed my bar towel at him. "You got this?"

"Yeah, I think I can handle the *zero customers*, dick-licker."

I gave him the finger as I left the bar to go in search of Claire.

It wasn't hard to find her, though. She was set up on the couch in Mara's office, which was in the back corner of a marketing firm a few streets up from the bar. Mara had taken over the office manager job

Lucian had suggested, and discovered that she loved it. The company was a marketing and branding firm local to the Ketchikan area, and they were expanding quickly, taking on more and more accounts as their reputation grew. There'd been talk of Mara buying in as a partner eventually, but for now, she was managing the office and enjoying it. It was different work from what she'd done in San Francisco and Seattle, apparently, but it was low-key and she really seemed to thrive on it, so Zane was happy because she was happy.

It also walking distance from the converted warehouse Zane was renovating—well, that Zane was lassoing all of us brothers into helping him renovate. Most of the complicated, technical stuff was being done by Bax and Xavier, but the easier stuff like laying tile and slapping up sheetrock the rest of us did on our downtime. It was almost done, and looking pretty damn sweet, honestly. They had a shitload of space, lots of natural light, and enough bedrooms that they could have a dozen kids and not run out of places to put them all.

As expected, Claire was sitting cross-legged in the corner of the thirdhand couch Mara had in her office, laptop open, fingers flying on the keyboard, a giant mug of steaming coffee on the table near her elbow, giant bright red over-the-ear Beats on her head.

Mara was at her desk, two monitors set up side-by-side, a pile of file folders in front of her, the one on top open; she too had a big pair of headphones on her head. Neither of them noticed me right away, and I just watched them for a moment. Intermittently, one of them would cackle and glance up and they'd shoot each other a look, and then go back to their computers. I realized they probably had a messaging thread up, so even while they were each working and in their own headspace, they were still talking to each other, trading jokes or dirty memes.

I leaned a shoulder against the doorframe and stared at Claire, just to see how long it would take before she noticed me. Mara's desk faced the doorway, so she noticed me right away, but I touched my lips with a finger, and she hid a smile while trying to ignore me. It took almost two full minutes before Claire started to shift, getting the slightly uncomfortable feeling of being watched. At first she glanced up at Mara, but she was studiously tapping away at her keyboard, so Claire went back to her work. I continued staring, as quietly as possible, and finally Claire slid her gaze up to the doorway, and when she saw me, she actually jumped.

"Holy shit, Brock, what the fuck?" She slid her headphones down around her neck. "How long have you been standing there?"

I laughed. "Almost five minutes, babe."

She eyed me. "So. What's up?" Another long glance at me, and then she sighed. "Wait, let me guess, you want to talk."

"Yeah."

She nodded, closed her laptop, set her headphones on top of it, and stood up, following me out of the office with a wave at Mara. Once out on the street, she threaded her fingers into mine and nudged me with her shoulder. "So. 'Sup?"

"You feel like going for a little flight?"

She shrugged. "Sure."

We walked together to the dock where my seaplane was moored. My plan wasn't new by any stretch of imagination—I sure as hell didn't have several hundred grand for a brand-new one; mine was a Piper Supercub from the late 1980s, heavily rebuilt by the previous owner, an older airshow pilot I'd gotten to know on my second national airshow tour. He'd sold it to me for a steal, since he'd been retiring and wanted to get rid of pretty much everything he owned so he could retire onto a sailboat with his twenty-years-younger wife. It had a brand-new engine, recently recovered wings and fuselage, a new prop, and some nice updates and upgrades to the mechanicals. It was a wide body, which meant it sat four as opposed to two, which was nice. I didn't do any cargo hauling, so I didn't need the cargo space, which was another reason I'd gone with this particular aircraft, since a lot of Supercubs or similar models only sat two to accommodate more cargo.

My aerobatics aircraft, a fifteen-year-old Staudacher, was currently in storage in Juneau, which was sad. I missed aerobatics, missed the rush, the adrenaline, the excitement.

Yes, I owned two planes. The Staudacher had been my first major purchase, and it had set me back almost a hundred and fifty grand, but I'd saved every penny—except for the cost of flying lessons—that I'd ever made working all year long and two jobs over the summers from the time I was fourteen. I'd saved up enough to put over half down, and Dad had cosigned a loan for the rest.

As soon as I took ownership of that bird, I set out to become a stunt pilot. I'd made some contacts with aerobatics pilots at the airport while taking lessons, which is how I'd gotten into it in the first place. I had the talent, and with a lot of aerobatics training I acquired the skills and, before long, I was performing at airshows around the Northwest, and eventually across the country. I'd quickly paid off the remainder of the loan and before long, I had a decent nest egg saved up, which I'd used to buy the Piper so I could fly in and out of Alaska without having to bother with the local airport and the long drive to the bar.

Claire climbed into the copilot's seat, buckled in and donned the headset while I went through the preflight. In no time, we were airborne and heading north. Unsurprisingly, Claire seemed in no rush to push me to talk. I followed the sound north, keeping an eye out for a likely spot to put down. It was a bright, warm, sunny day, and I had it in mind to anchor offshore somewhere and sit on the float with a fishing pole and talk. Zane had lit a fire under me and I was determined to get to the bottom of things with Claire. As restless and energetic as she was, she enjoyed fishing with me off the floats, and it had become one our favorite ways to kill a few hours on a Saturday afternoon.

After a quiet thirty-minute flight, I set down a few hundred yards away from the shores of the Muffin Islands, a spray of rocky, tree-covered islands near a set of other larger islands north of Ketchikan. It was a fairly remote spot, beautiful, lush, green, and peaceful. I threw out the anchor and let the plane drift backward until I felt the hook bite into the seafloor.

Claire already had the tackle box open and was setting up our poles while I shut down the engine. We rolled up our jeans around our knees and dangled our bare feet in the cool water, lines angled out, bobbers floating, the sun shining, a long warm breeze ruffling our hair.

"This is more than just a fishing trip, right?" Claire asked after a few minutes of silence. "I'm behind on work, but I figured this was important."

"I can't help feeling like you're suppressing something," I said. "Your dad's passing, what your mom told you…you don't just waltz away unaffected from that kind of thing."

"Maybe I do." She tugged on her line to set the bobber wiggling on the surface.

"Nope." I glanced at her, assessing; she wasn't shut down, but she wasn't liking this topic, either. "You're suppressing."

"So? Why can't I suppress it?" She shot me an angry look. "Do I have to tell you every little thing I'm thinking and feeling? And if I don't, it automatically means I'm unhealthy and suppressing? Is that it?"

"Claire, I'm just worried. You lost your father, and you learned your parents had been lying to you your whole life."

"And I'm supposed to be moping around crying, now? I'm supposed to sit on some therapist's couch and spout all my weepy emotions because Daddy didn't love me?"

I sighed. "I mean, well…yeah, kind of."

"That's not me, Brock, and if you don't understand that about me by now, then you haven't been paying attention."

"I *have* been paying attention, which is why I'm even doing this. I don't want to push you any more than you want to be pushed, but I know you're feeling things you're not letting out and, I'm sorry babe, but that's not healthy. If you don't want to talk to me—"

"I'm not seeing a therapist, Brock, so don't even finish that statement."

"Okay, okay, fine. Then talk to me."

"And say what?" She tugged her pole upward again. "I mean, for real, what is it you want me to say? 'Oh, I'm *so* sad, I'm *so* confused, I don't know who I am.'" The last sentence was delivered with such intense sarcasm it fairly cut the air like a razor. "Fuck that. I'm dealing, okay?"

"I just—"

"I know, I know. You just *care*," she said, interrupting me again. "You want to help. I'm grateful, Brock, I really am. But I'm fine."

Her bobber dipped, bounced, and then sank under the water, and she stood up on the float, angled the tip of her pole upward and cranked the reel, pulling in a giant fish. I scooped it up in the net, worked the hook loose, put it on a stringer, and she cast her line out again.

"Nice catch, babe. That thing has to be damn near a foot long."

She grinned at me. "I'm winning…again."

I rolled my eyes at her in fake annoyance, because that was an inside joke between us: she always caught more fish than I did, for whatever reason. It was fucking annoying, but also kind of funny, because she'd never been fishing until I took her out a week or two after we first met.

She'd hated it at first, but once she learned to settle in and enjoy the peace and just hang out with me and talk, she started to get into it. And then she'd caught her first fish, a four-pound monster, and she'd been…hooked—fishing puns for the win. And now, whenever we went out, no matter how many fish I caught, she always caught more than me.

"If Brennan was still alive—" I started.

"NOPE!" she shouted over me. "Not going there, Brock. Don't care. He's dead, Dad's dead, and I don't really give much of a fuck about either of them."

"Claire—"

"Wanna know how I'm dealing, Brock? I'm gonna chuck it in the fuck it bucket and move on."

"Come on, Claire." I sighed. "You're being stubborn."

And again, her bobber sank and she hauled in another fish. Bigger than the last one, too. This time she unhooked it and ran it onto the stringer, while I watched in a not-so-fake annoyance.

"What the fuck is your secret? Seriously."

She rubbed at the crotch of her jeans. "Pussy magic."

I stared at her. "The hell does that mean?"

"It means I have a pussy, so I'm just better at everything than you." She stuck her tongue out at me. "Girls rule, boys drool."

"Wow. *That's* mature."

She snickered. "You're just getting pissy because you know it's true."

"I'm getting pissy because you're being ridiculous."

"And if I wasn't ridiculous, you wouldn't be even half so attracted to me."

I laughed. "I can't argue with that, actually."

"That's right. See, Brock? I'm winning!"

I snorted, shaking my head. "You're something else, Claire Collins."

"Let's play a game," she suggested, jerking the tip of her pole upward a few times.

"Okay…"

"I bet I'll catch another fish before you get your first. And if I do, you're not allowed to ask me how I'm feeling, or what's wrong, or why I'm not emoting about my dad, or any of that bullshit. You just forget it."

"And if I catch a fish before you do?"

"I'll see a therapist. *And* I'll blow you on the flight back."

"That seems lopsided."

"Deal or no deal?" She held my gaze, her eyebrow quirked.

I sighed. "Fine. Deal."

She held out one hand for me to shake. "For real. No asking."

"Fine, I agree," I said, shaking her hand.

As soon as I let go of her hand, she started cackling triumphantly. "SUCKER!" she shouted, and stood up and started reeling in like a madwoman.

I stared in disbelief. "Are you for fucking real?"

She kept cackling as she hauled in yet another monster fish. "I had it on the line the whole time!"

"You're evil."

"Yes I am."

I restrained the urge to growl, or haul her over my knee and spank her. Which, on second thought, she'd probably enjoy. "That's not fair. No deal."

"Oh no, no no no. You shook on it! No takebacks." She tossed her pole into the plane and pointed her finger at me. "You wouldn't break your word, would you, Brock Badd?"

"You cheated!"

"And?"

"That negates the deal."

"No it doesn't. You'd have known I had a fish on the line if you'd looked at my bobber. Not my fault you weren't paying attention."

I had an image in my head, now: Claire bent over my legs, her sweet, sexy ass bare for me, my hand descending to spank her ass until those hot little cheeks were all red and she was begging me to stop, or to fuck her.

And damn it, now that I had the thought in my head it wouldn't leave. The idea of having Claire's bare ass under my hand, taking my punishment like the bad girl she was…damn. *Damn*. I had to do it, and somehow I knew she would probably get off on being spanked.

I glared at her, and then, on a whim, grabbed her wrist, threatening to yank her off balance and into the water.

"Brock! Don't!" She tried to resist, but I had her wrist in a firm but gentle grip, keeping downward pressure so she was one solid yank from going swimming. "Brock, I swear, do *not* get me wet. This is my favorite sweater, and my phone is in my pocket. I swear to fuck, I will never speak to you again if you pull me in."

I kept up the pressure. "Pull your pants down."

She froze, staring at me. "What?"

"You heard me." I transferred my grip on her

wrist to my other hand so I could set my pole in the plane, and then latched onto her ankle. "One heave, and you're swimming. Pants around your ankles."

"Why? What are you gonna do?"

"You never know. Now, pants down, Claire."

She moved slowly, never taking her eyes off me. She unzipped her jeans, shimmied them down around her ankles. "Okay."

I quirked an eyebrow up. "Underwear too."

She hooked her fingers in the sides of her neon green thong and tugged so the scrap of fabric was pooled down with her jeans. "Now what?"

"Lay face down on my lap."

"What if I fall in?"

"I won't let you."

"Promise?"

"I'd never break a promise to you, Claire." I held her gaze, letting her see the truth.

She moved gingerly, slowly and awkwardly shuffling toward me. I grabbed her waist with both hands and guided her down, keeping her balanced as she flattened her belly onto my thighs. "What's your plan here, Brock? If you want to fuck me, you're missing a few minor details."

"Not planning on fucking you," I said, palming her ass cheek. "At least, not yet."

"Then what are you—" She broke off with a

startled shriek as I smacked her ass cheek. I wasn't exactly gentle, either. The *crack* of my hand across her butt echoed across the water, and she lurched forward. "FUCK!"

I held her down. "Be still."

"What the hell is this?"

I spanked the other cheek, and she shrieked again, lurching so the plane rocked. "This is what you get for cheating."

The other cheek again, and now the pale, creamy bubble of her ass was pinking, and she was whimpering, gripping my jeans with both hands clawed like talons. I rubbed gently over the pink spots with my palm, and she began to loosen her grip. And I struck again, smacking harder than the last time, hard enough that she was jolted. I didn't give her a reprieve, but spanked again, and she whimpered, sounding like she was biting her lip. The whimper wasn't of pain, though. Oh no, I knew my girl.

"You like this, don't you, Claire?" I demanded in a rough voice, caressing the reddening flesh.

"No," she groaned.

I slid my fingers between her thighs and found her slit, dipped a finger in. "You're soaked, Claire. Your pussy is dripping." I spanked her again, twice on one cheek, but more softly. "Don't lie to me."

She writhed on me, and I tightened the grip of

my arm around her middle, keeping her pinned down onto my legs. "Your weak little spanks don't turn me on," she growled. "You're gonna have to spank me a hell of a lot harder than that."

"Is that right?" I murmured.

I sucked the juices off my fingers noisily, and she craned her head over her shoulder to watch me as I licked my fingers. Slowly, gently, I caressed her ass cheeks, one and then the other in soothing circles with my palm. And then, without warning, I spanked her again, once, twice, three times, and each smack was harder than the last, and she was moaning, shifting her hips, shrieking with the smacks and moaning in between them.

"Harder."

"Harder?"

"You hit like a bitch. Spank me harder." She grinned at me over her shoulder. "Is that what you wanna hear? Spank me harder, Daddy."

So I spanked her harder, alternating cheeks until the flesh was red and angry looking and she was gasping and writhing. And that's when I slipped two fingers inside her soaked pussy and spread her juices over her clit and rubbed the engorged flesh there until she was humping my fingers and groaning, shuddering.

Then, when I knew she was seconds from coming, I lifted her into the back seat. "Time to go," I said, standing up.

She stared at me, her jeans and underwear around her ankles, her skin flushed, cheeks pink, hair a mess, eyes wide, surprised, shocked, confused, still shaking. "Wait, what?"

I shot her an evil smirk. "That's it. Time to go."

"But—but I was—goddamn it, Brock!" she howled. "I was right there!"

"I know."

"And you're just gonna stop? You're going to leave me like this?"

"Yep." I hauled in the anchor, and then dried my hands on my jeans before climbing behind the controls.

She stayed in the back seat for a stunned moment, staring at me in anger. "You bastard." I glanced back, and she had two fingers between her legs. "Who needs you? I can come without you."

I reached back and pinioned her wrist. "Nope. No coming without me, remember?"

"Goddamn it." She shook my grip off and pulled up her thong and then her jeans. "This is your payback, huh?"

I winked at her and clicked my tongue. "Can't put anything past you, can I?"

She closed the door, secured the poles and tackle box, and slumped into the copilot seat. "You suck."

I went through preflight, and then started the engine and took off. When we were airborne and heading back toward Ketchikan, I shot a look at her. "You like being spanked."

She gave me a dirty glare. "Yeah, well, see if I let you do that again."

I laughed. "Oh, you'll let me."

She lifted one eyebrow. "You think so?"

"I know so."

She crossed her arms over her boobs and huffed. "Fuck you."

"I keep my promises, Claire. You cheated, and I got you back. You want me to finish you off? I can have you coming all over my fingers in seconds. Slip those pants down and I'll show you how fast I can make you come."

"But?"

I shrugged. "But you have to agree that you cheated and that it doesn't count. I won't ask about anything again if you really don't want me to, but you have to promise that you'll talk to me, that you won't keep things bottled up like you have been."

"Why are you pushing this so hard?"

"Because you mean more to me than just about anyone on this planet, and I know you're feeling things you're not expressing, but you're too damn headstrong and stubborn to talk about it. You'd rather push it all down and pretend it doesn't affect you. And when it comes down to it, you don't really trust me."

"I do too trust you," she argued.

"Then talk to me."

"I don't know how." She unbuckled the five-point seat belt, unbuttoned her jeans and shoved them along with her thong down around her knees. "Now—finish me off."

"Apologize for cheating and I will."

She sucked in a deep breath, closing her eyes in supreme irritation, and then let out the breath and met my gaze. "Fine." She lifted her chin. "Brock, I apologize for cheating. Can you forgive me?"

I held the aircraft steady with one hand and reached over with my other hand, dipping my middle finger inside her and then pulling it out to flick my fingertip against her clit. "I forgive you, Claire."

She moaned, and then sucked in a sharp breath, throwing her head back and closing her eyes in bliss. "My ass hurts so bad it's hard to sit down."

"I liked seeing your tight little ass all red and splotchy."

Her eyes flicked open. "That was the hottest fucking thing I've experienced in a long time."

"You like it when I spank you, don't you?"

She lifted her shirt up to pinch and roll her nipples between her fingers. "*Fuck* yes."

"You want me to bend you over my bed and fuck you from behind while I spank you, don't you?"

"I want that so bad, Brock!" She was writhing in the seat, grinding against my flicking fingertip. "I want you to spank me until I beg you to stop and then I want you to fuck me doggy style and keep spanking me. I want to feel your big hard hand on my ass cheeks, and I want to be so sore I can't sit for days, because every time I sit down I'll think about you spanking me and fucking me."

My cock was raging inside my jeans, bent double against the zipper, aching. "Fucking hell, Claire. You're such a dirty girl."

"Brock, baby—" She broke off to moan breathily, rolling her nipples between her fingers, riding the edge of orgasm. "You have no idea how dirty I can be, Brock. No fucking idea—oh god, oh god, oh god!"

She thrashed, fucking herself on my fingers, screaming like a banshee as she came. By this point, I was so hard inside my jeans that it was actually painful. Once Claire was finished coming, I tugged at the zipper of my jeans so my dick could straighten out a little bit. The movement caught Claire's eye, and she reached for me, still breathing hard.

"I feel like maybe it should be your turn, huh?" she said.

I put both hands on the yoke. "I wouldn't stop you."

She reached into my jeans and pulled my cock out. "You liked spanking me as much I liked being spanked, I take it?"

I nodded as she stroked me lazily in one hand. "Hell yeah, I did."

"What made you do it?" She rubbed her thumb over the tip, smearing pre-come. "I didn't think you were the kinky type."

"I'm not typically. But I was so pissed at you I thought about spanking you as a punishment, and I realized you'd probably just like it, and then I couldn't get that image out of my head."

She met my gaze, her fist gliding loosely around my shaft, her touch gentle, affectionate, unhurried. "Well, I don't approve of you punishing me, but I do approve of being spanked like that. Feel free to take me over your knee whenever you want. I might protest, but that's half the fun, right?"

"You totally earned it and you know it."

"I don't like being pushed, Brock. I'll talk when I'm ready, *if* I'm ever ready. Some things are just…"

"Off-limits?"

"No," she said, slipping her other hand into my pants to cup my balls. "Some things are hard for me to even think about in my own head, much less talk about. This is one of those things. I may not ever be able to really talk about it, and pushing me is just going to piss me off."

"I get that, and I respect that. But don't bullshit me, okay? Don't block me out and don't fuck with me. Like when you tried to use sex to get out of going to the hospital. That shit doesn't fly with me."

"Sometimes you don't listen to me, and I have to get your attention somehow."

I was finding it hard to focus on the conversation and flying at the same time. "I don't listen to you when what you're saying is bullshit."

Now both of her hands were around my shaft, slowly pumping, and her eyes were on my cock, and her tongue was sliding back and forth across her lower lip, an adorable little signal of hers that she was getting ready to use her mouth. Adorable, but also a Pavlovian thing for me, as in, when I saw that tongue stick out and lick her lower lip like that, my already-hard cock went even harder because I knew I was about to get her hot wet mouth on me.

Oh…yep. There she went. She set aside the headset and bent over me, and I hissed and clenched my fists around the yoke as she took me into her mouth, her wet heat sinking around me.

One of the first things I learned about Claire was that she had absolutely zero gag reflex. None.

And this was something she was always very eager to demonstrate on me. Imagine my shock, that first night together, when she got me hard and spent a few minutes using her hands, and then had bent over me and took my cock into her mouth, and then just kept taking. I mean, I'm a pretty well-endowed guy and she's a pretty petite girl, and I was in no way expecting or anticipating her to take even half of it when she started sucking.

But she'd glanced up at me with a little grin, as if she knew she was about to blow my mind, and then she'd sunk her mouth down my shaft until her lips touched my balls and her nose bumped my belly, and I wasn't even sure where it all was, or how she was capable of such a feat. She didn't always deep throat me, though. She liked to save it for when she really wanted to make it special.

Like now. She cupped my balls in her hands and massaged my taint—one of her favorite things to do to me, for some reason—and then, with that hot little smirk, she took me all the way.

"Holy fuck," I groaned.

She bobbed on me slowly, backing away a little farther every time, and then taking me to the hilt again. She had me flexing, groaning, and her mouth was suctioned around the head, her tongue sliding against me, sucking hard. I hissed, feeling the orgasm rising in me.

"Gonna come soon," I warned.

And now, with my warning, she deep throated me and then backed off until I popped free of her mouth, and she licked the tip, and then took me all the way again. And again. And again. Faster and faster. No hands, just my cock sliding wet and slick past her lips until I felt the pressure boiling inside me, hot and wild and undeniable, and I groaned, letting my hips flex.

"Oh fuck, fuck, fuck—" I snarled, my eyes narrowing, need blasting through me. "Now, Claire...I'm gonna come—right *now*."

She didn't slow down; if anything, she sped up. Took me as deep as I'd go, and then as I released she backed away, taking my come in her mouth and swallowing it with a loud gulp before sinking down on me again, eyes wide, nostrils flaring, tongue flicking and flitting and licking and swirling. Another hard blast wrenched through me, and now she backed away to wrap her lips around the head and sucked hard as I groaned and flexed and kept coming. She swallowed frantically, her fists around my cock sliding and pumping as her mouth sucked, and I felt myself getting dizzy from the power of the orgasm she'd pulled out of me.

I forced myself to focus, to keep the craft steady

in the air, keeping the nose up and the wings level.

"God*damn*, Claire."

She lifted up, and a droplet of my come slid down from the corner of her mouth. I wiped it with my thumb, and she grabbed my hand, licking my thumb, then pumped my cock a few times until more come seeped out, and she licked that away too, as if savoring the last of an ice-cream cone, and then she tucked me away and re-zipped and buttoned me.

Claire sat up and donned the headset. "It never ceases to amaze me how much semen you produce, Brock," she said, buckling up once more.

"You do it to me, babe."

"To you, or for you?"

I shrugged. "Both."

A few minutes of silence, and then she glanced at me. "I really am sorry, Brock."

"I know. It's okay. Just be real with me, okay?"

"I'm trying."

The rest of the flight back was normal, with normal conversation, normal silences, everything totally normal.

And yet...I still had an uneasy feeling.

EIGHT

Claire

Dru, Mara, and I were in the "family booth" at Badd's, the one closest to the kitchen and the service bar. It was the one booth in the bar that was always reserved for family and friends who weren't working and who wanted to hang out, It was a popular spot in the evenings, especially on the weeknights when Badd's wasn't as busy. There were always at least two or three people in the booth, and usually more than that squeezed in, with a pitcher of beer or a bottle of something going around. Tonight was a weekend, so all hands were on deck—all the brothers were working: Zane, Sebastian, and Brock were behind the bar, and Bax was at the door carding, the twins and Lucian were waiting tables, and Xavier was in the kitchen slinging booze food.

It was well past midnight, and the place was crowded wall to wall with people, three deep waiting for drinks and all the tables were full. One of the recent improvements the brothers had made to the bar was keeping the kitchen open through closing, with a limited deep-fry-only menu available after eleven. Since most other bars closed their kitchens at eleven, this brought even more traffic to Badd's, since who wouldn't want French fries or chicken fingers with late night booze? The after-hours menu was designed by Xavier and it featured items he could sling by himself and serve in extra-large paper cups, which meant no extra dishes to manage. It was a pretty genius move, actually. Their liquor sales had skyrocketed in tandem with food sales, and now even on weeknights the bar was pretty packed, and on weekends it was pretty much insane from open to close. It didn't hurt that the brothers were all sexy as hell, something the female patrons really appreciated.

I sipped from my glass and watched Brock shaking a martini, frowning absently, thinking about the way he'd caught me unawares with his bullshit interrogation.

Let's go for a flight, Claire, he says.

Let's sit on the pontoon and TALK, Claire, he says.

Let me pin you to the wall about your most private, personal, painful inner thoughts and feelings, Claire, he says.

I was truly pissed about it. Could he not just give it a rest?

Gahhh. The more I thought about it, the more pissed I got. I mean, where did he get off, thinking he could just drag everything out of me? What? I'm supposed to just spill everything I'm going through just because we're dating? Um, no. Thanks, nice try, but no. That's not how I work. I'm a very private person when it comes to my feelings. I've let him get closer to me than anyone else in my entire life…I've told him stuff NOBODY knows, not even Mara. Isn't that enough? He was there for me when my dad was dying, and yeah, he was probably right in that I'd eventually be thankful he had made me go. Because of his insistence, I'd discovered a truth which I would have otherwise spent the rest of my life not knowing. But right now…I wasn't thankful, I was *pissed*. At Brock, at Mom, at Connor, at Brennan, at myself, at life.

I was sitting in the corner of the booth, wedged in next to Mara, with Dru across from us. I was slamming whisky, neat. I hadn't bothered to count, since I was just kind of pouring them haphazardly from the bottle of Johnny Black Zane had dropped off...but the bottle had started out full and was now half-empty. A LOT of whisky, especially for a smaller chick like me. Thankfully Xavier had wandered out, saw how much scotch I was drinking, and returned promptly with a cupful of fries sprinkled liberally with Cajun seasoning and another cup full of chicken tenders and mozzarella sticks. All of which I was gleefully hogging. It was soaking up the whisky nicely, but I was still pretty well sloshed.

Okay, I was hammered.

But I had no intention of stopping. I tossed back the last swallow from my tumbler and poured another measure, sloppily with both Mara and Dru eyeing me and then each other, meaningfully.

"SHUT UP," I slurred loudly. "I don't need your silent judgment."

Mara sighed. "We're not judging you, Claire, we're just..."

"We're worried, honey," Dru finished.

"I'm fine."

"You're—" Mara started.

"Drunk," I cut in. "Yes. Very much so. But I'm fine. Toooooootally fine."

"Claire." Mara said my name in the tone of voice she reserved for when I was being obtuse. "You've been drinking whisky for two hours."

"I'm having *fun*," I snapped.

"You don't even *like* whisky, and plus, you haven't said a single word since we sat down."

"I'm *having FUN!*" I insisted, more loudly.

"You're eating *fried food*," Mara said, as if suggesting I was doing something illegal.

"I was hungry."

"You *never* eat fried food, Claire."

I growled. "Oh, for fuck's sake." I shoved at Mara until she slid out. "I don't need this shit."

I stood up, wobbly, and started to walk away. I got two steps before I spun around and grabbed the bottle and the tumbler, and then turned away again. And then I stopped, transferring the tumbler and bottle to one hand and then snagged the cups of food, glaring at Dru and Mara as if daring them to try to stop me.

Mara watched me for a second. "Where are you going?"

"OUTSIDE," I snapped. "Where there's no one to get on my case."

I threaded my way dizzily through the kitchen, where Xavier just watched me stumble past him to the service door, which he'd propped open with a milk crate to let in the fresh air and the cool evening breeze.

There was an old Formica-covered table out there

beside the dumpster, with a cluster of mismatched, cast-off chairs—lawn chairs, old wooden restaurant chairs, old bar stools. I slumped into the nearest seat and carefully set down my fuck-everyone-and-every-thing supplies, and immediately shoved half a mozzarella stick into my mouth. Mmmm, cheesy, deep-fried goodness. I knew I'd regret this later, because my stomach would very painfully and violently remind me that I hadn't eaten fried food in years, but shit, the amount of whisky I'd already had was going to be punishment enough. Why not add to the agony with some delicious in the moment?

I tossed back more whisky, and ate a handful of fries while mentally berating Dru and Mara. Even in my own head I knew I was being drunk and stupid, but I couldn't help it.

After a few minutes, Xavier came out with a pint glass full of beer, a white-and-green striped bar towel tossed over one shoulder and a stained white apron tied around his waist. He sipped his beer, and then eyed me, hesitating.

"Don't start, Xavier," I mumbled.

He didn't say anything, just quirked any eyebrow at me, and then took my glass from me, ignoring my protests, and then tossed back a healthy swallow before returning it.

Another few minutes of silence, and I couldn't

handle it anymore. "What, Xavier? What do you want?"

He shrugged. "I'm just taking a break, that's all."

I eyed him. He was a damn sexy kid, Xavier Badd. Tall and lean, wiry, with the signature Badd chocolate-brown eyes and messy dark hair, he was the most hipster of his brothers, always wearing tight jeans and retro T-shirts, like Atari and Galaga and original Nintendo and shit like that, retro-geeky stuff. He left his hair long and messy on top and cut close to the scalp on the sides. He was a super-sweet kid, and very eccentric which made him funny and unpredictable, plus he was fun to talk to and fun to mess with, since he was obviously a virgin.

He was wearing black Dickey work pants, much-stained, clearly meant only for work, and a faded black T-shirt with a red dodecahedron on it designed to look like a nucleus with electrons and such swirling around it—it was a D20, in gamer parlance, a dice used by Dungeons and Dragons players. The shirt looked old as hell, with holes in it and evidence of a lot of wear and tear. Much-loved, obviously.

"Bullshit," I said. "Let me guess…someone sent you to keep an eye on me."

He blushed, glanced down at the table, tracing idle patterns on the surface in the moisture left behind by his sweating pint glass. "Nah, I just—"

"You're a bad liar, Xavier," I said. "Pro-tip? Don't do it, you have too many tells."

He laughed, nodding. "I know. My brothers make fun of me for it."

"Who sent you?"

He shrugged. "Everyone?"

"Everyone?"

"Yeah, well, Mara told Brock that you'd come out here, and he was unable to leave the bar, and Mara said you were being…" He trailed off, uncomfortable with whatever she'd called me. "She said you were being difficult."

"Oh horse-shit. That's not what she said."

"No, but I'd rather not repeat it."

I laughed. "Now I'm curious. What'd Mara say, Xavier? It's not gonna hurt my feelings. We talk like that to each other and about each other, it's just how we are."

He was so fun and easy to mess with: I was wearing a low-cut V-neck T-shirt, no bra, so I leaned forward casually. He did his damnedest to not look, but he kept accidentally directing his gaze to my chest.

He glanced away, then looked at my eyes, and blushed. "You—your…" He let out a breath and leaned way back in his chair, tipping back on the back legs, and took a long swig. "You're messing with me, aren't you? You're using your feminine wiles on me."

I burst out laughing so hard I spewed whisky all over the table, and then dissolved into hacking. When I could breathe again, I laughed some more. "Oh my god, Xavier—holy shit, honey. Feminine wiles? That's the funniest thing I've ever heard in my entire life." I reached out and grabbed his wrist, meeting his gaze, worried my laughing had hurt his feelings. "You are so adorable it hurts, you know that?"

He frowned at me. "Adorable. That's wonderful."

I tilted my head at him. "You say that as if it's a bad thing."

"It is. No guy, no *man* ever wants to be cute or adorable, and that's what everyone calls me. It's the kiss of death. The moment a girl thinks you're so *cute* or *sooooo* adorable…" He drew his finger across his throat. "You're done."

"I didn't mean it like that."

"You didn't mean it to be condescending, no. I know that. But it was still…dismissive.

"I get a lot of shit about being a virgin. And partially, yeah, it is a decision I have made intentionally, because that's something I do not want to give away cheaply. I want it to have meaning. That's the story I tell everyone, and it's true."

"But?"

He shrugged. "But I'm also just…" A sigh, and another shrug, an uncomfortable one. "I'm not good with physical contact. Not with anyone. I *want* to have sex—with the right woman, someday hopefully soon—but…sometimes I'm scared I won't be able to. I'm worried my hypersensitivity to touch will make it impossible. What then? I remain a virgin the rest of my life?" He poured some Johnny into the tumbler and drank it. "Nikolas Tesla voluntarily remained a virgin his whole life, so as not to be distracted from achieving the maximum potential of his intelligence. Maybe that's what I'm doomed to be. I'll probably die like him, too—alone, poor, with my accomplishments only recognized long after my death."

"No, Xavier. I really don't think that's likely."

He wouldn't quite look at me. "But what if I can't ever go through with it?"

"I don't know. I can't really answer that." I hesitated. "I'd like to say that you'll find the right person and it'll work out for you. I mean, I'm not you, I don't have your issue with touch. But I went through some things that made me not want to ever do that, or to allow anyone to get that close to me. But I did, and even though it was kind of hard the first time, I got over it, and it became something I really enjoy. Maybe for you it'll be similar. I mean, hopefully you won't ever go through what I did, but I'm just saying you'll maybe have to just take it slow, take it one step at a time, with the right person, acclimating yourself to letting that one person inside your walls, letting them have that part of you."

"That makes sense, I guess."

I stared at him for a moment. "Damn you. That was a nice deflection." I took a sip of scotch and said, "Now. Tell me what Mara said. I won't be mad at you *or* her, I promise."

He sighed. "She said you were being a stubborn, obnoxious, impossible little bitch who wouldn't know a good thing if it literally bit you on the ass."

"I *do* know a good thing, but I haven't been able to get him to bite me, yet."

Xavier blushed again.

"She also might have tossed the word whore around a few times," Xavier said, not quite looking at me.

"Sounds about right. You can go back in there and tell all of them that I don't need a babysitter. I'm an adult and I can do what I want and they can all go fuck themselves. Tell Mara I said to remember that she's a commitment-phobic sissy just like me, so she especially can kiss my ass."

"Why am I giving them these messages?" Xavier asked. "Why not tell them yourself? Are you going somewhere?"

"I don't want to see anyone right now. Least of all Mara or Brock."

"I must admit, I do not understand any of this."

I laughed again. "Because you're beautifully and wonderfully innocent, honey-buns." I touched his wrist again, a brief contact. "Let me tell you something: when you fuck someone, it's just fucking. No complications, no mess, no bullshit. But once you start giving a shit, that's when it gets messy. You gotta be really sure you want that mess, kiddo, because once you start giving a shit, you can't take it back."

"You act like you can separate…fucking someone from caring about them." He hesitated over the F-word, which made me want to clasp my hands together under my chin and go *awwwww, how cute.*

"That's because you can."

"How?"

I shrugged. "It's just sex, just bodies and hands and sweat and spit and dicks and pussies. Peg A goes into Slot B, repeat until orgasm, it feels good, go home. Simple." I polished off the last of the fries with another shot of whisky, and holy motherfucker, I was wasted. I'd have hell to pay when I stood up, but for now, I was wallowing blissfully in the haze of being sloppy drunk.

"But…*but*—when you start doing stupid shit like *caring* about people, sex isn't just sex anymore. It's not just feeling good anymore. You can't just give a shit once and then be done. Oh *nooooo*, you have to *keep* giving a shit. Perpetually. And you have to allow the other person to give a shit about you. That's the worst part."

Xavier's frown was so puzzled, so thoughtful, so delightfully innocent my heart hurt. "Why would letting someone care about you be bad?"

"Because then they have the power to hurt you, and not just a few little hurt feelings, but the really deep down fuck up your life kind of agony. And that shit sucks, okay? It just sucks. I do not recommend it."

"It seems to me that pain heals, even if you never totally forget, even if you have scars, literally or metaphorically." Xavier's eyes met mine. "Pain will heal. But loneliness, isolation, the pain of not having anyone who understands you, not having anyone you really trust, not having anyone that can…be your person, I suppose…I would think that would be worth the risk of pain."

The innocence, the hope, the genuine kindness in his big chocolate-brown puppy dog eyes was way too much for me. I shook my head in irritation and stood up carefully.

"That's because you've never felt either one, Xavier." I flattened a palm on the table for balance and drained the last swallow of whisky in the glass, and noticed that the bottle was down to three-quarters empty. "But I'm black-out wasted and cynical, so

I wouldn't listen to me if I were you."

"You don't sound very drunk," Xavier noted.

"I'm one of those drunks who never looks, sounds, or acts as drunk as they really are. Make no mistake—I'm completely obliterated right now."

"So where are you going?"

I shrugged. "I dunno."

"Should you walk around alone if you're as drunk as you say you are?"

"Yes. I should," I said, picking my steps ever so carefully out of the alley toward the sidewalk.

"I'm not so sure I agree, Claire." He stood up and followed me. "You could get lost, or fall over and be hurt. Why don't you let me get someone to go with you?"

"BECAUSE I WANT TO BE ALONE!" I shouted. "I don't need a fucking babysitter!"

"I'm not trying to babysit you, Claire, I just—I'm worried about you."

"Yeah, well I'd say get in line, but it'd be a pretty short fucking line."

"That's rank nonsense," Xavier snapped, sounding more irritated than I'd ever heard him. "And on the behalf of myself, my brothers, Mara, and Dru, I take offense to that statement, and the insinuation behind it. The line is actually fairly long, at this point. There's not one person in that bar that wouldn't go out of their way for you, and you know it." He kept pace with me. "But what do I know? I'm just a cute, innocent virgin."

"XAVIER!" I heard a male voice shouting. "WHERE THE FUCK ARE YOU? I GOT ORDERS!"

"I didn't mean to hurt your feelings, Xavier. You're a gorgeous person, inside and out." I waved him away. "Now go. I'll be fine."

He eyed me warily, thoughtfully, and then turned and went back to the kitchen. I set out down the sidewalk, stumbling a little here and there. And with each step, I realized exactly how clobbered I was; it became harder and harder to put one foot in front of the other, harder to see straight, or see one of anything.

I wasn't sure where I was going, or why. All I knew was that everything hurt.

I didn't want to care about Brock. I didn't want him to care about me.

I didn't want to answer any more damn questions. I didn't want to think about my mom, or Connor, or whatever the fuck the other guy's name was, Brendan? Brandon? Brannon? Something like that. Fuck him, whatever his stupid Irish name was. Fuck him for dying. And fuck Connor for taking Mom back when he clearly wasn't up to the task of loving another man's baby.

Fuck both of them, for not being there for me.

Fuck Mom and Dad—*Connor*, I mean—for lying to me my whole life.

And fuck Brock for forcing me to go watch my stupid lying dick of a father-figure die, and thus learning the truth. Would have been better to have gone the rest of my life just thinking there was something wrong with me that prevented him from loving me. Knowing the truth fucks my up whole life in so many ways I don't even understand.

I abruptly stopped walking, wobbled, stumbled, and found a solid vertical surface at my back and slid down to a sitting position. Waves chucked and slapped nearby. I peered around and made out blurry white shapes of boats. I was at the docks, then? I couldn't really tell, and didn't care.

I didn't want to care about anything.

Fuck Brock for making me care about him, about me, about my past, about my future, about anything.

"Claire?" I heard a voice.

I ignored him.

"CLAIRE!" he shouted again.

"Stop shouting," I said. "I'm over here."

I heard the sound of running on the dock and then Brock was kneeling in front of me. "Claire, goddammit. What are you doing?"

I shrugged. "I dunno. Sitting here?"

"You're about to fall into the water."

"That's okay. I can swim."

"You're hammered."

"So I can swim hammered." I peered up at him. "You can fuck off. I don't need you."

"Yes, you do." He lifted me to my feet and guided me away. "Now, come on. You need to lie down somewhere."

"It's *lay* down, actually, not *lie*. And I don't wanna *lay* down. Leave me alone." I shook his hand off me, glared blearily around to find the apartment above the twins' recording studio where Brock was currently living, and thus, so was I.

"Claire, just let me walk you home."

"Seattle is a long walk, buddy."

He was silent for a few steps. "Not what I meant."

"I know what you meant." I felt the anger coming back, and while deep down I knew it was irrational and unfair, I was too drunk to care, too drunk to filter. "And I meant what I said."

"You're drunk and upset. We don't have to talk about this now."

"Talk about what, Brock? You think I could ever make this podunk little piece of shit town *home*? Get real." I tried to walk faster to get away from him, but only managed to weave an even more unsteady line.

"Damn it, Claire. Just stop," he said, trying to catch me in his hands again.

"Stop what?" I shook him off again. "Quit grabbing me. I'll stop pretending, how about that? Here's me not pretending anymore. This shit between us is done. It's over. It was never going to work, and you were a dumbass if you thought it could. We had some good sex, but that's all it was ever going to be."

"That's not true. You're just spooked."

"Spooked? What am I? A skittish horse? Fuck you. I'm not spooked, I'm done acting like I can do a relationship. I'm too fucked-up for relationships. Too fucked-up for you. Too fucked-up for…for everything." I felt his hands on my shoulders, turning me, guiding me, and I couldn't remember where I'd been going, and couldn't see which of the spinning doors I was supposed to go through, or how to make them stop spinning so I could grab the handle, so I let him guide me. "Fuck you. Fuck this. Fuck us. Fuck me. Fuck everything."

"That's a lot of fucking."

"Yeah, and that's all we were, Brock—a lot of fucking."

A door opened, somehow, and I heard my footsteps on a carpeted floor, saw the shapes of drums and guitars and a piano and microphones all jumbled together, and then there were stairs under my feet, and Brock was partially carrying me up them. I closed my eyes for a minute, and felt myself tripping, because my legs were getting mixed up. And then I was floating, floating in a pair of strong arms. God, his arms were nice. Yummy, and strong, and sexy, and I really did like them. I patted his bicep.

"You have nice arms," I said.

"Thanks."

I tried to open my eyes, and only managed one. His jaw was set, and his brow was furrowed. "Uh-oh. Bwock is aaaang-gwee," I said in singsong baby talk. "I maded him mad."

He laughed, and the furrows smoothed out. "You're just fucked-up."

"I know, and that's why this won't work."

"Yes, it will."

"No, it won't."

"Do you remember what you told me? That night in Michigan, before your dad's funeral?"

I shook my head. "No. But I'm sure it was a bunch of bullshit."

"You told me that a shit-storm was coming, and that you were going to try to break up with me, and that I shouldn't let you." He set me down on his bed, and then I heard his door close.

"That was drunk-me."

"And you're drunk now."

"Right. So I'm saying, drunk-me is an idiot and you should never listen to her." I put one foot on the floor to stop the spinning, keeping my eyes closed and focusing on keeping the contents of my stomach inside me.

"Exactly. Which is why you can say whatever you want right now, because you're drunk. It still hurts to hear you say it, even if I know you're drunk and don't mean it, but I'm not letting you sabotage us."

"I'm sorry it's hurting you, but I'm not saying this just because I'm drunk. I'm saying it because it's true. I don't want to keep doing this."

"Doing what, Claire?" His voice was soft, wary.

"Us. Caring about you. Letting you in. Dealing with your endless fucking *questions*." I made my voice as deep as I could in an attempt to mimic him. "'Hey, Claire, let me haul you away from work and trap you on my airplane so I can try to make you talk about your feelings, because I'm Brock and I'm *sensitive*.'"

I heard him make a sound that seemed conflicted. "Claire...fuck." He sighed, and stood up. "Go to sleep. I have to go back to work. We'll talk when you're sober."

"No, we won't."

"Why not?"

I pointed at the ceiling. "Because I'm leaving in the morning. Going back to Seattle."

"Why?"

"I told you. Because I'm done."

"Claire—"

I waved sloppily. "Go away. Go work. Buh-bye."

"Fuck." Another frustrated groan. "I have to work. I can't do this with you right now."

"Good. Don't. There's nothing to do, anyway. So it shall be written, so it shall be done."

"You're not leaving until we talk."

"Can't tell me what to do."

"I'm not, I'm just—"

I opened both eyes, which sucked and was a mistake, but made it work as a kind of cross-eyed glare. "GO—*AWAY!*"

"Goddammit, Claire."

"Yes, I'm fully aware that I'm being stupid and irrational and a bitch. Don't care. Go away." I felt my stomach lurch, and stumbled off the bed.

Brock slung open the door, guided me through it and to the bathroom, and then I fell to my knees on the toilet, heaving my stomach out. I felt Brock behind me.

"Fucking hell, Claire. How can I leave you like this?"

"Simple," I grumbled. "Use your stupid feet and walk away. I'm fine. Don't need you. Don't need anyone."

And hork, hork, hork. Burning, painful, nasty whisky vomit.

"I'm not leaving you here."

"Send one of the girls. I won't die before they get here. Probably."

"Not funny."

I peered at him. "Just go, Brock. I can puke without you hovering over me. I'm not gonna choke."

He left eventually, slowly, hesitantly. I ignored him, but the pangs in my heart told me I was making a mistake.

I pressed my cheek to the cold porcelain, which was gross but I was too wasted to care. After some amount of time I couldn't measure, I heard a door open and feet shuffling, and then sensed someone nearby. I peered dizzily from one eye, and saw Dru.

"Mara was too pissed to come, huh?"

Dru shook her head. "No, I volunteered. I thought maybe someone you don't know as well might be better, all things considered."

"I'm fine."

"Yeah, sure, sweetheart. Whatever you say." She winked at me, and then sank down to sit beside me.

"I am."

"I'm not arguing."

"Then why are you here?" I asked, fighting off a wave of nausea.

"Nobody likes to puke alone."

"I do."

"You're a sucky liar."

"Funny, I just said the same thing to Xavier."

"He is a terrible liar," she said, laughing. "And you're not much better."

"I'm not lying, though." I couldn't fight it anymore, and gave in to more puking. When I was finished, I eyed her as steadily as I could. "I really would rather be alone."

"No you wouldn't. You're just telling yourself that."

I groaned in frustration. "Nobody is listening to me."

"Because you're talking bullshit, honey, that's why. We all love you, and we don't want to see you like this."

"Everybody gets wasted sometimes. Have you even *met* the Badd brothers?"

"This is different and you know it."

"Fucking hell." I sighed. "I don't need this shit. I'm too drunk, and I just don't even care." I glared at her again. "Dru, babe, if you want to sit around and make sure I don't choke on my own vomit, then fine, that's your call. But I don't need a fucking lecture about how to live my life."

Dru lifted her hands in surrender. "Fine. I'll just sit here and keep my mouth shut."

"Perfect," I snapped.

I was being such a bitch, and I knew it, but I couldn't find the wherewithal to care. I felt another wave coming, and this time I didn't fight it. Another few minutes passed in silence, and I didn't puke again, and figured I was done. I tried to stand up, but my limbs were all confused and tangled, and up wasn't up, and I only managed to fall backward against the wall.

"Fuck. I need help getting to bed."

Dru helped me to my feet, guided me to Brock's bedroom, made sure I got into the bed, and then came back with a trash can. "In case you need to puke again." She left and came back with two Tylenol and a bottle of red Gatorade. "Take these and drink as much as you can."

I sat up and clumsily twisted off the top of the bottle, then managed to get the pills into my mouth and the bottle to my lips without spilling. I swallowed the pills and sipped the Gatorade until I was full. Dru took the bottle and recapped it and set it beside me.

"Scoot over," she said.

I rolled toward the wall, which was the side I normally slept on anyway. The world wasn't spinning as badly anymore, now that the whisky was mostly out of my system; I was exhausted, suddenly.

"Thank you, Dru," I mumbled.

"I've never had any real girlfriends," she said, "so

this is kind of fun. I might make you return the favor at some point."

"If I'm around."

"Why wouldn't you be?"

"Nothing. Never mind."

"Claire, what are you thinking?"

"I'm tired. I'm going to sleep."

Dru patted my hip. "You run, he'll just chase you, you know. Those boys don't know the meaning of giving up."

"I don't wanna talk about it."

She laughed. "I get it. It's scary."

"You have no idea what I'm feeling."

"Obviously not. But I'm not any better about this stuff than you are. I just know it's worth it, once you let it happen."

"Not going there with you, Dru. Sorry." I tried to shut her words out; I didn't want advice, I didn't want help, I didn't want any of it.

I just wanted to sleep. I wanted to not be drunk anymore. The fun had worn off and it was just painful and tiring and difficult and unpleasant. The real pain was in my heart, though. And the constant caring of all these people was exhausting. The only person who had ever given a shit about me was Mara, and we'd had a policy of not discussing heavy history. We'd helped each other through whatever bullshit we were going through at the moment, but for both of us, the past was best left in the past, and if we didn't want to talk about something, neither of us ever pushed it. I was there for her; she was there for me. And if we were being stupid about something, we called each other on it.

This was different, though. This was...*everything*. My past, my present, my future. It was all tangled up and everything hurt and nothing made sense.

Fuck, I couldn't handle it.

I tried to shut the thoughts out and just let myself drift on the waves of intoxicated exhaustion, until sleep finally rose up and sucked me down.

Sweet sleep, sweet peace of nothingness.

NINE

Brock

THANK FUCK: CLAIRE WAS PASSED OUT IN MY BED WHEN I finally finished work at 3:30 a.m. I shed my smelly work clothes and climbed in beside her, wrapped myself up around behind her, spooning her. Tugged her closer, my hand on her belly. She made a soft noise in her throat and wiggled her butt against me, tangled her fingers with mine.

I felt a bolt of relief, knowing that unconscious, at least, she still cared about me. The scene earlier had scared the shit out of me. She'd really sounded like she meant to leave, and I wasn't sure how I'd handle that. I really cared about Claire. More, I…I was in love with her. The thought of loving her, of being *in love* scared me stupid, made my heart hammer like a tribal drum. What was I supposed to do with that? I couldn't tell her that, not now. Not with everything she was going through. Not when she couldn't even see her way to talking to me about fucking *anything*. But the thought was out there, now. Echoing in my head, resounding in my heart. It was true, wasn't it?

Goddammit.

I opened my eyes and stared her face, in partial profile. Those cheekbones, her eyes closed, her expression at peace, her mouth slack. So beautiful. Passed out drunk, stinking the sour smell of old alcohol and sickness, she was still so beautiful to me. I saw how messed-up she was, how fucked-up she felt. The revelation her mother had laid on Claire had done a number to her, and she didn't know how to handle it.

Plus, I was relatively certain she was coming to the same realizations about her feelings for me as I was about her right now, and that was only terrifying her all the more.

Not to mention, I still felt like there was some element of our sex lives that was bothering her—something that she wasn't able or willing to put into words.

Fuck, so many layers, so much complication, and I didn't know how to sort through any of it. What do

I say to her? How do I get her to open up to me?

What if she left?

What if she didn't return my feelings? What if really was just good sex for her? Admitting to myself that I was falling in love with her was scary enough, but to tell her, to give her that power over me? I wasn't sure I could do it unless I was sure she felt the same.

I felt sleep claiming me, and I let it, clinging to her as tightly as I dared.

I dreamed. I dreamed of Claire, I dreamed she was naked, clinging to me, breathing in my ear, sounding tearful. I dreamed I was inside her, and she was facing me on her side, her thigh thrown over mine, and she was writhing against me, taking me bare inside her, gasping as she came, gasping as I came.

I dreamed she pulled away, and lay against my chest, breathing hard.

I dreamed the ragged gasping of exertion turning to tears, and that she buried her face in my neck and sobbed like I'd never heard her sob before.

I'm sorry, Brock. You deserve better than me.

No, Claire. I deserve you.

Go back to sleep, Brock.

I am asleep. I'm dreaming.

That's right, honey. You're dreaming.

I felt the bed shift, in my dream.

I'm sorry—I'm so sorry. Claire sounded like she

was in utter agony, and I just wanted to shelter her, comfort her, protect her.

She sounded far away.

Let me love you, Claire.

I can't—I can't. I don't know how.

Just try.

I have been. I'm sorry, but I can't do this anymore.

Yes, you can. You can't give up.

I am giving up. I'm walking away. It's what I do. It's all I know.

Learn something new, then.

It's too late.

It's never too late.

Goodbye, Brock. I'm sorry.

Goodbye? What do you mean, goodbye?

Silence. Dream-silence. Total and complete.

The dream shifted, became darkness, became the hoot of an owl, the chirp of a cricket. An unsettling sense of something wrong.

Eventually, the unsettled sense of something wrong became so strong that the dream seemed more like a nightmare, a sense of something wrong, something in the darkness that wasn't right. An absence.

A void.

Wrongness.

I felt the grip of sleep relax, felt it slip away. A bird chirped, and I felt the sun on my face from my bedroom window. I stretched, yawned, and my eyes fluttered open. I rolled over to glance at the clock: 9:45 a.m. Why was I awake? What had woken me? Why did I feel like something was wrong?

And then I turned back to the wall.

The bed was empty, except for me.

"Claire?" Maybe she was in the bathroom.

I got out of bed, and realized I was naked; I'd gone to bed in my underwear, I distinctly remembered taking off my jeans and T-shirt and socks, and collapsing into bed behind Claire in my boxer-briefs. She'd been fully clothed, wearing a purple V-neck and tight jeans.

I slipped on some shorts and checked the bathroom—empty; I checked the kitchen—also empty; the other guys' doors were closed, and she wouldn't be in there anyway.

She wasn't here.

I went back into my room, and realized her overnight bag was gone. Her pile of dirty clothes was gone from the corner where she tended to toss them. Her toiletries bag wasn't in the bathroom. Her pile of shoes was gone, including her Brooks running shoes, which she never went anywhere without. Her phone charger was gone from where it was always plugged in the outlet below mine.

Fuck.

FUCK!

She was gone.

She'd left.

It hadn't been a dream.

"You fucking coward, Claire," I muttered.

No note. Just a goodbye fuck while I was half-asleep and thought it was a dream. Seriously? That's how she left me? Anger rippled through me.

I snatched my phone off the nightstand and rippled the charger out of it, and dialed her number. It went straight to voicemail.

"Hey, this is Claire. Leave a message. Except you, Brock. Please don't make this any harder than it has to be."

I composed a text: **Why are you doing this?**

But then I deleted it.

Please come back.

Delete.

Eventually, the only thing I could see my way to sending was a single word: **Why?**

I didn't receive an answer, and knew I wouldn't.

I checked flight times: there was a 10 a.m. commercial flight to Seattle out of Ketchikan, which meant I wouldn't make it to the airport in time to catch her. I had to meet her in Seattle, then.

I took a shower, and tried not to panic.

I ate some breakfast, and tried not to hate her.

I texted the boys to say that I would be gone until I figured out this shit with Claire, and then headed out to the docks. I readied my Piper for flight and took off, heading for Seattle at top speed.

A little over two hours later, I received clearance to land at Kenmore Air Harbor. I took a taxi to her apartment, only to receive no answer when I buzzed, so I figured she wasn't back from the airport yet. There was a cafe across the street whose windows faced her apartment building's front door, so I claimed a table by the window and sat with a cup of coffee and watched her door.

Two hours later, still no Claire.

I called Zane, and he answered on the fourth ring. " 'Lo? What's up, Brock?"

"I'm here in Seattle but it doesn't look like she's coming back to her apartment. I was hoping to talk to Mara real quick."

"Shit. Okay, here she is."

"Hi, Brock."

"Did you know she was going to leave?" I asked.

"No, of course not. She was super drunk last night and when she's like that, she usually spouts a bunch of bullshit she doesn't mean."

"Last night was different, though."

A sigh. "Yeah, last night was different."

"She's not home in Seattle and she's not

answering me. Her phone is off, and I don't—I don't know where else she'd go."

"I don't know. Maybe back to Michigan? Now that her dad has passed, it's possible she'd go back to see her sisters. Especially if she's having trouble figuring out what to do about you guys." A pause. "She just...*left*?"

"When I woke up this morning she was gone, and her stuff is all gone."

"Did she leave her running shoes?"

"No, those are gone, too."

"Damn. For Claire, home is kind of just wherever her Brooks are."

"I know." I groaned, rubbing my face with one hand. "This is bullshit, Mara."

"I'm sorry, Brock. She's going through a lot, and I don't think she knows how to deal with any of it."

"She won't talk to me. I could help her, even if it was just listening and being there."

"She doesn't even talk to me about this kind of thing, though, and I'm her best friend."

"Did she tell you about what her mom told her?" I asked.

A pause. "Sort of. Just that her parents had lied to her all her life, but she wouldn't talk about what." Another pause, and I heard Mara suck in a sharp breath. "Holy shit. He wasn't her biological father, was he?"

"Nope."

"Who was?"

"A guy named Brennan O'Flaherty. He died before Claire was even born. That's the only reason Claire's mom even got back together with Connor. Claire doesn't seem willing to consider him her dad, anymore. She's just been calling him Connor."

"Holy *shit*, Brock."

"I know."

"No, you don't understand how bad that's going to fuck with her head. It's going to throw everything she thought she knew about herself into question. We never talked much about this stuff, but I know enough to be certain she has very serious daddy issues. This is only going to compound them."

"Plus I think she's falling in love with me."

"Yeah, that's not going to help."

"No shit," I said.

Another pause. "You feel the same way?"

"Yeah."

"Then you can't give up."

"She's not making it easy."

"Nothing about Claire is easy," Mara said.

"Well…?" I said, my tone of voice making it a joke.

Mara laughed. "Oh my god, you're terrible."

"I'm really pissed off at her, Mara. Like, I've never been so angry at another person in my whole life." I slammed back the last of my third cup of coffee. "I'm going crazy. I don't know what to do."

"Find her."

"Anywhere else she might go besides Michigan? You guys lived in San Francisco for a long time, didn't you?"

"Yeah, but I don't know if she kept in contact with anyone from down there. We had a circle of friends, but none of them were, like, real friends. More just drinking buddies, work acquaintances, and such. I don't know of anyone she'd feel comfortable crashing with."

"I'll have to try Michigan, then. If you hear from her, call me, will you?" I asked.

"Of course. But Brock, she's my best friend. If she asks me not to tell you where she is, I'm not going to. I hope she doesn't do that, but I can't betray her trust in me."

"I'd never pit you against her for my sake. She might, though. Right now, I feel like she's capable of just about anything."

"I know," Mara said. "That's what scares me."

A terrible thought occurred to me. "She was suicidal once. You don't think she'd…"

"Fuck me," Mara breathed, but then she

hummed a negative. "But no, I don't think she's there. She's not depressed, she's just...scared and panicking and mixed-up. She'd run away where she thought you wouldn't go, wouldn't find her. And if you do find her, she's going to put up a hell of a fight."

"If I can find her, be face to face with her, I think I can figure this out."

"I think your best bet is her sisters."

"Thanks."

"I want you for her, Brock. I'm really hoping you find her and convince her to give you guys another shot."

"It's not another shot. Nothing's over. She's just panicking, like you said. I just have to make her see that this is worth it."

"I know it is for me, with Zane, and this is scary as hell, being pregnant with his baby."

"You feeling okay, by the way?"

"Eh. Peeing a lot, hungry all the time, and I can't eat red meat anymore, for some reason." She sighed. "I just get sick thinking of it. It's weird. But I'm craving guacamole like all the fucking time, and I've never liked that stuff until now. Pregnancy is weird."

"My brother taking good care of you?"

"The best. He barely lets me out of his sight long enough to wipe my own ass."

"Good," I said, laughing at the visual of Zane

hovering around like a protective mother hen. "All right. Time to hit the skies for Michigan. Again."

I paid my tab and trotted across the street and up to her building. I buzzed, and buzzed, and buzzed. No answer. I buzzed a different door.

"Yes?" A gruff male voice.

"My girlfriend accidentally locked me out of 4-B, I just need to get back in."

"Oh. All right."

The door clicked with a buzz, and I went in and trotted up to Claire's apartment. Knocked on the door, and waited, listening. Silence. There was a gap under the door, light shining through from the rare sunny day in Seattle; I didn't see any movement to indicate she was on the other side, ignoring me. I knocked again, and waited some more.

The door across the hall opened, and an older black woman poked her head out. "Nobody's been there for a couple weeks, so you might as well spare your knuckles, honey."

"She didn't come home early this morning?"

"I'm an early bird, been awake since five, and ain't nobody come through. I'd have heard, since these walls are thin as paper."

I sighed. "Okay. Thanks."

She closed her door and I left, and took a taxi back to Kenmore. I topped off my fuel tanks and then went through preflight and headed southeast for Michigan. Several hours later, I was in a rental car heading from the Oakland County International Airport in Waterford to Claire's mother's house in Huntington Woods.

There were three cars in the driveway, and I couldn't remember how many there had been before. I sat in the rental car parked at the curb, trying to figure out what to say, if she was here. Eventually, I knew I would just have to wing it. I climbed out of the car and went up to the front door. Knocked.

Moira answered. "Hi, oh—Brock? This is a surprise. I was expecting a friend from church."

"Is Claire here?" I asked.

Moira shifted her weight to her other foot, clearly hedging. "I, um—"

I could see past her to the staircase—I saw Claire's overnight bag on the third step from the bottom. "She told you not to tell, I'm guessing, so you don't have to. I see her bag right there. Just…tell her I'm here, please?"

"She's out running with the girls. They went out after dinner."

"Can I come in and wait for them to come back?"

Moira hesitated again. "She's in a difficult place, as I'm sure you can appreciate."

"I know. But she left pretty abruptly, and there are

a few things we still have to talk about. If she won't see me, if she tells me unequivocally that this is really over, then I'll leave. But I need to see her."

"Okay. Come in, then, and I'll make some tea."

"Thank you."

Claire was capable of running well over ten miles at a time, so I knew I had a wait in store. I'd already spent the whole day looking for her, and would wait as long as I had to.

I settled in at the kitchen table with a mug of powerfully strong black tea, making uncomfortable small talk with Moira.

TEN

Claire

I WAS IMPRESSED WITH TAB AND HAYLEY. I'D SHOWN UP unannounced, and immediately changed into my running gear. Tab and Hayley had begged to go with me, and I'd agreed only after they said they both ran a lot of miles together. And so we ran. I set a punishing pace, with my earbuds in and *Lemonade* on as loud as I could handle it. I'd put in nine miles in record time, and Tab and Hayley had kept pace, although they were both fighting to stay with me.

I couldn't stop, though.

If I stopped running, I'd start thinking. And

thinking was the last thing I could handle right now.

I pulled out an earbud and turned back to the girls, who were a few yards behind me. "I'm going to keep going. You guys should go back."

Tab put on a burst of speed to catch up. "You can't outrun your problems, Claire." She tugged out both her earbuds. "Literally or metaphorically."

"Yeah, well...I'm sure as hell gonna try." I put my earbud back in and took off, leaving them both behind.

Funny how well I knew this neighborhood, even after all these years. I could still navigate the twists and turns and know exactly where to go to extend my route by another mile. My feet just...knew. So I ran, and I ran, and I ran.

The girls were lagging behind now, but they were still following, refusing to give up. And, truth be told, I felt better knowing they were back there. They hadn't asked a single question, they'd just run with me, just been there, and damn if that wasn't exactly what I needed.

No questions, no interrogations, no demanding I *open up*.

Dammit, dammit, dammit—don't go there, don't go there, *do not* go there. Don't think about Brock.

Fuck, I just thought his name. His name conjured images of his face, and his hands. Of him, this morning, mostly asleep. How he made love to me. That's what it was, too. I had to admit it. I couldn't deny it. He'd *made love* to me. Soft and sweet and slow, sleepily, clutching at me, moving with me in perfect sync. Thinking he was dreaming.

God, I hated myself. I fucking *hated* myself for how I'd handled that. I was a goddamn coward. A pussy. I'd let him think he was dreaming, and I'd taken the goodbye pleasure I'd needed and had run off in the early hours of dawn. But...I didn't know how to figure it out. I couldn't do it. He was falling in love with me, and I didn't know how to love. I knew I was feeling the same way but...I just couldn't. It was too scary. Too much. Too hard.

And he didn't know about the other things I wanted, sexually. How much I wanted him to spank me and bite me and tie me up and do all sorts of dark, dirty, bad things. I didn't even really understand *why* I wanted that stuff, why I craved it. A psychologist would probably trace it all back to Dad—to Connor, and all that, but I wasn't interested in psychobabble analysis. Fuck all that.

But I wanted it. I wanted him to put his big strong hands around my throat and squeeze while he fucked me and I wanted to come when he let go, gasping for air as I exploded around him. I wanted to be tied up at his mercy. I wanted...fuck. I wanted too much, and he was too pure, too good. He liked sex; he was *amazing* at sex. He knew how to read my body, how to touch me, how to make me come. He was so generous, always making sure I came before he did, usually two or three times. He liked to fuck me everywhere. He was adventurous, but not...kinky.

And I am.

And also...love?

That was too much.

I was running all-out, full-on sprinting. I wasn't even aware of where I was, just that I was panicking, my legs pumping crazily, lungs burning like fire, breathing ragged, heart slamming so hard it was dangerous. I realized I was on my mom's street, nearing the house. I pushed myself as hard as I could, and when I reached the mailbox, I slapped it as I let myself stumble to a stop, gasping, hands on my knees, chest heaving. A full two minutes later, Tab and Hayley arrived at a much slower pace, sweaty and gasping.

"Damn, Claire," Tab said. "You finished that entire last mile at a seven-minute pace."

Hayley just stared at me.

When I could finally stand upright and breathe somewhat normally, I realized there was a newer model Taurus parked at the curb that hadn't been there when we'd left for the run.

"Whose car is that?" I asked.

Tab and Hayley both shrugged.

"I don't know," Hayley said. "Mom mentioned she had a friend coming over today."

I sighed in relief. I couldn't handle Brock. I'd burst into tears and probably slap him and be angry and say a bunch of hateful shit I didn't mean, simply because I didn't know how to handle his overly emotional bullshit. Not when I was as fragile as I felt at the moment.

I followed Tab and Hayley into the house, wiping sweat out of my eyes with the back of one wrist. I heard Mom say something to my sisters as I moved through the den toward the kitchen. The next sound I heard was the three of them speaking softly and then the front door slammed shut.

The kitchen table was in the corner, so when you walked in from the den, you had to turn to see it completely. Which meant when I walked into the kitchen and went straight for the fridge for a bottle of water, I didn't stop to look at the table, to see who was there with Mom. I just assumed it was Mom's friend.

I twisted the top off the bottle and braced one hand on the edge of the sink as I drained half the bottle, still fighting to breathe normally.

Mom had gone silent, and so had her friend.

My skin crawled, suddenly, the back of my neck tingling, my spine going cold. Goosebumps broke out over my skin.

No.

NO.

I turned.

"Have a good run, Claire?" Brock asked.

Fuck, he was hot. I couldn't help but notice, appreciating the faded, light-wash blue jeans, combat boots left unlaced so the tops slouched open and the hems of his sort of but not really tight jeans sagged into the opening of the boots. A plain black V-neck T-shirt, tight and stretchy around his perfect body, highlighting his rippling abs and thick pecs and broad arms. He had a faded, dirty yellow baseball cap on, a black patch on the front with "PIPER" in white embroidered lettering, the bill curved just enough, and a pair of aviators hanging from the V of his shirt.

His eyes burned into me, mocha brown, *pissed…* and deeply hurt.

Fucking gorgeous.

My throat seized.

My hands started shaking.

"Brock." My voice sounded…tiny, and as scared as I felt. "Hi."

"Hi?"

He stood up, and I realized exactly how big and strong he really was, and how tiny I was in comparison. I wasn't afraid of him, but—oh hell, yes I was; not physically, I knew he wouldn't ever hurt me, but—shit. I was just scared.

"*Hi*?" he repeated, stalking toward me. "After the way you ran off, that's all you have to say?"

I stood my ground. "Don't. Just don't, Brock."

He tilted his head to one side. "Don't what?" He stopped when barely an inch separated us, and I had to stare up at him. "Don't be pissed at the cowardly way you left? Letting me think I was dreaming? Letting me wake up and find you gone? I've spent most of the day in the air, trying to figure out what I could have done differently, and I—I can't come up with anything. I'm so fucking *angry*, Claire."

"We're not doing this."

"Yes, we fucking *are*," Brock snarled.

The bitter, shaking anger in his voice rattled me to my core. I shrank away from him, curling into myself at how angry he sounded. Brock was even-keel, always. He was unflappable. He never freaked out. He never got angry. He was the most stable person I knew, which was part of what was so attractive about him to me—I could always count on him to be just… *him*. Cool, calm, collected, and beautifully handsome no matter what.

And now he was so angry he was literally shaking.

"Back up, please," I said. "You're scaring me."

He ground his jaw, but didn't back off. Instead, he grabbed me by the hips and lifted me off the floor, sitting me on the counter. He took my jaw in one hand, pressed my head back against the cabinet, and he kissed the ever-loving hell out of me. His grip on my jaw was a vise, painful. I relished the pain of his grip, succumbed to the kiss, to the brutality of it. There was no love in the kiss, only claiming. Domination. Punishment.

It turned me on so hard I felt my pussy gush with damp hot need, clenching in anticipation.

He didn't disappoint. Brock reached down and yanked my tiny blue Spandex running shorts down around my knees, rolled up my pink running bra. He had his jeans open in a flash, and then, before I could so much as suck in a breath, he was slamming into me. He filled me in one hard, rough thrust, driving his cock into me to the hilt, so hard I gasped. He palmed the back of my neck with one hand, grabbed my wrists in the other and pinned them against the cabinet over my head.

Oh…oh *fuck*.

He pulled out slowly, until I thought I was going to lose him, and then he fluttered a few times, short shallow teasing nudges, and then…he *fucked* me. He drilled me so hard it hurt, and his grip on my wrists was painful, and his hand on the back of my neck was fierce and harsh, keeping my head tilted back so I was forced to look up into his eyes.

"Look at me, Claire," he snarled.

"I am," I whispered.

He pulled out again, and this time he fucked me even harder, no warning, no teases, no making me come first, just a wet pounding of his cock into me. God, so good. The pain told me I was alive, that this was real. His anger was terrifying and his power was delicious. The dominance was intoxicating, so deeply, intensely heady that I could barely breathe for the perfection of this. His cock filled me so beautifully, the powerful thrusts so hard and rough and brutal and unflinchingly possessive that all I could do was wrap my legs around his waist and accept what he was doing to me.

His hand left my neck and cupped my breast, then he pinched my nipple with throbbing, piercing power to the rhythm of his fucking, and the harder he pinched the higher and hotter the pressure inside me built. I wanted to touch him, I wanted to flick my clit, I wanted to kiss him—but he would allow none of that.

I struggled against his hold on my wrists, and knew that he wasn't letting go. So I thrashed as hard I could, genuinely struggling to get free, tugging against his hold as hard as I could, with all my strength. I growled like an animal, snarling and raging, my hips writhing helplessly and furiously against his pounding thrusts. I craned my neck, stretching toward him, trying to get my mouth on him, my lips, my teeth. I'd bite him, I'd kiss him, I'd lick him, but he stayed out of reach. I thrashed, and he held me in place. He pinched my nipples, one and then the other, so hard I squealed from the pain of it, and yet the pain only made me fuck him back even harder, and he felt it, he knew it.

I growled in my throat as he fucked me, and I couldn't help but stare up at his unflinching gaze, and couldn't help the anger that flashed through me, the hate, the self-loathing, the pain, the hurt, the confusion, and everything else inside me that was all too tangled up to name or sort or understand.

The anger.

So much anger.

At Dad, at Brennan, at Mom, at the world, at Brock.

He didn't say a word. He just fucked me with brutal, punishing power, and I fucked him right back with all the anger I had, and we were both growling and grunting like snarling wolves fighting over a scrap.

He held my wrists and he palmed my back and jerked me closer to the edge of the counter and fucked me with complete abandon, and I could only cling to him with my legs and arch my back and move my hips as much as I could and take what he wanted to give me.

He pressed his forehead to mine, and his breathing was ragged, hissing through clenched teeth. "Take it, Claire."

"Oh—oh god."

"No. Say *my* name."

"Brock! Oh god, Brock!"

"Take it, Claire. Take it all."

"Yes! Give it to me, Brock!"

"You feel it?" His breath was hot on my lips, his body hard against mine, his cock slamming relentlessly, driving me to an orgasm so powerful I could feel it shaking through me even before it really crested. "You feel us?"

I sobbed as it crashed into me, through me. Words were impossible, breath was impossible, thought was impossible.

"Claire—*do…you…feel…US?*"

"YES!" I shouted. "I feel us, Brock, I fucking feel us, goddammit!"

He pulled me hard against him as he prepared to come, and his palm cupped the back of my head to cushion the blow as he slammed my head against the cabinet and kissed me as hard as he was fucking me.

"What is it you feel, Claire?" he demanded.

"Us, Brock. I feel us."

"No, that's not good enough. Say it. Say what it is."

I sobbed again, harder than ever, tears running down my cheeks, my breasts heaving against Brock's hard chest. I shook my head, struggling against him, denying his words, denying his truth, refusing his demand.

"SAY IT!" he shouted, and I felt the power of the words in the vibration of his chest and in the ringing in my ears.

"NO!" I shouted back.

He fucked, fucked, fucked, and I felt his cock throb inside me, buried deep, and I clenched around him with my own violent orgasm, screaming shrilly, and then snapping out to sink my teeth into his lip as he came with me. I felt him come hot and wet inside me.

He pounded into me, spurting even more. "Say it, Claire."

"NO!"

"Coward."

I sobbed, pressing my forehead against his, tears on my face, dripping down my chin, knowing he was right, knowing exactly what he was demanding I say. But I couldn't.

He came, and he came, and he came. So much semen. He slammed into me one last time, and I felt his come squirt out around his cock onto my outer labia, dripping down my taint. And then, when he was done coming, he sagged against me, nestling his head against my shoulder, nuzzling his nose into my neck. His hand released mine, and I couldn't help myself. I buried my fingers in his hair and rested my head back against the cabinet, no longer sobbing but still crying.

"Claire, please. Fucking *say* it. I know you feel it."

"Say what, Brock?" Stupid to pretend I didn't know what he meant, what he wanted. It was my last-ditch defense, though.

He groaned, a sound of utter despair and frustration. "Don't play stupid, woman. Not with me, not about this."

He was still buried deep inside me, still hard. His come slid out of me and down into the crack of my ass. He breathed on me, breathing hard, face buried in my neck, words muffled.

I stroked him, his hair, his broad shoulders. I had to. I couldn't *not* touch him. I couldn't *not* comfort him. Not when he was like this.

A sob broke free from me. *"Love,"* I whispered, my voice barely audible.

He lifted his head to meet my eyes, and I saw utter agony in his eyes. "Say it again."

"Love." I spoke loud and clear. "That's what I feel. For you. From you. *Love*. Fucking love. LOVE!" I shouted. "Is that better?"

"Claire."

I spoke over him. "You think me saying it is going to make this work? Like the word has some kind of magic to it? Like I'm just going to suddenly be less fucked-up because I've admitted that I'm in love with you?"

"There is magic, yes." He held on to me, as if to prevent me from running away again; smart man. "There is absolutely magic in the word. When you mean it, when it's real? When it's down deep, in your blood and bones? Yeah, there's magic in admitting love. Is it going to fix you? No. It's not that kind of magic."

"Then what's the point?" I asked.

For the first time since seeing Brock, I became aware of where I was—in my mother's kitchen, on her counter. Naked. With Brock's dick inside me, his semen dripping out of me. I'd screamed and cried and shouted and sobbed. He'd yelled and roared like a lion, and the back door was open, the neighbors less than fifty yards away. I wasn't sure where Mom or the girls were. The only thing I remembered was her talking to the girls when we first got back, and then hearing the front door slam. I hadn't even stopped to consider them, but I still didn't care. Not now. There was too much else to care about.

"What's the point?" Brock asked, his voice rough and low. "The point is *life*. The point is, no, I can't fix you, or your life, or your issues. It's not my place to fix them. I'm not trying to. I never have. I never will. That's *your* job. It's my place to just fucking *love* you, no matter what. It's my place to *be there*. To listen, and hold, and kiss, and love, and fuck, and talk, and take charge when you need me to. Back off when you need me to. The point is love—Love is its own point."

I shook my head. "I don't know anything about this stuff."

"And I do?"

"I don't know. You seem to."

"I'm just as scared as you, Claire. This whole thing is just as big and weird and all-consuming for me as it is you." He cupped my face in both hands, and I met his eyes again. The anger was gone, re-placed by...shit, I don't even know. A lot. "I don't know one thing about love. Except that I want it with you. Which means I'm not going to just give up. I'm not going to just you let sabotage us or run away from me just because you're fucking scared and mixed-up and have shit going on that I can't fathom. I've had my own heartbreak and hurt, Claire. I lost my mom when I was a kid. I lost my dad as an adult, and I wasn't even there for it."

He sighed and rested his lips on my forehead for a

moment before continuing. "I lost my best friend in a plane crash. We were flying together, doing a tandem Half Cuban Eight, and she…I don't know. She caught the tip of my wing with hers at the inverted downline. I managed to right myself, I still don't know how, but she didn't. I watched her crash. I watched her hit the ground and die in a ball of flames."

"Holy shit, Brock," I breathed. "I never knew."

"I don't talk about it. Not sure even my brothers know. The point is I've been hurt." He glanced up at me. "I said she was my best friend, because that's what she was. But she was also my fiancé. I wasn't going to tell anyone. We were going to fly to Vegas and get hitched by Elvis the day after the airshow. But then she died. And I haven't been able to…to let anyone get close ever since. It's just been casual fun. Until you. And that's all you were supposed to be, but then…I just knew it was more. From the start, I knew you were a hell of a lot more than one night of casual fun."

"Why didn't you ever tell me?" I asked, my voice a whisper.

He pulled out of me, finally, and I slid to my feet, knees shaky. He bent and lifted my shorts into place, tugged my bra down. Picked me up and carried me like a doll outside to the matching red Adirondack chairs. Set me in one, and took the other, not letting go of my hand.

"I've never told anyone," he said, eventually. "Not because it was a secret, but just because it was… it was *mine*. I didn't want to make a big thing for my brothers. They were all over the world doing all sorts of different stuff, and they'd all want to meet her, and I just wanted to have something be only mine for a while. You've seen how my brothers are, always in your face and in your business. And it's even worse now that Bast and Zane have women in their lives. I don't know. I just didn't want to share her."

I struggled to fathom what he was telling me. "You were in love with her?"

He nodded. "Yeah."

"Tell me about her?"

He breathed out shakily. "It's still hard. Her name was Beth. She was one of the most talented aerobatics pilots I've ever met. I mean, there aren't many women in the field anyway, but she was…she was *amazing*. We started out as friends, but it became something else, and then we realized what it was and…we kept it quiet.

"She wanted to elope and then bring me to meet her family—apparently she was the black sheep of her family. They wanted her to be a housewife or something, some hoity-toity upper-crust family from the East Coast. She wanted to fly, so she ran off and learned to fly." Another shaky breath. "It was a freak accident. She was so careful, so precise, so talented. A gust of wind, or a blink of an eye, a missed cue, I don't know. Her wingtip caught mine, and she just couldn't correct in time. I couldn't stop it. Couldn't save her. Couldn't do shit but watch her plane crash and burn."

"Goddamn, Brock."

"I landed as they were putting out the fire. I—I pulled her body from the wreckage myself."

I gasped, feeling a pang of agony for him. "I'm so, so sorry, Brock."

"I didn't fly for three months. Drank myself into a stupor for most of that time. And then another pilot dragged me out of my trailer and forced me to dry out, drove me to a shrink, and told me to get my head out of my ass. So I did. But flying…it's never been the same. Not without Beth. Dad died not long after and I came back here. Met you."

"You miss her?"

He nodded. "I do."

"You really loved her, huh?"

He breathed out a trembly breath. "So much." He turned his gaze to mine. "You want to know something, though?"

"What's that?"

"Yeah, I loved her. Yeah, I miss her. But what I

feel for you…it's so much more than anything I ever felt for Beth. That's what makes this whole thing crazy. I loved her, I really did. But you…what I feel for you surpasses that by an infinite amount."

"How is that…how does that even work?" I asked.

"I don't know. I just know she loved life and she loved love, and she would have wanted me to keep living and love again. I don't have any qualms or doubts about that. When I'm up in the air, flying the Piper, I feel her, sometimes." He squeezed my hand. "There. That's the one thing I've never told you. And now you know. And you know why I'm not going to give this up easily, no matter how much of a pussy you are about it."

"That's not fair."

"You ran off in the middle of the night, Claire."

"It was early morning, actually."

"Whatever. You fucking ran. You fucked me, and you let me think it was a dream." He held my gaze. "That's cowardice. I know you're scared, Claire, and I'll say it again—I fucking *get it*, okay? I'm not expecting you to just be suddenly fine about us, or your family situation, or anything. But you owe me more than what you did to me this morning. If you seriously, legitimately cannot handle us—if you can look me in the eye right now and tell me you don't love me and that you don't want to ever see me again, I'll walk. I'll walk away right now and you'll never see me again. But you owe me that much, Claire. You don't get to vanish like this was a one-night stand with a random stranger."

Panic. Deep, dark, overwhelming panic. He'd just fucked me the way I've always wanted to be fucked. He *took* me. He used me. He punished me. I'd never, ever in my life been so thoroughly and beautifully and roughly used like that, and I wanted it every single moment of every single day for the rest of my life.

But he wanted more from me.

He wanted LOVE.

The man I'd called Dad never loved me.

The man who'd conceived me had never even known I existed.

My mother…I supposed she loved me, in her way. But she also couldn't look at me without thinking of what she could have had with Brennan, what she lost. Sure, she spent nearly forty years with Connor, but it was passionless. They'd never kissed in front of us, never acted as if they couldn't keep their hands off each other. They were friends, they were life partners, but…it wasn't *passion*. And I never felt loved.

How could I show Brock what I'd never felt?

I didn't even know what love *was*.

Was it letting him fuck me softly and gently, in a

bed, and pretending I liked it? Was it the soft, melty feeling I got sometimes when I looked at him? Like my heart was expanding and I couldn't handle how hot he was, how kind and thoughtful and sensitive and powerful he was?

How was I supposed to love him?

I hated myself. I hated how badly I'd hurt him, this morning.

And I was selfish enough to want to keep him for myself. I wanted him at my disposal, in my bed, in my life. He made me a better person. He made me feel good. He made me feel beautiful.

But what did I give him? Aside from a world-class BJ and a high-rev libido, what did I have to offer? I was a fucking mess. I didn't know who I was. I didn't know what I wanted from life. I liked programming and running, but…what else was there? I liked sex. I liked to be dominated the way he had just now. I liked to be used like the dirty whore I was, because that's all I felt like I was worth.

FUCK.

There it was. That was the reality. That was the deep-down truth I'd been avoiding for so long: I wasn't worth being with a man like Brock.

Tears trickled down my face as the truth seeped through me. It hurt. It hurt so bad, but it was also a relief to finally be able to admit it to myself. I wasn't worthy of him. It wasn't about love or sex or how he fucked me or what I wanted. It was just the basic reality that I wasn't good enough. I'd never been good enough. Not for Dad, not for Mom, not for myself, not for anyone, and certainly not for a damn near perfect human being like Brock Badd.

He was watching me. He saw my tears. He saw the pain.

"Claire?"

I shook my head. "I can't."

"Can't what?"

I slid off the chair and knelt in front of him, taking both of his hands in mine. I met his gaze steadily with my own. "I can't do this, Brock. I just can't. I don't know how. You tell me to just...*try*, like it's so easy. But I don't even know where to start. I'm selfish enough to not want to let you go, but...I'm no good. I'm too much of a mess. And I just...I fucking—I can't do this, Brock. I'm sorry."

"Say it, then." He stared at me unblinking, unflinching, but I saw the agony in his eyes. The anger. "Fucking say it."

I shook my head. "I can't say that, either. That I don't feel...something for you, that I don't want to ever see you again—neither would be true. But I also can't do this. Not now, at least. Not yet."

"Then what are you saying, Claire?"

I broke into a sob, my eyes squeezing shut as tears sluiced down my cheeks. I let go of his hands and buried my face in his legs, shuddering and shaking. "I don't *know*, Brock! Just that I *can't*! I don't know how to love you! I don't know how to even *like* myself, for fuck's sake, so how I could I possibly be woman enough to love you? I'm not that woman. I want to be, but I'm just *not*."

"So you want to love me, but you don't know how, and you're not willing to try? Is that what you're telling me?"

"If that's how you want to hear it, then sure. It's not about not being willing, it's…FUCK! I don't know how to even say it so you understand!" I pushed away, stood up, tried to stop my shoulders from shaking, my breath from catching. "I can't do this with you. I can't be with you."

"Yes you can, Claire."

"No, I can't." I turned around and faced him, so he couldn't say I didn't say it to his face. "You deserve more than what I'm capable of giving right now, Brock. I can't be with you. Not yet."

"Not yet." He stood up and moved so he was inches from me, looking down at me. "That means you might be able to in the future?"

I shrugged. "Maybe? I can't promise you anything right now. I'm too fucked-up. This thing with my—with Connor, and my mom, and everything, it's too much. And you on top of it? Wanting me to love you, wanting me to be this woman who can just be...I don't know, something I'm just *not*...it's more than I can handle." I backed away from him. "You're pretty much perfect, Brock. You've got it all. You're gorgeous, you're smart, you're talented, you know what you feel and how to express it, you can just talk about things that I don't know how to even express within myself, and you're just...you're sweet and sensitive and affectionate and understanding, and—and yet you can come in here and take me hard and fast and fuck me so good it hurts...you're perfect, Brock. And I'm—" I backed away another step. "I'm not. I'm so far from okay that I don't even know what it looks like, what it's supposed to feel like."

"I'm not perfect, Claire."

"I know, I mean, nobody is actually perfect and I get that. But to me, for all intents and purposes, you pretty much are." He needed the words, and even though it cost me the last shred of sanity and dignity I had left, I gave them to him. "I don't deserve you, Brock."

He laughed. Actually fucking laughed, the bastard, and moved toward me. "That's the stupidest thing I've ever heard, Claire. For real. Nobody *deserves* anybody else. You can't...*not deserve* someone."

I backed away again, keeping distance between us so I didn't dissolve into tears, or break down and give in to wanting him. "Intellectually, I understand that. But don't you see? The problem is that, logical or not, it's how I feel."

He spun away, yanking his hat off and scrubbing his hand through his hair. "Claire, I—how can I make you see yourself the way I see you? How can I fix this?" He sounded agonized, his voice rough, throaty, almost tremulous. "I don't understand where I went wrong."

I sobbed again. "You didn't, Brock! I—I absolutely hate using this stupid horrible cliché, but...it's not you, it's me. You've done everything right."

"So why...why can't we work through your problems together?"

"Because I don't know how to be a *we*, Brock. I don't...I don't know what else to say, how else to put it. I just can't do this with you. I just can't."

He replaced his hat and turned to face me. "So that's it? There's nothing I can say? Nothing I can do?"

I shook my head. "I don't want it to be this way. I don't want to hurt you." I closed my eyes, tasting tears. "But no, there's nothing you can say. Nothing you can do."

"You want me to leave."

I nodded. "It's best, for right now."

"You're staying here?"

I shrugged. "I don't know. I don't know anything." I tried to stop crying, but couldn't. "I'm sorry, Brock. I'm so sorry."

He lifted his aviators and slid them onto his face, hiding his eyes. "I just have to say two things, for the record."

I crossed my arms over my chest, hugging myself. "Okay."

"One, I want you to know that I think this is complete bullshit. I think you're wrong, and you're just too scared of being abandoned to let me in. And two, I'm in love with you." He kept his distance, hands shoved into his hip pockets. "I told you I'd leave you alone if that's what you really want, so that's what I'm going to do. I'll give you time, I'll give you space. But I think you're wrong. I think you're underestimating yourself, selling yourself short. And me, too, for that matter. But I'm not going to try to talk you into being with me. Either you want it, or you don't."

I'm in love with you.

GODDAMMIT. He had to say that? *Now?* Fuck. Fuck, fuck, fuck, fuck, *fuck.* Not fair. So not fair. Because I knew I was doing the right thing. If I tried to have a relationship with him right now, it'd be a disaster for both of us.

But fuck me, this hurt so bad. I couldn't stop

crying, and I could tell he was fighting it, too.

"I'm sorry, Brock," I said, in a broken whisper. "I'm so sorry."

"Me too."

"You have nothing to be sorry for."

He shook his head, but more because he seemed unable to find words. He backed away, heading for the side gate. He let himself out, pausing before latching the chain-link gate behind himself. "This is fucking bullshit, Claire. I hope you know that."

I shook so hard with sobs that I couldn't stay on my feet. "I'm sorry."

"I'll wait. You change your mind, you find your way through whatever it is you're going through that you can't share with me, I'll be there on the other side." He backed away another step, digging a set of keys from his hip pocket. "You know where to find me."

I didn't get a goodbye from him. He didn't look back. He got in the rented Taurus and drove away. He didn't peel out, didn't do anything crazy, but as the back of the car pulled away, I could see his head and shoulders from behind. He yanked his hat off and tossed it angrily, then slammed his fist on the steering wheel a good half dozen times, so hard it was a wonder the wheel didn't break. Then his hand disappeared in front of him. Wiping his face, maybe?

The idea of Brock crying shredded me. I didn't want this. I'd never wanted this. This was exactly why I never did the emotional connection thing. This was why I just fucked 'em and chucked 'em. No emotions, no mess, none of this bullshit emotional agony.

Fuck this.

Fuck Brock for forcing me into this.

It wasn't just him, though, was it? It was me, too. I let this happen.

I collapsed into the grass and gave into wracking sobs.

At some point, Mom found me there, and sat in the grass with me, and her silent presence was almost more than I could bear, but also not enough.

Nothing was enough. Nothing could heal this.

And it was all my fault.

ELEVEN

Brock

WHAT A FUCKING DAY. IT WAS WELL PAST MIDNIGHT before I finally made it home to Badd's. I'd had to stop to refuel and to eat. I hadn't been hungry, but I knew I couldn't fly on an empty stomach, so I forced myself to eat a burger and some fries at a diner near whichever local podunk airport I'd stopped at. I wasn't even sure where I'd stopped—I'd been functioning on autopilot, going through the motions.

All I knew was pain.

I'd told her I loved her…

And she'd let me walk away.

That was all I could fathom. All I could think about, all the way to Ketchikan.

I stumbled into the bar, haggard, exhausted, and feeling like I'd been beaten up. I made my way to the service bar, where Zane was mixing drinks for Lucian. They both took one look at me and swore, almost in unison.

"What the fuck happened to you?" Zane asked.

"She dumped me."

Zane's eyes went wide. "She...*what*?"

"She fucking dumped me. Said she couldn't do it. She didn't deserve me." I shook my head. "I don't wanna talk about it. Just...give me a bottle of something."

"What's your poison?"

I shrugged. "Don't fucking care. Something that'll burn this shit out of me."

"Burn what out of you?" Lucian asked, his voice quiet, his eyes seeing far too much.

I stared him down, unwilling to let him see how badly I was hurting. "Everything."

Zane returned with a bottle of Johnny Walker Black Label and a tumbler. I took the bottle, ignored the tumbler, and lurched upstairs. Sinking into the couch, I flicked on the TV, tuned it to something with boobs and explosions on HBO, and set about drinking myself into a stupor.

I was more than halfway through the bottle when Sebastian, Zane, and Lucian showed up. Zane plopped onto the couch on one side of me, Bast on the other, and Lucian sat on the coffee table facing me.

"Why the fuck did she break up with you?" Bast asked.

I peered at him. "Because she's stupid."

"Brock, come on," Zane said. "This isn't you."

"Yes it is." I slugged off the bottle, taking three long swallows.

"You're the smart one, the stable one. You're not the drink yourself out of your problems brother." Bast took the bottle from me, took a swallow, and passed it to Zane, who took a drink and passed it to Lucian, who took two swallows and handed it back to me.

At which point it was mostly empty, so I knocked the rest out with four long pulls. "You don't know shit about me."

Lucian took the empty bottle from me and set it aside. "Explain that statement."

I was fucking hammered, now. I rarely drank more than a few beers or a glass of wine or whisky now and then, and never like this, not after...fuck, I couldn't even think her name.

Yet when I opened my mouth, words just sort

of fell out. "I was engaged, you know. Before I came back."

All three stared at me.

"You fuckin' what?" Bast demanded. "Say that again."

I swiveled my head sloppily around to stare at him, nose to nose. "I...was...en-*gaged*. Like, gonna marry someone."

"And you never told any of us?" Zane snapped.

"Who was she?" Lucian asked.

I shook my head. "Need more whisky for that question."

"You've had enough, I think," Zane said.

"Fuck you, Zane," I snarled. "You don't decide when I've had enough."

Lucian met Zane's stunned gaze; I never snapped, never snarled, rarely even got irritated. This was a side of me no one had ever seen. Whisky-wasted and heartbroken Brock was a monster.

Bast stood up, went into the kitchen, and got a bottle of Blanton's from the cabinet over the fridge. He uncorked it and set the fancy cork on the counter, probably so I wouldn't break it. I took a slug of the bourbon, and then another, and finally handed it back to him.

I heard a door open, and Dru shuffled out of their room, wearing a white button down of Bast's, blinking sleepily at us. "Whass goin' on?" she slurred, still half-asleep.

"Brother time," Bast said. "Sorry if we woke you."

She smiled at him, one eye closed, the other squinting. "I woke up to pee and you weren't there." She squinted at me. "Brock? Hi, honey. You okay?"

I shook my head. "Nope."

She shuffled to me and pressed a kiss to the top of my head. "I'm sorry."

"Women are stupid," I mumbled. "You excluded."

"No, I can be stupid too, and so can men." She turned and shuffled back to the bedroom. "I expect you to be on that couch in the morning, Brock. I want to make you pancakes and give you my stupid woman's opinion on another stupid woman."

"'Kay." I waited until the door was closed and then eyed Bast. "She's pretty amazing, bro. You got lucky."

"I married *way* up, man. I'm a lucky fuckin' bastard, and I got no intention of ever letting her go." He slapped my shoulder. "Now. As the ladies say, dish."

"Dish?" I couldn't remember what that meant.

Lucian took a pull off the bourbon, and then fixed a look on me. "Talk. Who were you engaged to and what happened?"

I took the bottle from him and drank until my

throat burned. "We trained with the same aerobatics instructor. She was better than me. Better reflexes, a more instinctive feel for things. Just…better than me in every way. Yet she looked at me like I'd…like I'd hung the moon and stars. It was…seeing her look at me that way was like a drug. I couldn't get enough." Another long drink, because this was the second time I'd spoken of this in one day, and that was more than I'd talked about it in a long time. "I wasn't keeping it from you out of, like, spite, I just…I wanted it to be mine for a while. You know?"

Bast nodded. "I gotcha, bro."

Zane nodded too. "Yeah, I know what you mean."

"She crashed," I said. "I watched her crash. I pulled her charred corpse from the wreckage with my bare hands."

"Jesus, dude," Zane said. "Having been around burned bodies, I know exactly how horrible that is."

"Her name was Beth."

Zane lifted the bottle in salute. "To Beth," he said, and then drank.

Bast and Lucian did the same in turn, and I followed suit, although I didn't say anything. I couldn't.

"So what are you going to do about Claire?" Lucian asked.

I shook my head and shrugged. "Hell if I know.

There's nothing I *can* do. She said she just…can't do it. Can't be with me. That she's too messed-up."

"She *has* been through a hell of a lot," Zane said.

"I know, but why can't she figure it out while being with me? I could help."

Lucian cleared his throat, and we all looked at him. "Sometimes, being alone to figure yourself out is the best thing for everyone."

"Doesn't feel that way," I grumbled.

"Of course not," Bast said. "I'm sure that shit hurts."

"I told her I loved her," I admitted.

"Damn." Zane clapped a hand on my shoulder. "And she still dumped you?"

"Yep." I closed my eyes and sighed. "What really sucks is that I can't even wish none of it ever happened, because it was amazing."

"I wouldn't give up yet, Brock," Lucian said.

"What if she never figures herself out? What if I…what if she—" I groaned instead of finishing my thought. "Fucking sucks. It just sucks."

My brothers were around me, keeping me from floating away on a river of whisky. I let myself drift, and eventually I felt hands lower me to a reclined position, and then pull my feet up on the couch. A blanket covered me.

"You're good brothers," I mumbled.

A deep laugh. "Shut up and go sleep, you drunk dickhead," Zane said, laughing.

"You're…dick." I couldn't manage anything else, and then I passed out.

I woke up to the smell of frying bacon, brewing coffee, and pancakes on a griddle. I cracked an eyelid, and caught an eyeful. Bast had Dru pressed up against the counter's edge, facing away from him, his arm around her waist—and judging by the way the muscles in his arms were moving, he was fingering her. She had her hands braced on the counter, her head thrown back. He was in a pair of gym shorts and nothing else, his tats bathed in the morning light filtering in from the window over the kitchen sink.

I cleared my throat so they'd know I was awake; the sound of my own voice made my head throb.

Bast pulled away from Dru and put his back to the counter while Dru rearranged her clothing and emerged from behind him.

"Hi, Brock." Her voice was far too bright for this early in the morning.

"Ung," I grunted.

Bast rumbled a laugh. "Hungover, huh?"

I managed to pull myself to a sitting position,

and immediately regretted it. The world swam, and my head throbbed, and my mouth was full of cotton balls, and I wanted to die. "Shoot me."

He just laughed. "Nah. We like you too much. How about we feed you instead?"

I stood up and shuffled into the bathroom for an epic piss, the kind that lasted for a solid minute and required a hand braced on the wall. When I emerged, there was a plate of pancakes and bacon on the table with a mug of steaming coffee. My head throbbed, but my stomach told me to eat. So I sat, and tried a piece of bacon.

"Crispy, almost burnt," I said. "Perfect."

Dru laughed. "I had to learn how you Badd brothers like your bacon. I grew up eating it floppy. Meaty, as my dad calls it."

I shuddered. "That's not bacon, then, that's just a sin."

"Amen to that," Bast said. "Bacon should be just this side of black, and so crumbly it just dissolves in your mouth."

"Damn straight." I tried the pancakes, and discovered that those were damn near perfect too. "Jesus, Dru. You do breakfast like a pro. Thanks."

She plated pancakes and bacon and put it at the place next to me, and then shoved her husband into the chair, pausing to kiss his temple. "My dad is a cop.

Breakfast was often the only time I got to see him, so I learned to make breakfast count."

"I like your dad," I said. "He seems cool."

She smiled at me. "I like him too. He's actually considering taking his retirement and moving up here."

"That'd be cool," Bast said. "He have any desire to work in a bar?"

She laughed. "You know, he just might. Hell, he's spent enough time in bars that he should know the ropes already."

A few moments later, she had her own plate of food and mug of coffee, and now it was the three of us chowing down in companionable silence. The food was exactly what I needed, reducing the severity of my hangover by several degrees. When we were all done eating, Bast cleared the dishes, poured more coffee, and set another pot to brewing.

"I hope you don't mind, but I filled Dru in," Bast said to me.

I shrugged. "None of it is a secret."

"I'm so sorry about your fiancé," Dru said, sympathy in her voice.

I nodded. "Thanks. It was…the hardest thing I've ever been through." I glanced at Bast. "How I was last night? That's how I was pretty much constantly for a good three months."

He shot me a look of shock. "You flew like that?"

I shook my head gingerly. "Hell no. I grounded myself after Beth died. Couldn't stomach the thought of getting back into a cockpit again."

"How'd you get yourself clear of it? Obviously you're flying again." Bast sipped coffee, tapping the table with a thumb and forefinger.

"A buddy literally dragged me out of my trailer and into his, forced me to dry out, and then took me to a therapist. I resented it at first and was an asshole about it since I was in booze withdrawal, but I went back the next week, and the next."

"So a few months back when I was being a dick and said you'd probably been to a shrink, and you said yes, you actually had…" Bast prompted.

"That was why. I saw Dr. Patel every week for two months. Three months of drinking myself to blackout every single day, two months of sobriety and therapy, and another month of working around aircraft and pilots…it was a full six months before I could even sit in the cockpit again.

"When I finally went up, it was in a trainer plane with a double set of controls and my buddy was in the plane with me, and good thing because I had a legit panic attack. I kept seeing Beth's plane go down. Her wing catching mine, toppling and spinning, hitting the ground, and going up in flames. Her body, all—fuck." I squeezed my eyes shut against the memory, felt both Bast's and Dru's hands on my shoulders. "Took me another three months of easing into it before I could fly on my own again. In a weird, freak turn of events, my first performance after her death was on the one-year anniversary of her death."

"Goddamn, man. That's fuckin' rough." Bast's hand squeezed my shoulder. "Why the fuck didn't you call us in? We're your fuckin' brothers, dude, we shoulda been there for you."

I shook my head. "Couldn't. At first, I was too ashamed of how clobbered I was getting every single day, and I didn't want you guys to see me like that. Then it was because I wanted more time to heal before I told you. And then...too much time had passed for me to be like, yo, guys, guess what?" I got up and poured us all more coffee, and then resumed my seat. "After that, I just didn't want to bring it up, couldn't handle the thought of talking about it."

"I guess I don't blame you," Bast said. "Wish you'd have told us though."

Just then Zane pounded up the stairs, drywall repair equipment in hand. "I've come up to re-mud those holes our dear idiot brother Bax pounded into the walls a couple weeks ago. They need to be mudded properly before I paint everything." He left the door at the top of the stairs open, and I knew he was listening.

Dru was eyeing me thoughtfully. "I have a question, which may or may not be out of line."

I sipped coffee, holding up a hand to forestall her. "I'm not an alcoholic. I chose to drink that way because I didn't know how to deal with Beth dying, and with the guilt I felt even though it wasn't my fault. It was too much pain and I couldn't handle it, so I drank myself stupid. I didn't touch alcohol again after Eddy pulled me out of my trailer, not for—god, how long? Eighteen months? A long time. And when I did, it was with Eddy so he could kick my ass if need be.

"I was scared of that same thing, that I'd be an alcoholic. But I'm not. I know my limits. I usually don't like drinking more than a few at a time. Being hammered to excess, like last night, it reminds me of that period of time, and I hate that side of myself. I'm a nasty drunk. I like a drink now and again, and I can stop myself whenever I want. Last night was a choice. I guess when extreme pain hits, it's the only way I know how to escape it."

"Well, thanks for answering my question and being so honest about it," Dru said. "Now I'm going to have a shower and get cleaned up. I'll see you guys later."

"You lived in a trailer?" Bast asked.

I nodded. "When I wasn't flying from show to

show, I had an Airstream I lived in, hooked up to an old Power Ram. I'd just bum around between shows. I've driven all over this country, and what I haven't driven through, I've flown over—especially in the Pacific Northwest."

"You still have the trailer?"

I nodded again. "It's in storage, along with my aerobatics plane." I traced the rim of the mug with an index finger. "It's down in Juneau. I've thought about bringing that stuff up here, using the airport here, spend some time doing the old tricks, and the trailer would come in handy for weekend getaways or something."

"That's what I was thinking," Bast said.

"Maybe you and I and Bax can drive down, leave Zane and the others here to run the bar. You and Bax drive back, and I'll fly my Staudacher up."

"Sounds good."

Zane popped up at the top of the stairs, drywall mud smeared on his forehead, working on the hole Bax had made near the door frame. "So...you and Claire are really done, huh?"

"Seems like it."

"Why, do you think?" he asked.

I studied the bartop. "She's scared. Messed-up. All that shit with her dad not being her dad, everything she's been through, she just...can't handle being with me right now, she said."

"Ah. The old 'it's not you, it's me' bullshit, huh?" Zane said.

I nodded. "Pretty much. I'm not sure it's completely bullshit, though. It sucks, but I get the feeling she was telling the truth. But she's also just scared of being in love."

Zane glanced at me, dipping the scraper into the mud. "That's really what it is for you, huh? For real?"

I shrugged. "Yeah."

"And for her?"

"She won't admit it, but I think so, yes."

Zane kept his gaze on the drywall he was mudding, but spoke to me. "Well, it may suck, but you just have to wait for her. Either she'll figure her shit out, or she won't. And if she doesn't, then you'll just have put on your big boy undies and get over her. It'll hurt, and it'll take time, but it'll all work out."

I gaped at him. "Okay, then, Dr. Phil."

Zane laughed. "What? I have a little bit of wisdom stored away, okay?"

"From your extensive experience in long-term relationships?" Bast said, laughing.

Zane lifted the scraper. "You know I can bury this in your chest from here, right?"

Bast held up his hands. "Just sayin', man. You're

an ex-Navy SEAL, not a love expert."

Zane's gaze darkened. "Tell another soul and I swear I'll bury you two fuckers, but…when I was bored, which was a lot, I'd read romance novels on a Kindle. You can only read so much Patterson and Grisham and Clancy, you know? I bought some steamy romance shit by accident, thinking it was something different, and I figured what the hell, I'd paid for it, might as well try it. And to my surprise, I enjoyed it. And that shit is actually fun to read, and pretty informative."

Bast and I stifled laughter. "Fuck you, dude. You're pulling our chains," Bast said, past coughs of restrained laughter.

Zane kept mudding, and then he was done, and joined us at the breakfast bar, stealing my coffee, which was now cold. "No, it's true. Don't believe me, I'll show you my Kindle."

"Hard to believe you even *own* a Kindle," I said, "much less that you'd read *romance*."

"Hey, that shit gets downright erotic, okay?" He twisted the mug in circles. "When you're alone with a bunch of dudes in the ass-end of Kandahar waiting out a bunch of asshole guerrillas, you want something to take your mind off the boredom. My Kindle fit nicely in my gear bag and I could load it with hundreds of books, and then easily stow it when it was go-time. Whenever I was somewhere with decent Wi-Fi, I'd buy dozens of books at a time so I had them ready when I wanted to read. It's like having your own library in a piece of plastic barely bigger than my own hand."

I conceded with a laugh and raised both hands. "Okay, okay. I just would never have guessed."

"Well, no shit. That was the whole point. Not even the guys in my squad knew about that." He chuckled. "They'd never have let me live it down, had they found out."

I let out a breath, slowly. "So, I just wait, huh?"

Zane clapped me on the back. "You went after her. You said your piece, so she knows how you feel. The rest is up to her."

"Fucking sucks." I sighed.

"Fucking sucks," both Bast and Zane agreed in unison.

Dru came down, then, dressed, hair twisted up in a damp knot, a mug of coffee in hand. She waved her hand at her husband and Zane. "Shoo, boys. I want to talk to Brock."

I thunked my head on the counter. "Oh, yay. More *talking* about shit."

Dru laughed. "I'll do most of the talking, don't you worry. I've also invited Mara over for extra moral support."

"Yippee. Is it too early to get drunk again?" I asked. Dru didn't laugh, though, instead she eyed me suspiciously. "I'm kidding, I'm kidding. I have no desire to drink right now. Except maybe more coffee."

Zane and Bast left to go down to the bar, leaving me alone with Dru, who made us a fresh carafe of coffee, which she used to fill my mug, and then Mara breezed in, belly bump first.

"Damn you both for having coffee when I can't," she said, awkwardly climbing into a high-top chair, sipping from a giant Tervis full of ice water with half a dozen lemon slices floating in it. "I'm allowed a single eight-ounce cup of coffee a day, and lemme just say, that is nowhere *near* enough."

"I can't imagine not being allowed to have coffee," I said. "Would it help if I didn't have it around you?"

Mara laughed. "It's coffee, Brock. I'm not a recovering alcoholic, here." She leaned over and inhaled. "Just let me sniff it a few times."

I laughed as she inhaled the scent of my coffee, and then went back to sipping from her pink-and-leopard-print Tervis via a foot-long pink straw.

"That there is a whole hell of a lot of water, Mara," I said.

She rolled her eyes. "Don't even get me started.

I've already had one of these, and I've peed roughly fifteen times so far. I'll probably have to pee another fifteen times just while we're talking."

I sipped coffee, and then kicked my feet up against the front of the breakfast bar, tipping back in my chair. "This feels like an intervention."

Dru chortled. "It kind of does, doesn't it?" She patted my hand, and adopted a soft, simpering, lisp. "Now Brock, I want you to know we're all here because we love you. There's no judgment here. This is a judgment-free zone, so you can say whatever you need to, all right?"

I went with it. "Hi, my name is Brock, and I'm a Claire-aholic. It's been—" I glanced at my watch, "sixteen hours since the last time I saw her."

Mara fiddled with her straw. "What happened, Brock? All I know is that Dru texted me saying you and Claire had broken up."

"She freaked and bolted on me." I rocked back and forth in the chair, feeling off-kilter and uneasy and trying to contain the pain. "You guys saw how she was the other night, wasted and being impossible. I thought it would pass, I thought she'd—I thought we'd wake up and talk it through. But when I got up, she was gone. Her stuff was gone. I flew to Seattle, but she wasn't there. That's when I called you. I flew to Michigan and found her at her mom's place. I was so pissed, you know? Like, what the fuck? She told me she couldn't do this anymore, couldn't do *us*. Nothing I said was getting through. She was just…I don't know. Already gone, in a way. I even told her I loved her."

"Damn." Mara poked at the lemon slices with her straw. "Not how I saw this going."

I laughed bitterly. "Yeah, me neither."

"So she was just like, this is done, it's over?"

I tilted my head from side to side. "Sort of. She kept saying she was sorry and that she didn't want to do this, but that she had to. I got the sense that she wasn't trying to close me out completely, like end us forever, just that she needed to…" I shrugged. "Figure herself out, I guess."

Mara ruffled her long, loose hair with one hand. "We all know she's been through a shitload, especially recently. But I can tell you she was never even sure she wanted a real relationship, but you guys just seemed to work, almost like it was…I don't know, inevitable, sort of. I don't think she even really thought of it as a relationship, as such. And then it became obvious that that's what it was, and she couldn't deny it, so it freaked her out."

"If she feels too fucked-up to be able to even know where to start," Dru said, "it would make sense that she felt like she had to put you guys on pause, more or less. Maybe try to think of it as a break rather than a break*up*?"

Mara said, "I think that's right, though. Give her some time and space."

I nodded. "That's what everyone is saying, and it makes sense. I understand it, but I don't like it."

Dru patted me on the back. "I wouldn't expect you to *like* it. But it might be a good thing. Once she has some time to chew on things a bit, maybe she'll be in a better place to be able to think about you guys, and you can keep going with your relationship and it'll be even better than it was before."

I sighed again. "Well, I think that's all I can really hope for, right now, I guess."

It fucking sucked, but it was what it was.

I pulled my phone out of my pocket, opened up the thread with Claire, and typed out a message.

I haven't given up on you, or on us. I need you to know that. Take time and space, if that's what you need. I'll be waiting on the other side for you. I don't expect you to even reply, just maybe let me know you're still alive every once in awhile, ok? Just know that I love you. I also don't expect you to feel the same way or say it back or anything. Just know it's true.

The message switched to "read" after a few minutes. The gray bubble with the three dots popped up, the dots rippled a few times, and then the bubble vanished. This happened twice more, as if she was trying to figure out what to say, but couldn't. Eventually, a reply popped up from her.

It was a single letter:

k

TWELVE

Claire

Dr. Liz Rivers was a younger woman, mid- to late-thirties maybe, with a cute brunette bob and delicate cat's eye glasses. Her soft, quiet mannerisms belied a sharply observant intelligence and a keen insight into human nature. I hated her as much as I loved her.

"All right, Claire. So your homework last week was to work on forgiving yourself." Dr. Liz gave me a gentle smile, one full of calm encouragement. "How do you feel that went?"

I shrugged one shoulder. "Okay, I guess. Quite

honestly, forgiving Connor was easier."

Dr. Liz nodded. "Of course. Forgiving ourselves is always the hardest thing to do. We often feel as if *others* deserve forgiveness, that *others* can earn or obtain or be given our forgiveness. But ourselves? Oh, no. That's much, much harder. That's why we've waited this long to work on this aspect of your therapy."

Dr. Liz continued, "How did you go about trying to forgive yourself?"

I shrugged again; I shrugged a lot around my therapist. "Um. I would think about all the shitty stuff I've done, and instead of letting myself feel like crap and get down on myself for it, I'd think about forgiving myself."

"Do you feel like it's working?"

I laughed, somewhat bitterly. "No, not really. I still feel like shit a lot of the time."

"When you say you feel like shit, what does that mean? Can you unpack that a bit?"

"I used people. Guys—men, I mean. I used them. I took what I wanted, and I made it all about me, and then I ditched them." I focused on the toes of my bright red Converse shoes. "It's not about the sex, exactly, or feeling like…like a slut. I'm okay with that. I've made peace with that—"

"Have you?" Dr. Liz, usually soft and quiet and sincere and kind, interrupted me, her voice sharp.

"*Have* you really made peace with feeling like a slut?"

I restrained the urge to either bolt or smack her. "Yes, doctor, I *have*," I snapped.

She was unfazed. "I'm not so sure I believe you, Claire." She made a note on her yellow legal pad. "The vehemence of your reaction makes me think otherwise."

I groaned. Five months of therapy—biweekly at first, and then after two months, weekly—you think I'd have learned by now not to bullshit Dr. Liz, since she always saw through it.

"FINE!" I huffed. "No, I'm not okay with it. I haven't made any kind of peace with it. I'm still fucked-up over it. I'm still fucked-up over getting pregnant and the miscarriage and being disowned, so hell, of course I'm not ready to...what? Forgive myself? Is that what I'm supposed to do? Part of me says I should just own my actions. Guys can be players and fuckboys, they can rack up one-night stand numbers in the double and triple digits and society thinks he's a big, swingin' dick badass because he can haul down major ass like a modern-day Casanova. But if I do the same thing, I'm a dirty slut. And I think that's bullshit. Guys talk about how many chicks they've banged, and they congratulate each other on it. If another girl hears that I've fucked...what, forty, fifty different guys? They look at me like I've got actual crabs on my face or some shit."

"You can't control others, Claire. I'm not interested in how others react. And if you ask me, I'd say
the guys who sleep with that many different women
deserve the slut label too. I'm not in the business of
labeling or judging, I'm just saying, if society is going
to put that label on promiscuous women, then men
who do the same thing deserve the label as well."

"That's what *I'm* saying!"

"I know, but my concern is with you. How you
feel about yourself." She tapped the tip of her pen on
the pad, and then flipped the pen around her index
finger. "The point of all this, aside from the general
need to deal with a lifetime of built-up issues, is to get
you to a mental and emotional place where you feel
ready to face Brock again, right?"

I nodded. "Right."

"Well, then, we can't get sidetracked by the injus-
tices of society. You made choices. You dealt with your
pain and confusion and abandonment and everything
else via sexual promiscuity. You chose to wall yourself
away from the world, you chose to keep your true
self hidden, and to never rely or depend on anyone.

"Understandable, and expected even, considering the way your parents handled things with you—
which, as I've said, is simply inexcusable." She flipped
the pen around her finger again, and then scrawled

something on her pad. "That past is yours, and you have to accept it. It is what it is. You cannot change it. Forgive yourself for it. Move on from it. Commit to making different choices in the future. Notice my phrasing there, Claire: *different* choices, I said, not *better*.

"The passing of judgment—whether on ourselves or on others—is a losing game—there is no winner. We are all flawed, and we all make choices we wish we hadn't. It's up to us and *only* us to direct our future, to decide what is good and bad for us.

"Obviously, this is predicated on a basic sense of right and wrong. Lying is wrong, murder is wrong, cheating and theft are wrong, embezzlement, extortion, all that is obviously wrong. But the personal choices that we make which do not fit so easily into neat little right or wrong boxes...how do you quantify the morality of those things? It is up to the individual, I believe. And for you, however you quantify the morality of your history of promiscuity, you have to make peace with it. You can't allow the past to have such a powerful hold on your present, because what has a hold on you *now* affects you in the future."

I thought about what she was saying. I realized that I had been judging myself all my life, and always found myself to be lacking. I let myself muse out loud. "I could never do right, for Connor—for Dad.

Nothing was ever good enough. No matter what I did, how well I did it, it was never enough. I was always treated as…less. Less worthy. Less…less inherently *good*. Like Tab and Hayley deserved God's grace and mercy—God's, and therefore Mom and Dad's—*they* deserved that, but I didn't."

I tapped my shoe on the carpet in a rapid, nervous pattern, because when my brain was firing this fast, my body had to move, too, even if it was just a tapping a toe or bouncing my knees. "I think I sort of absorbed Connor's judgmental view of myself. It was the way I was always treated, and so I treated myself that same way."

"That's a very important realization, Claire." Dr. Liz leaned forward, elbows on her knees, and fixed me with a sharp look from behind her glasses. "You deserve understanding—from others, but most of all from yourself. You won't ever allow yourself to succeed if you don't give yourself room to fail, and allow yourself understanding when you do fail.

"And I'm not even saying the choices you've made in your life are bad choices, or that you've failed in any way. I don't believe that, not at all. I think you've succeeded. You've come through a lot, and you're still here. You sought out help when you needed it most."

"But I hurt Brock along the way."

"Perhaps, but I think you did the right thing.

You knew you weren't in a place to be with him. It wouldn't have been fair to him, or yourself to have even tried to be in a significant relationship. You needed this time, Claire." She sat back once more. "You have made wonderful progress. I think you're on the right track with the understanding that you've been judging yourself too harshly. Continue along that path, and try to find your way to deeper self-forgiveness and understanding."

We talked about a few other things, and I answered honestly and openly, and then when my hour was up, I thanked her and went out to my car.

I owned a car now, which was kind of crazy. It was a Jeep Wrangler, bright blue, two-door, soft-top, four years old. I'd bought it from a guy that lived in my mom's subdivision, and he'd beefed up the engine and the exhaust, put on big, knobby off-road tires and a three-inch lift. Immediately after buying it, I'd gone on Amazon and ordered fluffy pink seat covers and a giant fake crystal shifter knob for the manual transmission stick, to girl it up a bit. It was a ridiculous, absurd, and insanely fun vehicle, and I loved it.

I'd relinquished my place in Seattle, had a company box up my stuff and send some to me and they put it the rest in storage. I quit my job at the firm and hung out my digital shingle as a freelance programmer, which had honestly gone a hell of a lot better than I'd expected. I was constantly busy and making really good money, but better than anything, I was working for myself, by myself.

I hung out with my sisters, and had lunch with my mother several times a week. Those lunches were a shock to me, because I discovered that I really did have a lot in common with Mom, and that I genuinely *liked* her, as a person. Now that Connor was gone, at least—and that was a weird realization to have. There'd been two full sessions with Dr. Liz spent dissecting that, what it meant for me and how I felt about it.

That was the other thing that was different for me: I'd tried half a dozen therapists until I found Dr. Liz; we clicked—she just *got* me, and I found her mannerisms and the questions she asked and the insights she provided to be genuinely helpful. She called me on my shit, but gently, and pushed me to understand myself.

I hadn't seen Brock in six months, but I'd texted him a few times, as requested, telling him I was still alive, still in Michigan, and still working on myself.

I had a month-to-month lease on an apartment not far from where Mom and the girls lived. But I hated my apartment.

I hated Michigan.

I missed Mara.

I missed Badd's, and the brothers.

And most of all, I missed Brock.

I'd been totally celibate for the last six months, not even using my vibrators on myself. Total sexual celibacy. It was utter hell…but it was good, too. It made me focus my time and thoughts on what counted: fixing myself, understanding myself, and forgiving myself. Getting to a place, as Dr. Liz said today, where I could be with Brock.

It was a bright sunny day, warm and beautiful. I had the top and doors off my Wrangler, Sia blaring from the radio, and for the first time in a very, very long time…I felt good. I'd made huge progress today, I could feel it. Understanding that I'd taken on Connor's disapproval—if not downright dislike—of me made it easier to see how I'd gone so long hating myself, refusing to allow myself to have anything good. The moment a guy got too close, he was gone, and that was assuming I even saw him more than once, or bothered to learn his name.

I drove for a while, letting the sun beat down on my skin, the wind ruffling my hair, big bug-eye sunglasses making me feel glam and gorgeous, one foot hanging out of the doorway onto the step. I let my mind wander, ruminating on everything Dr. Liz had said, everything I'd learned over the past five months with her.

After an hour of driving, I ended up in the parking lot of a suburban park, watching the kids play, and I realized I was done here. Oh, I'd have Dr. Liz refer me to someone in Ketchikan to keep up with the sessions, since I knew I wasn't *done* done, but...I felt ready to see Brock. Ready to have a conversation with him, ready to see if he was still willing to explore a future with me.

I kicked my feet up on my dashboard, pulled out my phone, and called Mara.

She answered on the third ring. "About fucking time you called me, whore," she teased, joy in her voice. "I miss you so much it's stupid."

"I miss you too, hooker-face." I heard myself sniffle, feeling oddly emotional. "So, guess what?"

She hesitated, sounding wary when she replied. "What?"

"It's time."

Another pause. "It's time?"

"It's time."

"No way." She was still skeptical and wary, not wanting to get her hopes up.

"Way."

"When?"

"Well, I don't have an exact time frame, but soon. Very soon."

"Can I tell anyone?" Mara's voice was hushed,

but was trembling with excitement. "Can I tell Brock?"

"No!" I shouted. "No. I'm driving there. I'll need the time to figure out what I'm going to say to him."

"Claire, I—"

"He's not…he's not seeing anyone else, is he?" I asked, interrupting her.

"What? Hell no. He barely leaves the bar, these days. Since Zane and I have the warehouse finished, Brock moved from the apartment over the studio into the one over the bar. He works, and he flies."

"He flies?" I wasn't sure what that meant. "He's always flown. He's a pilot."

"Well, yeah, but he brought his stunt plane up here, and he's been practicing a lot. If he's not in the bar, he's in the air. And no, he hasn't so much as looked at another woman." Mara hissed. "Shit, shit shit—ow."

"What?" I asked, panicked; Mara was due any day now. "What's wrong?"

"Oh, it's just the baby. He's kicking me right in the spleen, and it fucking hurts."

"You better not have that baby before I get there, bitch-nuts."

"Well then you better get your tiny ass up here, slut-muffin! I'm about to pop like a champagne bottle. My OB says if I don't go into labor on my own in the next week or so, she wants to induce me, otherwise little baby Badd will be too big for me have him vaginally without increased risk of needing a C-section. Plus, he'd tear me from hoo-ha to hey-ho, and that doesn't seem fun, to me."

"Tear you what-now?" I asked, faint.

"Apparently I have a small vagina, despite the fact that the rest of me isn't exactly small, which means a big baby might tear my perineum."

"Jesus, Mara. That sounds horrible."

"Yes, it does," she said, her voice far too cheerful. "But that's childbirth for you."

"Well. On *that* note, I'm going to let you go. I'll be leaving here in the next few days, so I should be in Ketchikan by the end of the week." I let out a heavy breath. "I love you, Mara. I can't wait to see you, and the others."

Mara sucked in a sharp breath. We'd toss out *love ya, bitch* now and again, but that wasn't that same as a heartfelt, insult-free statement. "Claire. Stop. I'm already a hormonal mess. Start in with that shit and I'm gonna be sobbing in about ten seconds."

"Okay, fine. I take it back. You're probably a fat whale and I hate you."

She sniffled, laughing. "That's more like it. Get up here. We miss you." She hesitated. "*He* misses you."

"Don't tell him. Don't tell anyone I'm coming, okay?"

"I won't." She sucked in a steadying breath. "Get here soon. Love ya."

"Bye, Preggo."

"Bye, Thumbelina." She hung up first, so I couldn't hit back, which made me laugh in affectionate irritation.

I left Michigan two days later, the few important possessions and bags of clothes packing my Wrangler to the roofline, and it took me four days of driving to reach Alaska; I made it to Ketchikan a little after four in the afternoon on the fourth day. I parked across the street a hundred or so feet down from Badd's. The door to the bar was propped open by one of the tall bar chairs, and Brock was lounging on the chair, his feet hooked around the chair legs, half of a grilled cheese sandwich in one hand, his phone in the other.

My breath caught at the sight of him, and my heart palpitated. He was more beautiful than ever. He'd bulked up some, his chest and arms looking a bit brawnier, his face fuller. His hair was longer too, as if he hadn't even bothered to have it trimmed since I saw it last. It suited him, the scruffy look. He hadn't shaved in a few days, and the heavy stubble on his jaw was a delicious shadow of masculine hotness.

He looked…sad, though. He was staring at his phone and frowning, letting out deep breaths every now and then. I wondered what he was looking at, what he was thinking.

I got out of my Wrangler, stretching and twisting to crack the kinks out of my spine. He didn't notice me. His attention was on his phone, the sandwich in his hand going to his mouth every now and then, his jaw flexing as he chewed. Even his jawline was gorgeous. God, I had missed that man. I had missed everything about him from his hands to his cock. I'd missed…fuck, I'd missed *everything*. But I was still scared—in fact, I was probably more scared now than ever.

I moved up the sidewalk in the direction of Badd's, on the other side of the street. I slid my phone out of the back pocket of my jeans and pulled up the text message thread with Brock.

Hey, I sent.

I leaned against the railing separating the sidewalk from the docks beyond, the sea at my back, and watched Brock. I saw the moment he got my message; his posture straightened, and he set his sandwich down on his knee, his brows furrowing even deeper, a heavy breath expanding his thick, broad chest.

Hi.

I hesitated, thought through a dozen different messages, but in the end, nothing I had to say could be said over iMessage. So I kept it simple.

Look up.

His head shot up, and his gaze fixed on me. He didn't react right away, just stared at me almost blankly, as if trying to absorb the fact that I was really standing there.

And then he shoved the rest of his sandwich into his mouth and washed it down with some beer from a half-empty pint glass he'd hidden on the ground behind the chair. He brushed off his hands and mouth, and stood up, slowly unfolding his big frame. His expression still revealed nothing, which I knew meant he was wary. He glanced both ways for traffic, and then strode slowly across the street, stopping a foot away from me.

My eyes swam with tears I wasn't ready to let fall. "Hi, Brock."

His jaw flexed, and his broad chest swelled, sank. "Hi, Claire."

"Um." I shifted from foot to foot; now that I was here in front of him, I had not a single fucking clue where to start. "Hi."

An amused grin chased across his features. "We did this already, babe."

Babe. God, it felt so good to hear that word from his lips.

"Yeah. I just—I don't know where to start." I sucked in a deep breath, blinking hard.

"Well, start by answering me a question."

"Okay." I let a breath out. "Shoot."

"Are you back?"

I pointed at my Wrangler, so full of random shit and boxes of knickknacks and bags of clothes that only the driver's seat was useable. "That's mine. So yeah, I'm back."

He eyed my Jeep, a silly grin on his face. "You bought a giant, tricked-out Wrangler?"

"What, you think I'd own a…a Camry or Sentra or something?"

He laughed, nodding his head and then shaking it. "Yeah, no, I can't see you in a Camry. That Wrangler absolutely suits you." He sobered, his gaze flicking back to me and holding there. "And us?"

"I…" Another stupid tear escaped; now that I was learning to feel and then deal with my emotions instead of suppressing them, I was a lot weepier than I'd ever been, especially when it came to Brock. Anytime I talked about him in my sessions with Dr. Liz, I'd go through half a box of tissues. "If you…if you still feel the way you did before, then…I would—shit, this is a hell of a lot harder than I thought it'd be."

"Claire."

I held up a hand, sniffing hard and blinking, staring at my toes in an attempt to get a grip, because if I looked at him too long I'd lose my shit. "Hold on. Just…let me work through this. I'm learning to let my emotions have space inside me. I'm not very good at it yet, but I'm trying."

"Claire." Again, patiently.

"I just—I've done a lot of work on myself over the last six months. You're probably gonna hear a lot of therapy lingo out of me, because I've been seeing a therapist." I wiped my eyes with both hands and looked up at him, then back down at my feet. "I'm going to keep going, my doctor down in Michigan referred me to someone up here. I'm still going to be a mess and I'm still working on some things, but I was hoping that if you still—"

"Claire." Another patient interruption. I heard a grin in his voice, and felt his fingertip on my chin.

I looked up, met his eyes, saw a world of emotion in them. "I'm trying to make amends here, mister."

He snaked a hand around my waist, curled his fingers into the small of my back and yanked me up against his hard body. "No amends to make. You needed to figure yourself out. We've got all the time in the world to talk about all that shit." His palm cupped my cheek, his thumb brushing over my lips. "You're here.

That's what matters."

My breath caught again, at the hardness of his body, the strength of his grip, the heat in his eyes, the love written on his face. "God, Brock. I've missed you."

He laughed, and bent down to brush his mouth against mine, a ghost of a kiss. "I thought about you and missed you every single day. It was horrible."

I wrapped my arms around his waist, clawed my fingers into the thick muscle of his back. "You remember the conversation we had, about not…about not masturbating?"

He quirked an eyebrow at me. "Yeah."

"I held to that."

"You have?"

I nodded. "There's been no one else, not even myself."

He let out a relieved sigh. "Me too, actually."

"How are either of us sane right now, if neither of us have even whacked off in six months?"

Brock's laugh was infectious. "I don't even know. I don't think I am, to be honest." His hands rolled over my shoulders, kneaded the back of my neck, and then slid and danced down to my ass. "It's been made worse by the fact that Bast and Dru are like goddamn teenagers, and the walls in that apartment aren't exactly soundproof."

I couldn't help laughing with him. "Poor Brock. That had to have been torturous." I leaned against him, my cheek to his chest, his heart thudding under my ear; despite his calm demeanor, his heart was hammering as hard as mine. "Can it really be this easy, Brock? I just show up and it's fine?"

"I've been waiting six months, Claire. It's been hell, I don't mind admitting." His fingers buried into my hair, which I'd let grow, so it was now a little past my jaw. "You're here. You want to be with me. Right? That's what this is, a yes to us?"

I nodded, stepping closer to him, feeling his erection behind his jeans against my belly. "Yes, Brock. I want to be with you. If you still love me, then—"

His hands tilted my face up toward his, and his mouth crashed down over mine, his tongue clashed and slashed against mine and over my teeth, and I could only kiss him back with a delighted, desperate whimper. His kiss was a welcome home, and an expression of how badly he'd missed me, and a declaration of how much he wanted me.

I broke the kiss, gasping for breath, resting my forehead on his chin. "Holy shit, Brock. You take my breath away, you know that?"

"I missed you."

"Clearly," I teased, and reached between us to trace the ridge of his erection. "Someone else missed me too, I see."

"Someone else is fucking dying right now, that's what. Someone else needs you so bad it's not even funny." His hands cupped my ass possessively. "If I wasn't by myself in the bar, I'd—"

"HOLY SHIT! Is that Claire?" I heard Bax's booming, gravelly, thunderous voice from down the street. "She's back! Hot damn! Maybe now Brock will stop being such a mopey little bitch all the fuckin' time."

Brock sighed in resignation, but didn't let go of my butt. "Bax, has anyone ever told you that you have absolutely zero tact what so fucking ever?"

Bax just laughed. "Yes, in fact, they have. Frequently. Tact is for politicians and pussies."

He stopped beside us, wearing a pair of black track pants and a white wife-beater, a pair of wrap-around Oakley's on his face. And holy fuck, if he'd been big before, Bax was positively colossal, now. Every inch of him was packed with heavy muscle, yet as he'd approached us, his step was light and graceful.

There were shadows of bruises on his face, though, under his eyes, as if he'd recently broken his nose or gotten black eyes, or more likely the latter because of the former, and his nose was crooked from having been broken and reset several times since I'd last seen him. He lifted a hand to shove his sunglasses up on top of his head, and his knuckles looked...

rough. Scarred.

And even though he'd always been the most beastly of the brothers, he was in some ways the most easy-going and playful.

Now though, he exuded a sense of...I wasn't sure. Threat? Danger? Not the way Zane did—you took one look at Zane and just knew in your bones that the man was lethal; Bax was different—the air around him was one of barely controlled and thinly veiled rage and brutality.

He scared me, and I don't scare easily.

Bax's gaze slid from me to Brock and back. He grinned at us. "Go on. Get out of here."

Brock frowned. "I'm behind the bar tonight. Till close."

"I know. I'll cover you. Your girl just came back." He wiggled his eyebrows, and then winked. "You gotta get...reacquainted."

Brock frowned again, brows scrunching, lines creasing the corners of his mouth. "Don't you have a...thing...scheduled tonight?" There was heaviness of meaning to that hesitation.

Brock waved a hand dismissively. "I did, but the match got rescheduled. Apparently the guy I was gonna fight got into a motorcycle accident, and they can't find anyone to take his place in time. Not anyone that could put up a half-decent fight, at any rate."

I tilted my head. "What are you guys talking about?"

"Not important," Brock said.

At the same time Bax answered, "I'm a prize fighter. Twelve matches undefeated." He thumped his chest with his fists like a gorilla. "They call me the Basher. Because any fucker who enters that ring with me gets fuckin' bashed to shit."

"Bax," Brock snapped. "Cool it."

Bax blew a sarcastic raspberry. "Yes, princess, I know you don't approve. Still don't give a shit."

"At some point, somebody's gonna enter that ring and take you down."

"I hope so. Winning all the time is getting boring. I could use a challenge." He clapped a huge, hard, heavy hand on both Brock's and my shoulders, angling us toward the bar. "Now. You two go upstairs and get it on like Donkey Kong before you start fucking right here in the street and, trust me, none of us want to see that shit. I got the bar shift tonight."

"You're sure?" Brock asked.

Bax whacked his brother on the back a little too hard, on purpose. "What, is this my first day or something? Yes, G-Q, I got it. Go. Diddle your woman while the diddling's good."

I laughed. "You're out of control, you big dumb ape." I slapped his arm, and it was like slapping the side of a cliff.

"Why yes, yes, I am." He nodded seriously. "Control, tact, sanity, the Baxter craves not these things," he said, in a truly horrible Yoda impression.

I didn't need to be told again. I tugged on Brock's hand. "Babe. He said he's got it. Let's go."

Brock eyed Bax one more time, suspiciously, and then shrugged. "All right. But if you need help—"

"I won't need help, dick lips." He waved us away in a shooing motion as we paused in the doorway of the stairs leading up to the apartment. "Now seriously get the fuck out of here before I change my mind."

Brock nodded, and then hauled me upstairs, taking them two at a time.

I followed him into his room, and he shut the door behind us, locked it, and then twisted to face me, ripping his shirt off.

I whistled appreciatively. "Damn, baby. Looks like Bax isn't the only one who's been working out."

He flexed for me, half-serious, half-joking. "Gotta channel my libido into something, don't I?"

I reached for his fly. "I've got a channel for your libido."

THIRTEEN

Brock

MY BACK WAS AGAINST THE BEDROOM DOOR, AND Claire was facing me. For a moment, we just stared at each other, sparks of sexual tension flaring between us, but also something else. It was like a Vulcan mind meld—we just totally, completely *got* each other in that moment. It was powerful, emotional, and completely open and honest.

Claire reached for the fly of my jeans, hunger in her eyes; I grabbed her wrist to stop her, remembering the last time we'd had sex together. I'd taken control completely and utterly, and she'd been consumed by paroxysms of utter rapture. What I wanted was to kiss her stupid and let her ride me until neither of us could walk. What she wanted, however, was for me to show her exactly how badly I'd missed her, how badly I needed her. I could see it in her eyes, in the hesitancy to make the first move.

I held her wrist, keeping her from touching me first. "Ah-ah-ah," I said. "I don't think that's how this is gonna go."

She frowned, a puzzled downturn of her mouth. "No? What do you mean?"

I let go of her wrist and stepped around her to sit on the edge of my bed. "Take your shoes and socks off."

She reached for the edge of her shirt. "Okay, I will, but first—"

"Nope." I held up my hand palm out. "Shoes and socks first."

"Brock, what's gotten into you?"

I gazed steadily at her, not giving anything away. "Just trust me, Claire." I gave her the slightest, quickest of winks. "Do what I tell you."

A slow, happy grin spread across her lips, and then vanished. "You just want me to obey, huh?"

"Exactly."

She nodded. "Okay. I'll bite." She wiggled a foot. "So. You want me to start with my socks and shoes, huh?"

I quirked an eyebrow. "It's a practical measure. Hard for you to wiggle out those tight little jeans if you're still wearing socks and shoes."

She giggled. "I suppose that's true." Claire reached down and started untying her sneakers.

"Turn around," I told her.

She huffed a little laugh, and then turned to face away from me, bending over at the waist to untie her shoes, presenting me with a lovely view her round ass, hugged by a pair of tight, dark blue jeans. She straightened and toed off her Converse, then bent again and balanced on one foot at a time to slip off her white ankle socks.

She turned back around to face me. "Now what?"

I wiggled my foot. "Now me."

She bent over again, and the V-neck of her button-down gaped open, giving me a little glimpse at her tits, unencumbered by a bra of any kind, as was typical. Just a glimpse of her tits as she bent over was enough to make my cock harder than ever, and it was already throbbing and straining at the confines of my jeans.

When my shoes and socks were gone, she lifted her palms up. "And now?"

"Your zipper. Slowly."

She flipped open the button and pinched the tab

of her zipper, making a dramatic show of tugging it downward.

"Take 'em off."

Claire shimmied her hips side to side, hooking her thumbs in the waist of the jeans, sliding them down past her thighs, and then kicking them off.

"Now your thong."

Her shirt ended just below her navel, showing off her yellow V-string. She turned to face away from me, staring at me over her shoulder as she bent to lower the thong past her knees, and then stepped out of it. God, her ass. So firm, so taut, a perfect round bubble of muscle, just squishy enough to have a nice little bounce to it. Pale skin, which would pink up nicely when I spanked her—something I intended to do, and soon.

But first…

She stood in front of me, facing me again, her pussy playing peekaboo from between her thighs. "Now my shirt?" she asked.

I shook my head. "Now you take off my pants."

"Demanding today, aren't we?" she asked, sassily.

I licked my lips. "I'm just getting started, babe."

She sucked in a breath. "Oh really?" A flick of her fingers had my button popped open, and then she was dragging the zipper down. "What else do you have in store for me?"

"Be a good girl and I'll show you."

"What if I want to be a bad girl instead? What then?"

"Bad girls get spanked, Claire. You should know that by now."

She lifted an eyebrow, and then took a step back from me, ripped her shirt off, and then crossed her arms under her breasts. "In that case, take your own pants off."

I laughed, stood up slowly, and stepped out of my jeans and boxers in one movement. "Bend over the bed, Claire."

She sucked in a deep breath, her eyes widening, her nostrils flaring, her thighs tightening together. But she shook her head at me. "No. You'll just have to make me."

I gripped my cock in my hand and nudged at the triangular apex of her thighs. "Oh, I think I'll enjoy that quite a bit."

She ground her jaw together and tried to stay stoic, tried to not react as I teased her with my dick. She held out for about six seconds, and then her thighs relaxed and she shifted her feet apart, flexing her hips forward. I pressed the head of my cock into the top of her bared slit, right where her clit was, and she whimpered. I rubbed myself in circles against her clit until she was moaning softly and her hips were moving.

And then I stopped, and when her eyes flew open and her mouth moved to whisper protests, I grabbed her by the shoulders, spun her around to face the bed, and pressed her upper half forward. To her credit, she managed to remember to resist.

"What are you going to do, Brock?" she asked, in a passable impression of fear.

"I might fuck you, or I might spank you," I said, "I haven't decided yet."

I slipped a foot between her feet and knocked her stance wider, then stepped up behind her and bent over her. My cock nudged against the seam of her ass, my thighs against hers, my chest against her back, all of me touching all of her.

I pressed my lips to her ear as I brought one of her wrists around behind her back and then the other. "You were a very bad girl, Claire."

She only barely stifled an uncharacteristically giddy giggle. "I was, wasn't I? I deserve punishment."

"It feels like you're mocking me, Claire."

She couldn't suppress the next giggle. "Would *I* mock *you*?"

In answer, I slipped two fingers between her thighs to find her slit, found her wet and hot and ready for me. I nudged the tip of my cock against her opening, and she gasped in anticipation. "Is this what you want?" I demanded. She nodded, and I spanked her ass cheek, once, hard enough that she squealed. "Answer me out loud."

"YES!" she shrieked. "Yes, I want that."

I slipped my cock in a little deeper, gripped her wrists together in my left hand and palmed her ass cheek with the other. I stayed like that, hesitating so she wouldn't know when it was coming, or what was coming. I waited until she got antsy, shifting beneath me, wanting me deeper. I flexed my hips ever so slightly, giving her a fraction of an inch more of my cock, and she whimpered, needy and breathy.

"God, Brock—*please*."

"Begging already?" I smoothed my palm against the soft flesh of her ass cheek.

"I haven't had your cock in six months, Brock. I need you so fucking bad." She wasn't playing, this time; the need in her voice was genuine, as was the desperation in her next words. "Fuck me, Brock. God, *please* fuck me. However you want. Take me however you want me, just give it to me. Don't make me wait anymore."

Without warning, I drilled into her, sinking my cock as deep as it would go in a single rough thrust and, at the same time, I spanked her ass with a loud, resounding *crack*. "You were the one who made me wait, Claire. Six months." I pulled out slowly, gently, paused to make her wait, make her anticipate and guess, and then I fucked in again, spanking her other cheek just as hard. "Six months I went without jerking off. I didn't look at a single dirty picture, not even the nudes you sent me way back when. You know how many painful hard-ons I had to suffer through? How bad my balls ached?"

She whimpered as I pulled back out. "I had to, Brock. I'm sorry. I'm so sorry. But I had to. For both of us."

I slid in and out of her in slow, gentle, delicate thrusts, teasing her—and myself. I sank in deep, bending over her, nibbling on her earlobe. "I know, Claire," I whispered.

And then I pulled out and fucked her again, harder than ever, spanking both sides now, one and then the other in quick succession. "But still. Six months, barely a word from you."

She gasped as I fucked her. "I know, I know. But if I let myself think about you, oh god—oh *god*—" She broke off as I fucked her again, harder and faster, three times in a row, spanking her with each thrust. "Fuck, fuck, that feels so good. I knew if I started talking to you, texting you, I'd give in. I wanted you every moment. I missed you every moment. God, Brock, I needed you so bad it hurt."

I pulled her backward a few inches and released her hands. "Touch your clit, Claire. Let me feel you come. Make yourself come around my cock."

"Keep doing what you're doing," she murmured, keeping her hands crossed behind her back, "and I will without needing to touch myself."

"Oh yeah?" I spanked her, and now the firm bubbles of her ass cheeks were pink from my hand, and she was writhing beneath me, pushing back into my thrusts. "Like this?" I used both hands, now, spanking one side and then the other, fucking her steadily in slow, measured thrusts.

She gripped the flannel quilt on my bed with both fists and arched her back, groaning and gasping, and then those sounds turned to breathy whimpers as she moved with me. "Yeah, god yes. Just like that. Don't stop, please don't stop."

I didn't stop.

I fucked her and spanked her until she was a thrashing mess beneath me. "Use your fingers, Claire. Come hard."

She slipped two fingers between her body and the bed, and I felt them moving, circling. It was all I could do to hold out. I wanted to come inside her like this. I wanted to let go, to fuck her mercilessly and come so hard I saw stars. But I had other ideas, better plans.

I gritted my teeth and clenched my muscles to hold back as she went wild beneath me, thrashing, screaming, her pussy clamping around me as she came. I nearly lost it, then, only barely managing to keep it back.

I wasn't ready to come yet.

She was still spasming and grinding when I pulled out and let her go; as soon as I released her, Claire slumped limp to the floor, clutching the bed and panting. She turned a gaze up at me, and then glanced at my cock, hard, glistening, pointing at the ceiling, bobbing as I breathed. "You didn't come," she said.

I shook my head. "No. Not yet."

"I want you to."

"I will," I promised. "Just not yet, and not like that."

She twisted to face me, then reached for me. "You want to come a different way, is that it?"

I held out my hands, palms facing hers, fingers spread out. "Hold my hands." She met my gaze and threaded her fingers into mine, kneeling in front of me. I gave her a smoldering stare. "Open your mouth for me. Taste us on my cock."

She parted her lips and angled so I could fill her mouth with my cock, and she tongued me as I slid in. Then she backed away, so I popped out. "God, Brock. We taste amazing."

I gave in to it for a moment, let her taste me, let her take me into her mouth, into her throat, let her twist her head this way and that, licking me and mouthing the thick shaft with her head tilted to one side, until I was groaning and growling with the need to come.

When I couldn't take it anymore, I tugged her to her feet. Met her gaze. "When I come, it's going to be inside you, your eyes on mine."

She caught her breath. "Brock I—"

I touched her lips with my finger, shushing her. "You know how often I've thought about this day, Claire? The day when you came back and said you wanted to be with me?"

"Probably almost as often as I did," she said. "I dreamed of this. What you'd do, what I'd do."

"I fantasized about it. I thought about taking you up against the wall, in the shower, bent over the bed, all the places we've fucked before."

"God, I want you to fuck me in all those places."

"And I will."

She slid a fist up and down my length, an idle, affectionate stroke. "But?"

"But the more I thought about it, the more I realized there was only one thing I really wanted, when I finally had you back, when I could finally bury myself inside you."

"What's that?" she asked, stroking me, whispering in my ear. "Tell me."

"You know, I remember the night we met very vividly. I remember each time we fucked that night, and where. And I remember each time and place we've fucked since." I let her stroke me, burying my fingers in her hair. "We've fucked in the shower, on the floor, you bent over the bed, up against the wall… anyplace there is to fuck, we've fucked. Except one."

She stilled, freezing. "Where?" she breathed.

"In bed." I nodded at the furniture in question. "We've been in the bed for sex exactly one time: the night we met, the third time we fucked. It was reverse cowgirl. You took longer to come that time than any of the others, but when you did, you came *hard*, and so did I."

She sighed. "That was amazing. And scary."

"We've fucked on your couch in Seattle. On the bar, downstairs. In my plane, and on the float of my plane. In the bathroom of more than one bar. You've sucked me off in almost as many different places. Up against the window of the hotel, remember that?" I breathed all this in her ear. "Yet we've never once had regular old vanilla sex in a bed."

She froze again, her hand clutching my cock. "In a bed means it's different. I never have sex in bed. I never have. It was a rule from the very first time, which was the last time, for me. Keeps it from…I don't know. I don't know."

"Keeps you, and them, from forming an attachment," I answered for her. "You don't like looking into my eyes and kissing me while we fuck, because then it's too much like something more than fucking."

"Right."

"That's it, isn't it?"

She ducked her head, and nodded. "Yes. It keeps me from letting it mean something."

"Even with me?"

"It meant something with you anyway. It always has. That's what scared me. Even when you took me hard and fast up against at a wall, it meant something. If you fucked me doggy style on the floor, it meant something." She remembered herself, and went back to stroking me; the depth of the conversation had allowed me to start slackening a little, and now her touch brought me back to life. "It's always meant something. And that night, we fucked reverse cowgirl on this bed, and I didn't even stop to think about it until I was nearly at orgasm, and it scared me, because it just felt so right, so easy, totally normal."

"You said it was a rule from the very first time?"

She nodded. "When I let a guy have sex with me for the first time after...all that other shit, it was in his bed. He didn't think anything of it—I mean, for most people that's just where you fuck, and I get that. But for me...it's just always felt too intimate."

I caught her wrists to stop her touching me. "Claire, I don't need you to—"

She shook her head, cutting in over me, reached up to cup my face in both hands. "No, Brock. You *do*. You deserve that from me—I owe it to you. And I'll give it to you, I swear I will. Because what we have, it's so much more than anything I thought even existed. After six months apart, the moment I saw you, the moment you kissed me, I just—*knew*." She looked up at me, her eyes boring into mine, glittering, burning, intense, and open.

"Knew what, Claire?"

"That I've been in love with you for…a long time."

"When you do think the moment was, when you fell in love with me?"

"The first time you ate me out." She wrinkled her nose and grinned at me. "That's not entirely a joke, either."

"And you've been fighting it this whole time?"

She nodded. "You scare me, Brock."

"How? Why?"

"Because you have so much power over me. I'm the actual dictionary definition of an independent woman, but you—you…" She paused, looked away, and then met eyes again. "You *own* me, Brock."

"I don't want to own you, I just want to be with you."

She laughed. "I know. That's why it's scary. Because what if you start wanting more than I can give? I don't know how to love. I've never really been shown true love—I don't really know what it looks like. Even what Mom and Dad had wasn't...I don't know—they loved each other, I know they did, they spent thirty-two years together. But their love was... weird. It wasn't something I would ever emulate. It was a relationship built on guilt and shame and convenience and a sense of doing the right thing by each other. I bound them together, in a weird way. But they weren't passionate about each other. They didn't *need* each other desperately...the way I need you."

"You came back, and you've admitted you want to be with me, that you fell in love with me a long time ago." I moved to sit on the bed. "Have you finally understood that all I want is *you*?"

"It means I'm trying." She shuddered, sighed. "It means I'll always keep trying."

She feathered her fingers into my hair at the back of my head, and pulled me down to kiss me, and the kiss was transformative, transportive, rapturous. More than teeth and tongues and lips, it was souls, hearts, and minds merging. She was giving me herself in the kiss. The conversation that went before had been a long time coming, and now it was consummated with this kiss. I'd gone slack, needing the words she was giving me more than I needed sex, more than I needed the release. And now, with the kiss, I still didn't need anything more than what it was, a slice of heaven made real, her hands clutching me with reverence and love, her mouth moving on mine, her tongue seeking mine, kissing me so deeply, so fervently, so passionately that it was...it was the truest expression of love Claire Collins was capable of creating.

She pulled away. "Lay down on the bed, Brock," she whispered.

I slid backward and lay down in the middle of the bed, my hands tucked under my head. She stood there beside the bed for a moment, staring at me, just breathing and just looking at me.

She was naked, and so gorgeous. Small breasts high and firm, dark areolae the size of quarters, plump nipples. Flat, toned abs, indents at her hips leading down to her pussy, dark pubic hair trimmed into a neat, short V. Strong, lean, powerful runner's legs. Her hair was its natural blonde, a few inches longer than it'd been last time I'd seen her, and she'd left it loose and a little wild, tossed and tangled by the wind as she drove with the top down of her ridiculous Jeep. I loved it, loved her hair like that, a few strands in her eyes, some tucked behind her ear, the rest left to blow wherever it wanted to.

I was hardening under her gaze, which was hungry, needy again, but now was rife with the new openness I wasn't used to seeing in her eyes. She wasn't blocking or suppressing or keeping anything in. She wanted me—shit, the girl was insatiable, so she *always* wanted me, which was the best thing in the world—but she also just...*loved* me. And was looking forward to showing me.

She crawled onto the bed from the foot end, prowling like a lioness up between my outstretched legs. She crawled over me, hands on either side of my hips, an eager, lascivious smirk on her lips, and then she took me into her mouth, and this time, it wasn't because I'd told her—playfully ordered her to—it was because she *wanted* to. If I hadn't been totally erect before, her sweet warm mouth took care of that in a heartbeat. She took me to the back of her throat, and then once again demonstrated her lack of a gag reflex, sliding me into her throat until her lips were at the base of my cock and her nose was touching my belly. She backed away and immediately pressed down again, and then started fucking me with her mouth around the root of my throbbing cock.

"Claire, Jesus—Claire, stop. I'm gonna come in a second—" I reached for her, pulled up and away. "I don't want to come in your mouth this time."

She let me fall out of her mouth, grinning up at

me. "Oh, I wouldn't have let you." She crawled farther up my body, until she was straddling me. "I'm on a hair trigger, and I wanted you ready for me."

"I'm more than ready," I said.

She sat astride my waist, ran a hand through my hair and then cupped the back of my neck. Leaned forward so her lips brushed mine, her breasts brushing my chest. Reaching a hand between us, Claire guided me to her entrance and she sank down onto me in a single smooth slide, no pause, no hesitation, no drawing it out, just a beautiful joining of our bodies. We both moaned in unison as her pussy swallowed my cock, and then I was fully seated inside her, her ass on my thighs, her mouth on mine, her weight on her shins on the bed.

"I've never done this before," Claire whispered. "Not like this."

"No?"

"Never like this." She clung to me, started writhing on me, her breath hot on the side of my neck. "I can see this being addictive."

She moved, lifting her hips and dropping them, rolling slowly, grinding on me. Taking me, using me to bring her orgasm to the surface. She hadn't been kidding—she was on the edge, riding me hard and fast within moments, gasping, crying out, and clawing her fingers down my chest as she detonated.

As she climaxed, she cupped my face with one hand and touched her trembling lips against mine, shuddering on top of me. "Brock, god…Brock."

"Claire—" I was getting close, her clenching clamping heat bare around me bringing me swiftly to that edge as well. "Claire, I love—"

She pressed her thumb over my lips and shook her head. "Not yet." She stared down at me, desperation in her eyes. "Don't say it yet."

I knew what she wanted, then. I saw it in her eyes, felt it from her.

I lifted up to kiss her, grinding my hips against hers. Ran my hands over her back, cupped her ass, pulling her against me as we moved together. She ended the kiss first, her forehead resting against mine.

"Brock," she whispered.

"I know."

I captured her legs with mine, clamping my thighs around hers, and rolled over without allowing our connection to break. And then, just like that, she was beneath me. Her eyes were wide, her breathing fast…

But she had a smile on her face, bright and bold and fearless and beautiful. She slid her arms around my waist and clawed her fingers into the muscle of my back, wrapped her ankles around the backs of my knees, and her breathing caught.

"Brock," she whispered again, happiness in her eyes, shining wetly.

"I know." I pressed against her, pushing deeper, and she gasped, lifted her hips against mine. "Me too."

She palmed my ass, pressed her forehead against my shoulder and then bit the side of my bicep, and began writhing beneath me, desperate for more. "Say it," she murmured, kissing the side of my jaw, then my cheekbone. "Now say it."

I laughed at the giddiness in her voice. "Hey, Claire." I braced one hand in the mattress beside her, used the other to brush her hair out of her face. "Guess what?"

Her smile shone up at me as our bodies moved in perfect incredible sync, hips meeting and retreating, breath coming hard and fast, her hands on my ass and my back and in my hair and everywhere, her legs hooked around mine and her feet stroking me wherever they could reach, our bodies so eager to caress and show as much affection as we could, because this was love.

"Hey, Brock—what?"

I sank into her, feeling her clamping around me, feeling myself unable to hold back any longer, feeling my heart expand and connecting to hers and merging with her skin and her soul and her past and our future.

I extended the moment as long as I could, not breaking eye contact as I brought us closer and closer and closer…

She was gasping, shrill and desperate, clinging to me everywhere she could, moving with me, and then her gasps turned to moans, soft, sweet, wild sounds as she clenched and throbbed around me, and then it was time, I couldn't wait any longer, I was bursting with the need to finally say the words to her and hear them back, violently desperate to release inside her after so long.

"I love you, Claire." As I said the words, I came, and the words became a chant. "I love you, ohhhh god, I love you."

Again and again and again, and Claire was crying, coming apart beneath me, sobbing and clutching at me wildly and kissing me in a thousand places with a thousand kisses each more desperate and crazed than the last.

"Brock, Brock, oh my god…*Brock!*" She screamed my name as she shattered, shaking, trembling, gasping. Her eyes flew open and locked on mine, tears running unheeded down her face, joy in every line and pore and movement. "I…I love you, Brock."

My breath caught, my throat closed. I bumped my forehead against hers, and she clutched the back of my head, her lips seeking mine. These were the words I'd been waiting to hear, and they meant so much to me that all I could do was utter her name, again and again. "Claire, Claire, Claire."

All I could do was pour myself into her and feel her lush tight body writhing beneath me, her hands all over me, her lips on me, her pussy clenching around me throbbing and clamping down so tight it was nearly painful as she came and came and came, milking my orgasm until it became something else entirely, more than just a release.

When I could come no more, I collapsed on her, and she laughed in pleased surprise, taking my weight. She stroked my hair and my back and my ass and my arms, just caressing, petting. Loving me with her hands.

I went to move off her, sure I was crushing her with my weight, but she held me in place. "No. Just... stay like this for a while. I..." She inhaled the scent of my hair. "I love this."

"I'm not too heavy?"

She shook her head, her hands moving over me, tracing my muscles. "You're perfect."

I don't know how long we stayed like that, me still buried inside her, my weight on her, her hands moving, our breathing slowing into a synced susurrus.

Eventually, she pushed at my shoulder. "Now switch." I rolled again, and now she was fully on top of me, her head tucked under my chin, her fingertips resting on my face. She lifted up to look down at me. "I want to say it again, when it's not the heat of the moment."

She gazed at me, a long silence growing as she allowed the feelings to move through her, the fear of putting herself in my hands, the joy, the bliss of being together after so long apart. "I love you, Brock Badd." Her voice was strong, her eyes searching mine as she said it.

She rested her head on my chest again, and I breathed in the moment, letting my hands now roam her skin.

After a moment, Claire lifted up again. "Aren't you going to say it back?"

I grunted a negative. "Nope. Gonna let you have that one."

She laughed. "Oh."

"It doesn't have to be a you-then-me sort of thing, Claire. It can be whatever we want it to be. Expressing love for each other however we feel like expressing it."

She slid off me to lay on the bed beside me, and took my slack cock in her hand. "So if I wanted to express my love for you like this?"

"Then I'd say, baby, I've got all night." I watched her hand move, teasing me to life. "I'd say, baby, let's get started on forever right now."

She laughed. "That was cheesy."

"You love it when I'm cheesy."

"True, I do love it when you're cheesy." She fondled me into erection, toying with me until I was achingly hard again. "I also love it when your come is leaking out of me, and I get your big fat cock inside me again and you come even more, and I spend the whole next day smelling like you, with your come dripping out of me every time I sit down or stand up."

She rolled on top of me, took me inside her, and this time, she rode me to completion, hers and my own. We hurried there, grinding together until she was breathless above me and I was pouring into her. Less than five minutes from start to finish, but her eyes never left mine, and we didn't need to say the words this time, we just needed to move together, come together, feel the intensity of our union.

Again and again, and again, all through the night. We slept, and we woke and we joined together, and we slept again. Dawn came eventually and I was inside her again, above her again.

We never left the bed.

I lost track of the number of times we each said I love you.

As it should be.

EPILOGUE

Evangeline

THE AIR IN MY FATHER'S PRIVATE JET WAS TENSE AND stifling.

"Evangeline." Father's voice was stern and stentorian and stiff with anger. "I just received word of your marks at Yale from this past semester. You still aren't applying yourself as you should be. At least not in the classes that matter."

"Well, you see, that's what's funny, Father. Your notion of which classes really matter differs from mine, as you may recall from our previous conversations on this topic." I stifled a tired sigh. "You're lucky

I'm attending those ridiculous, wretched classes at all."

"*I'm* lucky?" His thick, manicured, salt-and-pepper eyebrows rose toward his hairline. "You have things rather backward, I'm afraid."

We were in the midst of yet another maddeningly polite argument about everything we always argued about: my life, my choices for my career and my future, and the fact that Thomas Haverton was not the man for me.

"I have absolutely no interest whatsoever in politics *or* business, Father. This isn't new."

"Politics and business are your birthright and your inheritance, Evangeline. You cannot simply ignore the path life has set out for you."

I couldn't keep back the groan this time. "*Life* hasn't set out that path for me, Father, *you* have. And I'm not interested." I waved my French-manicured fingernails behind us, where Thomas Haverton—my father's protégé and the subject of much hopeful matchmaking—was fielding a conference call. "*He* is interested enough in the business for the both of us. You want someone to take over your place as CEO and president of du Maurier Enterprises? Give it to him. I don't want it."

"That's the plan already, my dear," Father said. "But I want the business to remain in the family.

Which is why I really think you need give the man a fair shake."

I bit my lip to keep from cursing at my father. "This is even older news than my apathy about business and politics. Thomas is a fine businessman and a worthy successor to your chair as the head of the board. But I have less than no interest in him romantically. I do not feel about him like that now, I haven't for many years, and I will never have those feelings going forward. Not ever."

Father had his chair swiveled to face me across the aisle. We were on board Father's private jet which, despite its massive size only boasted a total of six chairs, although each chair was a high-tech work of leather-wrapped luxury, featuring full massage capabilities, 360-degree swivel, a footrest, cup holders, AC, and USB ports, and could fully recline to become a bed. I was on the other side of the aisle, facing forward, perpendicular to my father, using body language to create a sense of disinterest in the topic.

"Evangeline, come now. He's a wonderful man. Smart, driven, successful, wealthy in his own right, and within ten years of your own age, not to mention his impeccable breeding and pedigree—"

"Yes, Father, he's a prize stallion, I'm sure." I rolled my eyes. "Good for you. If he's so wonderful, you marry him."

"You have been destined to marry Thomas Haverton since birth, Evangeline. It is fated. There can be no better match for my daughter."

The argument had the same effect it always did… none whatsoever, although I do admit I was being worn down, exhausted by their persistent efforts.

I'd broken up with Thomas Haverton at least three times, and yet any time I was home for a break or a weekend, anytime I had lunch with Father or Mother, Thomas showed up, and I got sucked back into his orbit. He showed up for our family vacations, showed up at birthday parties and business functions. I couldn't escape him, couldn't avoid him.

His long, sleek black Mercedes would show up outside my dorm at Yale and Raymond, his driver, would be behind the wheel, Thomas in back with his tablet and laptop and phone and slim leather brief-case, working as always. He and Father worked together and were so much alike it was scary. He should have been born into my family rather than me.

When Thomas showed up, he wouldn't go away unless I came outside. He'd have Raymond follow me at a slow crawl, and he would carry on a conversation with me regardless, and everyone would stare and whisper and point, and so I would get in just to stop the scene.

Invariably we'd end up at a private table at some

exclusive restaurant in the city, and he would order a four-hundred-dollar bottle of wine and then things went the way they always went. We'd get to the part where I was supposed to invite him up to my room, and I wouldn't, because I didn't want Thomas in my private space.

I'd slept with him a once or twice, years past. He'd been my first date, my first kiss; we'd gone from first base to second to third in gradual phases, and then I'd given him my virginity in his suite of rooms at the top of his parents' exclusive high rise in Manhattan after senior prom.

I'd cried, and he hadn't understood, and then he'd gotten drunk on champagne and I'd ended up calling Teddy, Father's driver, to come get me at three in the morning, my dress rumpled and ruined, my hair a wreck, my makeup a disaster, tracks of dried mascara on my cheeks. I'd had to explain to Teddy that Thomas hadn't hurt me, at least not like *that*.

That was more than three years ago now, and since then I avoided Thomas as much as possible. He just wasn't the man for me. As far as I was concerned, I had clearly broken up with him, but yet he persisted. He continued to propose with four-carat diamond rings and elaborate showpieces worthy of *The Bachelor*.

Why would he continue after being refused

three times? The answer was simple but hard to understand—it was because Father had promised him
that I *would* marry him. It just might take some time
for me to accept.

Father was stewing, now. Clenching his jaw, sighing prodigiously, and eying me furiously. "Evangeline.
This is maddening."

I laughed. "On this, Father, we happen to agree."

"So why must you insist on being so difficult?"

I stared at my father in irritated befuddlement.
"You mean, why must I insist on, oh, I don't know,
having my own personality? My own dreams and desires and plans that don't necessarily line up with your
vision for my life?"

"Precisely," Father muttered, without a trace of
any irony whatsoever.

"You are unbelievable."

"The feeling is mutual," I snapped.

A moment of silence, and then another sigh
from Father. "I just want the best for you."

"I know you do. But the best for me is the freedom to choose my own path in life."

"There are certain expectations that have been
thrust upon your shoulders, simply due to the family
into which you were born, Evangeline. You cannot
ignore the duty you owe your family."

"Why do you think I'm even attending those

stupid classes you've forced me into, Father?"

"You're barely passing. That hardly counts."

"A C-average isn't exactly barely passing."

"You're a member of MENSA, Evangeline."

I shrugged. "Perhaps that may be important to you, but it isn't to me."

"No child of mine should be seen to be maintaining anything less than their very best, and you are capable of far more than a C."

"I'm not in high school, Father. My grades are my business, not yours."

Father rumbled a sound of displeasure. "I'm paying for the classes, so it is my business, I rather think."

"Then I'll quit school entirely. Will that make you happier?"

Father shoved up out of his chair, anger in every line of his body. "You are simply impossible, Evangeline du Maurier."

I didn't reply, because there was no point: what I wanted didn't matter. I was simply expected to be the compliant daughter who accepted Father's plans for me, to accede to his wishes, to do as he instructed; Father knew best.

He was Lawrence du Maurier, owner, founder, president, and CEO of du Maurier Enterprises, a global complex of corporations and LLCs spanning industries from technology and communications, to medical research and arms development. He was also a former three-term senator, a man with connections to the highest levels of government, and the ears of lobbyists, lawmakers, and Congressional committees. He was an immensely powerful man, one who was accustomed to getting exactly what he wanted—because he always did, no matter what he had to do.

Halfway through my sophomore year at Yale, I'd changed my major from poli-sci to art. I'd dumped the politics classes, blew off the cushy internship Father had set up for my summer at a prestigious Boston firm, and had enrolled in painting classes, art history, and anatomy courses in the fall semester.

Father had been furious, of course. We'd quarreled. He'd cursed at me, I'd cursed back, he'd cursed louder, and I'd stormed off and spent my summer in art classes at the community college near our estate in Connecticut. Then, when I returned to school for the fall semester and visited the office to get my schedule, I discovered that Father had switched everything back to poli-sci. He'd even rearranged my schedule so I could intern at the Boston firm Thursday, Friday, and the weekend, the rest of my classes being crammed between Monday and Wednesday.

No amount of finagling from me had persuaded the enrollment office to change my schedule back, since Father was one of the biggest donors the university had. He always got what he wanted, and what he wanted was for me, his daughter, his only child, to major in political science.

He did not care that I *hated* politics, did not care that I loved art and that I was a talented sketch artist and oil painter. He was unmoved by the fact that the portfolio of art I'd put together on my own over the years had been good enough that the head of Yale's art department had arranged a private study program for me...up to that point I'd been self-taught.

Now it was my senior year, and I was technically majoring in poli-sci. But I was only barely scraping by in those classes, and I'd convinced the art department head to let me continue with the private study program, making me a double major. It had been my best political moment, honestly, when I'd outmaneuvered my father.

I gave him what he wanted, sort of, and more importantly, I got what I wanted. The win was that I half-assed the poli-sci classes, blowing them off as much as I dared in favor of time in the studio, painting. I passed the classes, maintained a C-average, but I was primarily focused on my art. And there wasn't a single thing Father could do, because I was giving him the poli-sci major, but he couldn't make me love it, couldn't make me want it, couldn't make me study harder, or attend class when I didn't want to.

It became obvious that my poli-sci skills were not what the Boston firm wanted and they quietly suggested to my father that I "take a break." Which was another win in my column, as far as I was concerned, since it freed up a large block of my time.

Then there was this vacation to Mallorca. It was a big deal, a yearly trip our two families had been making together for twenty-five years, alternating stays at our estate and the Havertons'. I knew that this year's trip would mean that Thomas would renew his efforts to convince me to marry him, and I would have no part of it.

After Father stormed away from our perennial argument, I returned to scrolling idly through my social media feeds, passing the time in stony silence as the jet traversed from Connecticut to Los Angeles, where Mother would meet us—she had been hosting a big fundraiser in San Francisco, and the Havertons' had been visiting a family friend on the West coast. Father arranged that we would fly out to LA, overnight there, refuel and restock the G6, then Richard and Elaine Haverton and Mother would join us, and we would all make the transatlantic flight together.

Mother and Father and the Havertons would visit and eat dinner and watch movies and drink way too much, and Thomas would make thinly veiled insinuations and drink champagne and try to get his hands under my skirt.

I had other plans, of course, but had no intention of sharing them with anyone. I just had to bide my time and wait for the best moment to make a break for it. I knew Father wasn't above essentially kidnapping me, if he had to. He would have Lance, Freddy, and Hassan firmly but gently prevent me from getting away. Which meant I had to be sneaky. I would need a distraction, if possible. It would mean making my escape without my luggage, since I couldn't see any way of retrieving it once it had been removed from the cargo hold.

I had my carry-on, of course, in which I had a full change of clothes and a pair black flats, but one outfit wasn't anywhere near enough. I had my credit cards, and the debit card, which drew off my personal account.

Years ago, I'd foreseen Father would try to manipulate me via money, so I'd forged his signature on some key documents, which had allowed me to transfer the sizable monthly cash allowance Father provided me with from the account he controlled to a private, secret one *I* controlled. I never transferred all the allowance, obviously, in case he ever looked at my spending habits. I'd learned to live fairly frugally, considering the fact that my allowance was six figures a year.

The frugal—for me—lifestyle meant I'd saved up a nice nest egg of money in an account Father knew nothing about, and couldn't touch even if he did, since it was at a totally different offshore bank in my name alone. It meant tiresome wire transfers every month, which meant secret visits to Father's bank, but it was all worth it.

The point was I could buy my own clothing, and anything else, when I got away from Father and Thomas.

The G6 was now making its final approach to LAX, and once we'd taxied to the private hangar, there would a limo waiting to take us to the condo in LA where we'd stay the night and wait for Mother and the Havertons to arrive.

I collected my things once I felt the wheels touch down, unbuckling, and trying to figure out how I would get away. I'd just have to play it by ear, I decided.

Fifteen minutes of taxiing, and then the jet halted, and I heard the bump of the stairs and the hissing of the cabin depressurizing as the door opened. From my window I could see the limo with the temporary driver, and the airport staff unloading our baggage into the trunk of the G-Wagen, which would transport it all to the condo and back again tomorrow. Not only did one not carry one's own luggage, one didn't even travel in the same vehicle as one's luggage.

Ridiculous.

I'd grown up with it, but it was still ridiculous. On my own at Yale, I cooked my own food, carried my own books, walked to class, studied in sweatpants, painted in ratty thirdhand clothes purchased from a resale shop. I did my best to make sure people didn't even suspect the kind of money and political clout I came from. Other students in the poli-sci program would absolutely *murder* to have the advantages being my father's daughter came with, but I had absolutely ZERO interest in a political career.

Thomas tried to take my carry-on from me. "Let me carry that, Evangeline."

I kept it out of his grip. "It's fine, Thomas, I can manage, thank you."

He took it from me anyway. "I'm attempting to be a gentleman. The least you could do is let me be nice."

"I appreciate the gesture," I said, "but it's not necessary. May I have my bag back, please?"

Thomas ignored me, keeping hold of my bag, tucking an arm around my waist with unwelcome familiarity. "I have reservations for us tonight at Abrakadabra Vinoteca. You brought some eveningwear, I assume?"

Typical Thomas, making assumptions. I reached over, snatched my bag from him, and put a foot of space between us as we walked across the tarmac to the waiting limo.

"Actually, Thomas, I have other plans."

"Oh." He frowned, dug out his phone and consulted his calendar. "I can move it to Saturday. We've dined there on numerous occasion, so I'm certain they'll accommodate us."

"You're forgetting that we are leaving tomorrow for Europe." I paused for effect. "You must know by now that I'm busy every day. Forever."

Thomas stopped, eyeing me in irritation. "Now really, Evangeline. Don't be ridiculous." He moved toward me. "You're dining with me. It's tradition."

I lifted an eyebrow. "Is that a command, Thomas?"

He narrowed his eyes at me. "If you like."

I snorted. "How well has issuing commands worked for my father, Thomas?"

He struggled to remain calm. "It's dinner, Evangeline. Why be difficult about it?"

"Thomas." I stood nose to nose with him, staring him down. "I do not wish to spend time with you. You can issue all the commands you wish, but I'm not going anywhere with you."

"We'll see about that," he huffed, and stalked angrily toward the limo.

"Yes, we shall," I said, more to myself, since he was now out of earshot.

If it weren't so enraging, the sense of entitlement Thomas felt toward me would have been comical. He thought if I didn't do what he wanted, he could just beseech my father, who would then force me to do what Thomas wanted.

The joke was on them, however; I wasn't about to be forced into anything, let alone a ridiculous vacation I wanted no part of, or dinners with Thomas Haverton, or days on end at a stifling, overly lavish estate sipping tea and munching on finger sandwiches and making banal small talk with people I didn't like.

I waited until Thomas and then Father were in the limo and then slid in and took a spot far from both of them, pretending to be absorbed in my phone, although all I was really doing was scrolling through my Instagram, looking at posts I'd already looked at a dozen times. Father and Thomas were discussing some client account, since Thomas worked directly under Father, was his protégé, and the son he'd always wished he had. Thus the pressure to marry Thomas—because once that happened he would truly be family and take over when Father decided to retire.

The limo took us to the condo, a forty-five-minute drive. Thomas and Father got out, and I followed them, and then stopped at the front doors of the condo building. "Oh, I've forgotten my phone in the limo," I said. "You guys go on in, I'll be right up."

Father frowned at me, as it was inconceivable that he'd ever forget his phone, since it was all but surgically attached to his hand. "Teddy, stay with her, please."

Make sure she doesn't escape, is what he meant.

I got back in the limo, retrieved the phone I had intentionally left behind. The driver had lowered the partition so he could lounge in the front seat. I slid across the seats to sit directly beneath the partition.

"Can you please take me somewhere?" I asked.

The driver, a middle-aged black man I'd never met before, eyed me suspiciously. "Ma'am?"

"I have a few errands to run. Can you take me, please?"

"I'm supposed to wait here, in case your father or Mr. Haverton need to go somewhere."

"They've got a meeting right now that will keep them busy for at least an hour and I won't need more time than that. Besides, where would they need to go?"

He shrugged. "Not my place to know."

I glanced at Teddy, who was standing by the door, waiting for me. I had a few more seconds before he'd come over to the limo to get me. I turned back to the driver. "What's your name, sir?"

"Shawn, ma'am."

"Shawn. Please. I've been stuck on a plane with

them for hours. I just need to get some air. Please. An hour or less. Please?"

"I won't get in any trouble?"

"I'll tell them it was my idea."

"One hour."

I grabbed his arm and squeezed. "Oh, thank you, thank you, *thank you*, Shawn! You have no idea what you're doing for me."

He turned around and put the car into gear. "Better not be nothin' illegal." He glanced back. "Close that door."

I slid across the seats again, met Teddy's eyes as I closed the door, and hit the lock button. Shawn pulled out into traffic, and I watched Teddy trotting after us, hands in his hair, realizing what I'd done. He was going to get it for sure, but he'd worked for Father for thirty years, and wasn't likely to be fired over this, since Father knew it was me being rebellious, not him being slack about his job.

I liked Teddy, but I needed my freedom.

Shawn drove away from the condo into downtown LA, and I realized that if I stayed in the city, Father and Thomas would find me. He had the power and the resources, and LA was a city he knew as well as he did DC and New York. He could have city detectives sniffing me out within hours. There was no doubt about that.

I had to get away, somewhere far. Remote. Unlikely.

"Shawn?" I asked.

He lowered the partition again. "Ma'am?"

"Can you take me to LAX, please?"

"Uh, I don't know if I can do that."

Cabs passed by, swerved around us, some stood parked on the curb. "Pull over, then."

"Ma'am?"

"If you won't take me, I'll take a cab."

He sighed, a low, discreet sound of irritation. "That ain't safe. Those bozos can't drive for shit." He sighed again. "Fine, but I'm gonna get fired for this for sure."

"I'll make sure Father knows it was all me, that you were just doing what I asked."

"Where you gonna go?"

I stared out the window as he made the necessary adjustments to get us on course for LAX. "I don't know. Somewhere far, far, far from here."

A few minutes of silence. "I went on a cruise once, with my wife and kids," Shawn said, apropos of nothing. "One of them Alaskan cruises. It stopped in this really great little place called Ketchikan. Quaint place, really beautiful. Has a deep harbor, so the big old ships can dock there, but it's a pretty remote spot."

"Are there flights there from LAX?"

"Not direct I don't think, but you can get there with a connection or two."

"That sounds nice."

"Like I said, it was a nice spot." He glanced at me in the rearview mirror. "It ain't fancy, though."

I laughed. "That's perfect, actually. I'm discovering I like things rather more simple than my father does."

"Ketchikan's your spot, then."

"Perfect. Thank you, Shawn."

My phone rang, and I silenced it. It rang again, and again, and again, and I ignored them all. Then text messages started pouring in from Father and Thomas.

Where are you?

Where did you go?

This is unacceptable, Evangeline Du Maurier!! That was from Father, of course. He'd used my full name, which was meant to indicate how mad he was, adding the two exclamation points for emphasis.

I shut off my phone.

I heard another phone ring, a standard imitation old school ringer; Shawn picked it up, and I reached through the divider to catch at his arm. "If it's my father don't tell him anything, Shawn. Please."

He eyed me in the mirror and then shut the phone off. "Who you running from, ma'am?"

"My father. And Thomas."

"Thomas?"

I sighed. "It's complicated." I waved a hand. "It's not, actually. My father wants me to marry him, and I despise him. Neither of them know the meaning of the word no. I'm not running away forever, I just...I need space. I need freedom. They suffocate me."

Shawn nodded. "You're not in trouble, though?"

I shook my head. "Nothing like that. They just want things from me that I don't want for myself, and they have no intention of ever letting me do what I want. I want to live life on my own terms, and they don't appreciate that."

"I s'pose they wouldn't."

He lapsed into silence the rest of the way to the airport. "Which airline, ma'am?"

I stared blankly. "Um. I don't know. I've...I've never flown commercial before."

This got me an amused stare in the mirror from Shawn. "They all the same, I guess. But if you're going to Alaska, you might as well take Alaskan Airlines. Probably got the best deals and the most flights."

"Alaska?"

Shawn laughed, then. "Well yeah. Ketchikan? It's in Alaska."

"Oh. Of course."

He laughed again. "It ain't Siberia, ma'am."

"It's not…like…a hunting camp or something? I don't mind simple, but I draw the line at rustic."

Another laugh, a deep guffaw as he pulled to a stop outside the appropriate terminal. "It's a regular old American city. Bars, restaurants, a movie theater, shops, B-and-B's, Wi-Fi, tourists. Nothing to be scared of. It's just…in Alaska."

I inhaled deeply. "Thank you, Shawn. Thank you so much, for everything."

He shrugged. "All I did was drive you around."

"True," I said, "but you drove me *away* from Father and Thomas."

Another chuckle. "Guess I did." He nodded at the terminal. "Follow the signs to the Alaskan Airlines counter. Ask directions if you need to. They'll help you."

I thanked him again, exited the limo with my purse, overnight bag, and phone. It was easy to find the right counter, and I was in luck as there was a fight leaving in a little over than an hour. I had just enough time to get to the gate. There was a several hour lay-over in Seattle, but I could wait in the airport. It was already after ten at night, and the flight was at eleven-thirty and would arrive in Seattle at a quarter after two in the morning, and then another flight left for Ketchikan at seven-forty that same morning.

The flight was uneventful, if less comfortable

than I was used to, and certainly lacked the privacy I was used to. I'd booked first class of course, but even that couldn't touch the comfort of a private jet. I was doing this on my own, though, and that was the important thing. On my own, for myself.

I had no idea what was in store for me, but it would be an adventure. *My* adventure.

My adventure started when I fell asleep at the gate in Seattle and missed the flight, which meant another six and half hours in Seattle, so I took an Uber to the city and spent the day seeing the sights on foot, browsing Pike Place and getting coffee from the original Starbucks. Another Uber back to the airport in time for the flight, and I got to Ketchikan at three in the afternoon.

I'd spent some time Googling places to stay, and had actually managed to book a room at a little bed and breakfast. I got a cab from the airport to the B-and-B, checked in, and promptly passed out. I didn't wake up until after midnight, and when I did wake up, I was wide-awake and knew I wouldn't be going back to sleep again anytime soon. So I set out on foot, hunting for somewhere to get a drink and something to eat.

Turns out there wasn't much, at that hour.

I wandered for over an hour up and down glistening, rain-wet streets, quiet and abandoned, the cute little shops all closed, restaurants darkened. As I walked, I Googled "late night food in Ketchikan" which brought up only a few results, a cafe which seemed like it was on the opposite end of the city from where I was, a couple all-night fast-food places, and a place called Badd's Bar and Grill. There wasn't much info or any pictures of the interior, but it had great reviews and seemed close to where I was. I opened up directions in Google Maps and followed them toward Badd's.

On the way, I saw light coming from an open door and streaming through a couple of windows, and heard the deep thud of bass and the cheer of a crowd, so I ducked in, indulging my curiosity.

It was wall-to-wall humanity, a seething mass of bodies, all yelling and jumping and screaming; at first I'd thought it was a concert of some kind, but as I got into the crowd I realized the music was more just background, and that the crowd was centered around something happening in the center.

I got shoved a few times, and some elbows in my side, and I realized most of the crowd were men, with only a few women here and there.

I was dressed in casual clothes, nice slacks and a

silk blouse, with my favorite flats—it was my backup clothing, easy to stuff into even a smallish bag and wouldn't hold wrinkles, but it was still nice enough that I stood out.

And I was getting a lot of looks.

Like, a *lot*.

Most of the men were dressed in dirty jeans and wife-beaters, or black T-shirts with vile images on them. The women were, for the most part, companions to the men, and I do use the term "companions" loosely.

What had I wandered into?

I pushed through the crowd, feeling trepidation growing inside me. I had the very distinct feeling that I shouldn't be here; I didn't belong here. My concern was strong enough that it began to turn into fear. But...I wasn't going to back down at the first sign of something different. I was here for an adventure, to discover life on my own terms. I couldn't do that if I ran off every time I encountered something different or uncomfortable, or even a little scary.

So I pushed through the crowd until I was close enough to see what was happening. I immediately regretted it. I'd made it to the front row, which put me, literally, ringside.

"Ring" was another loose term, though. There wasn't a ring, per se, just a roughly circular area cordoned off by stolen police barriers, the crowd all on the outside. Inside the barriers were two men. Both huge. Naked from the waist up, glistening with sweat. Blood dotted their chests and hands, ran down their faces from gashes and cuts, turning their faces to crimson masks. Their fists were taped, and they both wore shorts, one in blue and white, and the other in solid red, and they both wore special sneakers. One of the men, the one in solid red trunks, was significantly more muscled than the other, and seemed to be less bloodied.

My stomach turned at the sight of the blood, and I felt faint, but I couldn't look away. The bigger one— he was *huge*. He was a monster, a colossal bruiser of a man, shoulders like mountain ranges, arms thicker than most men's thighs, a trim waist and massive lat muscles, giving him an almost superhumanly exaggerated wedge shape. Instead of rippling, cut abs, he had a stomach that was so thickly muscled he looked capable of laughing off a kick from a horse.

And indeed, as I watched, his smaller and more bloodied opponent ducked, wove, and then cut loose with a brutal barrage of uppercut punches to Bruiser's midsection, each blow furiously powerful, his taped fists thudding and smacking with loud echoes like the reports of gunshots. And Bruiser? He took the hits without flinching or blocking, a grin on his face, and then scythed a mammoth fist downward with the force of a descending meteorite. It connected with the smaller fighter's cheekbone with a resounding *crack*, and the fighter stumbled backward...

He crashed into the barrier directly in front of me, so close I could smell his body odor, so close his sweaty shoulder smeared against me. And then Bruiser was on top of him, fists flying like rockets, launching one after the other in such fast succession the impacts seemed to create one sound—a crunching wet smack. My stomach turned at the sound, at the way the smaller fighter flinched and jerked at the crashing body blows.

I couldn't move away—I was now pinned in place by the crowd.

Bruiser's eyes flicked away from his opponent for a moment, and caught mine. It was an instant of eye contact, but I swear I felt a bolt of something pass between us, a spark, a recognition of sorts, even though I knew I'd never seen this man before. This close, he was more massive than I'd originally thought. I wasn't short, at five-eight, but he was several inches taller than me...Thomas was six feet even, and this man was probably two or three inches taller than Thomas. His face, even through the mask of blood sluicing over his features from a cut to his eyebrow, was chiseled and gorgeous. His eyes were wide and deep set, a vivid, arresting shade of Yellow Lab brown-gold; his head was shaved on the sides, with the top a little too wide to be a mohawk, more of an extreme version of an undercut. The hair itself was probably brown, but right now it was nearly black from being sweat-wet, tied at the back of his head. His jawline was craggier than Mount Fiji, and I've seen that in person. And his body? Good god. He could rival John Cena for raw, brutal, perfect bulk.

All this passed through my head in an instant, as our eyes met. His gaze flicked over me as fast as mine did over him, and a tiny smile curled the corner of his mouth, amused, derisive, fascinated, lecherous; a very complicated smirk, to be sure.

And then the moment was over. His opponent was recovering, pushing himself off the barrier, assisted by eager hands from the crowd, and then the massive, brutally beautiful Bruiser swung his fist in a lazy haymaker, connecting with a disgusting smack, and I felt hot sticky wetness spray across my face. I nearly vomited when I passed my fingers across my forehead and they came away red with blood.

Bruiser laughed—actually laughed out loud, and even his voice was attractive, in a raw, powerful way. Deep, raspy, guttural. His laughter was rife with amusement at my disgust. He could afford the time to laugh at me, because the blow which had sprayed me with blood had also dropped his opponent to the ground in a limp heap.

I shoved through the crowd as it howled its approval.

I heard a voice from speakers somewhere. "Winner by K-O is the one, the only...*BASHER!*"

Of course his ring name was Basher. I caught a lot more glares, stares, and more than a few catcalls as I pushed through the crowd to the doorway, gasping for breath when I made it outside. Inside, the air had been wet with sweat and humidity and excitement, leaving me heaving with disgust at the thought of breathing in the perspiration of so many other people.

Not to mention the fact that my face was sticky with a man's blood, drying into tacky clumps on my face. I didn't dare wipe at it, knowing it would just smear worse. I had blood on my fingers, and I looked down and saw that my cream silk blouse was dotted with blood. My slacks, at least, were maroon and didn't show blood very easily and could probably be salvaged, but my shirt was ruined.

I loved this blouse.

I nearly cursed, but didn't.

I swallowed my anger and fear and disgust, and hurried away from the doorway of the warehouse that had held the fight. I only made it a few steps when I felt a prickling on the back of my neck, a crawling down my spine. I glanced over my shoulder and saw four shapes behind me by a dozen or so steps, dressed in baggy jeans and hoodies, hands in pockets.

"Hey, sweetheart, slow down. We just wanna talk." The voice slithered with anticipation.

Yeah, they didn't want to talk. I hurried, desperate now to reach the bar and grill I'd been heading for originally. It should only be a few blocks away. A left turn ahead, then a right, and it would be on my left two blocks down, with the docks on my right.

I was nearly running, but it didn't seem to make any difference.

They were right behind me.

Fear clogged my throat; I was hyperventilating, gasping shrill sounds of terror.

"Come on, honey. Have some fun with us."

"Yeah, we can show you a *real* fun time."

No, no, no. Not like this. No.

I heard running steps, and then two were in front of me and two were beside me, hands grasping at my arms, at my waist, plucking at my shirt, reaching for my purse.

"Let go!" I shouted. "Leave me alone!"

"Awww, she don't wanna play," one of them drawled.

"I think we can convince her," another said.

"Not here, though," a third said. "Bring her into

that alley there."

I felt myself being lifted off the ground, and I kicked and screamed and thrashed, but a dirty, bitter-tasting hand clapped over my mouth. I kept screaming, the sound now muffled.

"Hold her legs," I heard.

"I got her arms."

"I saw her first, so I get first dibs," another voice said. Eager, vile.

"I got seconds."

"Eh, she's fine enough I don't mind sloppy thirds."

I was pinned down, thrashing and kicking and screaming and biting, seeing faces and figures, a scruffy blond beard, pierced ears, tattoos on hands, black sweatshirts. I heard the jingling of a belt buckle.

No, please, please, please.

I saw the face of Bruiser in my mind, and wished he were here. Why, I wasn't sure, but I felt like if he were here, he'd save me from this.

I clamped my thighs together and hooked one foot under the other. Hands pawed at my shirt, my slacks. I thrashed harder, making it as difficult as I could, fighting the need to cry. If I started crying, I'd stop fighting. No crying.

Absurdly, I could still feel the blood on my face.

"Fucking hold her, Brad. Jesus."

"I'm trying, but she's fuckin' strong, bro."

"Ya'll are fuckin' pussies." I heard a metallic *snick* and felt something sharp touch the side of my cheek. "Pretty thing like you, wouldn't want any scars would you? Hold still and we'll finish with you soon enough. Keep fighting, well...I won't kill you, but you won't be as pretty anymore." His voice was low and dark and quiet and terrifying, and I knew he meant it.

"Dude, Jimmy...this is supposed to be just a little bit of fun," said the first voice.

"Shut the fuck up, Brad," Jimmy said.

I went still.

I squeezed my eyes shut, prayed, begged silently as hands ripped at the clasp of my slacks.

And then I heard a sound...a choked gasp, and something like a watermelon hitting the ground.

"The fuck?" Brad's voice.

"Hey, man, back off. We found her first." This was the one who had told Brad to hold me still.

"Get the fuck out of here before I cut you to ribbons, motherfucker."

The laugh, then...I knew that laugh. It was the same amused, gravelly chuckle I'd heard when the blood had sprayed my face. Maybe my pleas had reached God after all.

"Drop the knife, pussy-boy." God, his voice. It sounded like the earth cracking open, like a boulder rolling through shale, crushing stones—rough, deep, powerful.

"Four of us, one of you, bitch." Jimmy again.

"Three, now."

"What'd you do to Tom?" That was Brad.

"Broke his fucking skull open, that's what." A shuffled step. "Maybe you don't recognize me."

"Shit! It's Basher!" Brad again.

"Still three on one," Jimmy said, his voice full of bravado.

I was frozen in place. Eyes shut, shaking all over.

Then my eyes flicked open, and I saw a massive shape blocking the alley entrance. Bruiser, standing in a pool of orange light from a streetlamp, still in his fighter shorts, but wearing combat boots and a hoodie, his face clean, the cut over his eye patched with a butterfly bandage.

His gaze went to me, and then flicked back up to the three men standing around me. There was a body on the ground, stilled, right beside me. I refused to look any closer.

Bruiser/Basher, whatever his name was—he had his hands in the pockets of his hoodie, casual, his body language relaxed. "Here's how it's gonna be, cocksuckers—I'm gonna count to three, and if you're not gone, I'm gonna start breaking bones." He pulled his hands out of his pockets, and his hands were still taped from knuckles to forearm, the once-white tape now pink-red with old blood. "One."

The three men, my would-be rapists, shuffled forward, glancing at each other, each silently daring the other to make the first move.

"Two."

"Jimmy, I think we should go," Brad said, his voice fearful. "We've all made bank watching this dude fight. I don't want any part of this shit."

"Then fuckin' run, you little pussy." Jimmy, the tallest of them, a long folding knife in one hand, stepped forward.

Bruiser tipped his head back, a pleased, feral grin on his face. His hands, loose at his sides now, curled into fists and then relaxed again. "Three."

I watched, I never took my eyes off him, but I still never saw him move. One moment he was standing in place, hands at his sides, utterly calm, and then there was a crunch and a body was flying backward. I watched Jimmy lunge, his knife slicing out. It hit nothing but air, because Bruiser was twisting aside, his fist crashing into another body. Not Jimmy's, one of the others. I heard another crunch, a cry of pain, and then Bruiser punched again to the same spot, high in the ribcage, and his fist went into the body a little too far—the cracking, crunching sound was ribs being shattered.

I felt my stomach revolt, but couldn't look away. I didn't dare move a muscle, I didn't want to be seen or be noticed. Jimmy still had the knife, and he might decide to use me as a shield. If I stayed still, hopefully the attention would stay on Bruiser, who was clearly more than capable of handling it.

The body with the broken ribs collapsed a few feet away from me, and his eyes went to me, hazed with agony. I didn't feel sympathy at all.

Bruiser moved again, and this time his foot swung—I watched it connect with the guy he'd first struck, who was just now getting to his feet, slowly, groaning. Bruiser's foot smashed into a kneecap, which went the wrong way, and then his fist darted out, and if cheekbones can break, that one did.

Now it was just Jimmy and Bruiser.

Facing off, the knife waving side to side in Jimmy's hand, and then it flashed forward with sudden speed. Bruiser twisted aside, but not fast enough—I saw the blade slice open his sweatshirt, heard him grunt in pain as the edge bit into his flesh.

And then Bruiser lashed out with his hand, grabbing Jimmy's wrist and twisting his arm away, and his other fist descended like a hammer, and I turned away just as Jimmy's elbow was smashed until it faced the wrong direction. I covered my face with my hands, but found myself peeking through my fingers as

Jimmy fell to his knees, groaning, breathless with agony. Bruiser stood over him, a mammoth predator, an avenging angel. One scything fist, and Jimmy's face was crumpled, his jaw hanging loose as he toppled to one side. Bruiser wasn't done—he planted a combat boot into Jimmy's torso, and I heard bones break yet again.

He spat a gobbet of saliva at Jimmy. "Pussy."

And then he turned his gaze to me, brows furrowing. I scrambled away as he prowled toward me—he'd saved me, yes, but what if he'd only saved me so he could have me for himself? I couldn't seem to find my feet, could only scrabble with my feet on the ground, my butt scraping across the ground as I tried to get away from him—only to catch up against the cold metal of a dumpster.

He crouched three feet away from me, and his face was…well, features like his couldn't be described as *gentle*, but his expression was soft and kind. "Hey, relax. I got you, Prada."

Prada?

He reached out, and I realized he was handing me my purse, my favorite, a black Prada handbag. I snatched it from him and held it against my chest, all the emotions I'd been refusing to feel crashing into me now, fear—no, raw terror—chief among them.

"Listen, you gotta relax. I won't hurt you." He

shifted a foot closer, his hand still extended in the same gesture I'd once seen Father's horse trainer use to approach a skittish colt. "Deep breaths, okay? Just breathe. You're fine."

I was hyperventilating through clenched teeth, couldn't catch my breath, lungs on fire, panic wracking me.

He was closer, now, close enough to touch, and his fingers pressed against the back of my hand. "Breathe, Prada. Breathe. You'll pass out if you don't breathe." He reached up with his other hand and brushed a lock of my long black hair away from my eye, and his brown gaze met mine, and something in his eyes soothed me enough that I could suck in a shuddery breath. "That's it, that's it. One more time. Good. Now just keep breathing, all right, Prada? Nobody's gonna hurt you."

I forced breath into my lungs and summoned my voice. "My name is Evangeline Du Maurier."

He smiled at me. "Nice to meet you, Eva."

"*Evangeline*," I emphasized. "Not Eva."

"Sure, sure. *Evangeline*, then."

"And you are?"

Another voice came from a ways away, distant. "Bax! Where you at?"

"Alley!" Bruiser—who seemed to be named Bax—called out, without taking his gaze off me.

I heard a footstep, and then the same voice, closer. "Shit, Bax. What the fuck, man?"

Bax was in front of me, so from the mouth of the alley, whoever was looking for him couldn't see me.

"That's my brother, Zane," Bax said to me. "He's one of the good guys. Like me, for the record."

Then he stood up and faced his brother, which gave me a look at him too. Six feet even, but almost as built as Bax, with his hair cropped close to his scalp, wearing jeans, a tight white T-shirt, and combat boots. "Seriously, Bax. You can't go a fucking hour without getting into some kind of trouble?"

Bax gestured at me. "In this case, the trouble was legit. These four pieces of shit were about to rape my new friend Evangeline."

The brother standing in the light was close enough that I could make out his expression, which went hard and violent. Baxter exuded violence, but his brother? His brother's presence seethed with a roiling, potent sense of impending death.

"And you left them alive?" His voice was so quiet it was frightening.

Bax shrugged easily. "I'm not you, bro. I'll cheerfully kick the ever-loving fuck out of people, but I generally try to draw the line at murder. Even in the case of attempted rape."

"Yeah, well...I don't." His brother took a slow

step toward the closest body, who was writhing in pain, groaning softly.

Bax's eyebrows shot up, and he moved toward me. "Hold on a second, there, Zane. Why don't we wait until I get Eva here somewhere else? I don't think she needs to see anything else at this point."

He lifted me to my feet, and his hand was huge as it enclosed mine, rough as sandpaper and powerful, but gentle. He hustled me out of the alley, but not before I took a backward glance at the men who had been about to rape me. Bax's brother, Zane, was crouched down, picking up the discarded knife, examining the blade, and then he grabbed the nearest body with his empty hand and rolled him to his back. I looked away before I saw anything else.

"Is...is he really going to...*kill* them?" I asked, after we'd turned the corner.

"You gonna cry at their funerals if he does?" Bax asked, glancing at me.

His arm was around my waist, keeping me upright, because I realized I was having trouble walking, and it was only Bax's arm that was holding me off the ground and keeping me moving.

I thought of their nasty, evil, eager voices and reaching, ripping hands, and what would have happened to me had Bax not shown up...and I shook my head. "He can have them."

Bax's laugh was dark. "That's what I thought."

"Won't he get in trouble?" I asked.

Bax shook his head. "I'm not gonna be asking any questions, but Zane was a Navy SEAL, so this kind of thing is what he did for a living. I'm not worried." He took my purse from me and held it by the black patent leather, hand-stitched handles. "Just don't think about it, okay? Don't give those fuckers another thought, and don't worry about my brother. He can handle himself just fine."

I think if any other male had tried to touch me, right then, I would have screamed. But for some reason, Bax's arm around my waist was comforting. Part of me was terrified of him, knowing what he was capable of. But I also had no doubts that he'd never put a hand on me to hurt me.

My stomach flipped, lurched. I closed my eyes to focus on not puking, but when I closed my eyes, all I could see was those faces, and I could feel their hands on me, pawing at my breasts, ripping at my pants. I sagged in Bax's hold, and shook away from him, collapsing downward. He guided me to a sitting position and I felt a wall at my back, and felt him beside me, close but not touching.

"Fuck." He sighed the curse word tiredly. "You're safe, Eva. I've got you. They're gone. They're taken care of."

I nodded, but it wasn't until I forced my eyes open that the images vanished, and even then I could almost feel their hands on me still, and I felt dirty. Grimy. Filthy. Breathing was hard.

Bax's eyes scrutinized me. "You're still freaking out, ain'tcha?"

I nodded. "Can't—can't breathe."

"Listen." He shifted so he was kneeling in front of me. "We gotta get you off the street. You need a drink, and you need a long hot shower and a change of clothes."

"But I don't have any other clothes."

He didn't ask any questions, which I appreciated, even though I would have, in his place. "Okay, well... if you trust me enough to come with me," he said, "then I can get you all that—a stiff drink, a shower, clean clothes, and something to eat, if you're hungry."

I met his gaze. My mind flashed to him in the ring, huge and brutal, smashing his opponent to the ground with vicious ease; I saw him devastating four men as if they were nothing, one of whom had been armed. But yet, I looked into his eyes, and I only saw someone who cared about what had happened to me. He seemed to genuinely care, deeply, about what I needed and wanted.

I worked myself to my feet, and managed a slow, steadying breath. "I trust you."

His grin was cocky and beautiful and kind all at once. "Thatta girl, Eva."

"My *name*," I snapped, "is *Evangeline*."

"And *my* name is Baxter Badd." He took my hand, bowed over it, and kissed the back of it, his eyes on mine, twinkling with amusement. "It's a pleasure to meet you."

One's heart most assuredly should *not* do flips this soon after what I'd just experienced, but for some reason, mine did.

Good Girl Gone Badd

Releasing AUGUST 4, 2017

Visit me at my website: **www.jasindawilder.com**
Email me: **jasindawilder@gmail.com**

If you enjoyed this book, you can help others enjoy it as well by recommending it to friends and family, or by mentioning it in reading and discussion groups and online forums. You can also review it on the site from which you purchased it. But, whether you recommend it to anyone else or not, thank you *so much* for taking the time to read my book! Your support means the world to me!

My other titles:

The Preacher's Son:
Unbound
Unleashed
Unbroken

Biker Billionaire:
Wild Ride

Big Girls Do It:
Better (#1), Wetter (#2), Wilder (#3), On Top (#4)
Married (#5)
On Christmas (#5.5)

Pregnant (#6)
Boxed Set

Rock Stars Do It:
Harder
Dirty
Forever
Boxed Set

From the world of *Big Girls* and *Rock Stars*:
Big Love Abroad

Delilah's Diary:
A Sexy Journey
La Vita Sexy
A Sexy Surrender

The Falling Series:
Falling Into You
Falling Into Us
Falling Under
Falling Away
Falling for Colton

The Ever Trilogy:
Forever & Always
After Forever

Saving Forever

The world of *Alpha:*
Alpha
Beta
Omega
Harris: Alpha One Security Book 1
Thresh: Alpha One Security Book 2
Duke: Alpha One Security Book 3
Puck: Alpha One Security Book 4

The world of Stripped:
Stripped
Trashed

The world of *Wounded:*
Wounded
Captured

The Houri Legends:
Jack and Djinn
Djinn and Tonic

The Madame X Series:
Madame X
Exposed
Exiled

Badd Brothers:

Badd Motherf*cker

Badd Ass

Bass to the Bone

**The Black Room
(With Jade London):**

Door One

Door Two

Door Three

Door Four

Door Five

Door Six

Door Seven

Door Eight

Deleted Door

Standalone titles:

Yours

Non-Fiction titles:

Big Girls Do It Running

Big Girls Do It Stronger

Jack Wilder Titles:

The Missionary

To be informed of new releases and special offers,
sign up for
Jasinda's email newsletter.

65272940R00227

Made in the USA
Lexington, KY
06 July 2017